INDEPENDENT LEGIONS
PUBLISHING

GREG. F. GIFUNE – BENEATH THE NIGHT
ISBN: 978-88-99569-25-9

1° edition paperback - October 2016
Cover Art by: Daniele Serra

BENEATH THE NIGHT

Summary

LONG AFTER DARK

1	Pg 3
2	Pg 16
3	Pg 37
4	Pg 54
5	Pg 72
6	Pg 88
7	Pg 105
8	Pg 129
9	Pg 148
10	Pg 165
11	Pg 180
12	Pg 190
13	Pg 195

THE RAIN DANCERS

1	Pg 201
2	Pg 216
3	Pg 228
4	Pg 239
5	Pg 253
6	Pg 264
7	Pg 277

ABOUT THE AUTHOR	Pg 282
AVAILABLE BOOKS	Pg 283

ACKNOWLEDGEMENTS

Thanks to Shane Staley and Eric Shapiro for their friendship and continued belief in my work. And special thanks to Alessandro Manzetti and everyone at Independent Legions Publishing for their kindness and support and for being such a joy to work with.

Greg F. Gifune

Beneath the Night

LONG AFTER DARK

For my sister Kimberley

"In a real dark night of the soul it is always three o'clock in the morning, day after day."

— *F. Scott Fitzgerald*
"The Crack-Up"

1

The rain began to fall just after three in the morning.

Accompanied by a violent wind, it gushed from dark skies, lashed the house and drenched the neighborhood with such ferocity the noise alone would've wakened Harry Fremont had he been asleep.

But Harry wasn't asleep. He was wide awake.

In fact, he hadn't slept since the night before.

From then on the flu had kept him awake and coughing, blowing his nose, battling a fever and enduring waves of head and body aches that just wouldn't quit. Unfortunately, that last night of sleep hadn't been particularly restful either, as he'd been plagued by a series of disturbing dreams and nonsensical thoughts that continued to replay and echo in his mind. He couldn't remember details but the nightmares and thoughts were connected, and he was fairly certain they all had something to do with first being pursued and then pursuing someone else, and ultimately, imprisonment in darkness. Though horrifying, he couldn't put his finger on many specifics, just elusive shadow memories of being lost in a labyrinth of dark corridors and wracked with pain as glimpses of lifeless lunar surface flashed before his eyes. His muscles still throbbed, but he couldn't be sure if it was residue from nightmares or merely a symptom of the virus raging through his system.

In the dark, sitting in a recliner in his den, Harry carefully attempted a deep breath, heard his chest wheeze, then felt a familiar itch at the base of his throat. Another wave of coughing was coming. He closed his eyes, concentrated and sat perfectly still, hopeful this might prevent it, but a sudden chill shot up along the center of his back and into his neck. He shivered, and the movement sent him over the edge and into a vicious coughing fit. By the time it finally wound down he was out of breath, his chest hurt and he was sweating profusely. More chills fired through him, his nose began to run and a sharp cramping pain stabbed him just above his pubic bone. *Oh no*, he thought, *not that too.*

He reached for a box of tissues on the coffee table. He'd blown his nose so many times in the last twelve hours the skin around and just beneath his nostrils had already turned raw and red. He delicately pressed a fresh tissue to his nose and blew. It didn't seem possible anyone's head could hold this much. It was endless, and now postnasal drip had kicked in, trickling down the back of his throat like liquid glue. Tossing the tissues aside with a defeated sigh, he slouched forward in the recliner and felt sorry for himself awhile. Not that it mattered any. Harry was alone in the house. He glanced at a small-framed photograph of Marlon, their dog. He'd died just a few months before, at twelve, of cancer. *God how I miss that little guy*, he thought. *If he were still alive he'd be right here next to me, like always.* Sometimes Harry still caught himself looking for his old friend even now.

Normally he would've been upstairs with Kelly, cuddled up tight and warm, the dog at the foot of the bed. But Kelly had left that morning for a three-day business trip to San Diego. Her position at a highend coffee company had always been an importantpart of her life, but since her promotion from middle management to Vice President of Sales a year before, her career had become increasingly intrusive in their daily personal lives. She worked much longer hours, and although her pay had more than doubled, the position also required a great deal of business travel. Harry was proud of his wife and her success, but disliked this newest development intensely, which led to several arguments between the two. In fact, they'd had words just hours before.

Kelly was staring out the tiny windows on either side of the front door while waiting for her cab to come and take her to the airport. As she so often did when upset, she purposely avoided eye contact. Harry had just begun to feel under the weather, but mistakenly assumed he was simply overtired and stressed.

"I'm just saying I don't like all this travel, OK?"

"We've been over this," Kelly said evenly. "We discussed this before I took the job, we discussed it after I took the job, and now we discuss it every time I have to get on an airplane. I don't like being away from home either, but longer hours and occasional travel is part of what I do now."

"*Occasional?* You went to Atlanta less than a month ago, and a week before that you were in Montreal for two days. Two weeks before that you were in—"

"What do you want me to do? Quit a job I worked a decade to get?"

"I want you to care about what this is doing to us."

She turned and looked at him, her normally pretty blue eyes narrowed and glaring. "What does that even mean?"

"It means sometimes you act like you care more about your job than our happiness."

"Don't you mean *your* happiness?"

"Sorry, I was under the impression my happiness was the most important thing to you, since yours is to me."

"Then support me in what I'm trying to do."

"And what is that exactly?"

"Now you're just being a jerk. I'm working my ass off to build the company to heights it's never seen before—you know that—and once that starts to kick in I'll be able to expand my staff and delegate more. Then I won't have to do all this traveling. I'll be able to send somebody else. Give it some time. I've only had the job a year."

"I'm getting tired of you never being here."

"I would think with all that's going on you'd be happy I'm doing so well." Kelly folded her arms across her chest, ruffling the jacket of her pinstripe skirt-suit. "Funny, I don't remember you bitching when my pay doubled and it helped make Garret's college bills easier, or when it helped us get the new house."

The words stung the same as if she'd slapped him in the face. "The sale of this house is primarily what afforded us the new one. And *my* job bought this house and everything in it. You know, back when you were just a receptionist, answering phones, fetching coffee and barely making enough for grocery money. My job paid for you to go back to college and get your degree. My job supported you and me and Garret for years, so spare me your—"

"Whatever, my cab's here," she said, bending down for her bags. "I'll call you when I land in San Diego. My hotel info is on the pad in the kitchen."

They stared at each other a moment.

"I love you, you know," she said.

He gave a guarded smile. "I love you too."

Kelly leaned in and kissed him. "We'll figure it out when I get home, OK?"

He nodded. "Sure."

"You look tired," she said as she hurried out the door. "Go to bed early tonight, get some rest."

He tried, but when his symptoms began they'd all come at once, attacking him as if from thin air and rendering any hope of sleep impossible. His nose clogged, his ears began to ring, he was suddenly freezing and achy and a headache had settled behind his eyes. Forced to accept the fact that he was coming down with either a serious cold or perhaps even a bout with the flu, he'd wearily rolled from bed and returned downstairs to the den. Angrily blowing his nose and cursing whoever had given him this crap, he watched television awhile and tried to take his mind off things. He rarely got sick, couldn't even remember the last time he'd had a cold, but on those scarce occasions when Harry *did* get sick, he got very sick. Clearly this was going to be one of those times.

By midnight he was exhausted, lightheaded and feverish, so he took some aspirin, shut the TV off and tried to sleep in the recliner.

That didn't work either. His body wanted to sleep, needed to sleep, but by then the incessant cough had joined the festivities and wouldn't allow it.

Rain battered the windows, the roaring wind escalated, the walls around him creaked and moaned, and something about these normally mundane sounds made Harry uneasy. More uneasy than they should have.

But he couldn't figure out why.

Again his thoughts turned to his wife. She'd called as promised from the airport to let him know she'd landed safely, but he'd been in the bathroom and the call went to voicemail. He checked his watch. San Diego was three hours behind Massachusetts so it was a little after midnight there, maybe she was still up. He pictured Kelly sprawled on a hotel bed watching TV, legs stretched out before her, a remote in one hand and a drink in the other, her hair mussed and makeup faded, suit jacket slung over the back of a nearby chair, blouse and skirt wrinkled, pumps kicked off to the floor below along with a tangle of pantyhose.

With a grunt Harry struggled up out of the recliner and over to the cordless phone on a small end table next to the couch. He dialed the voicemail and listened to her message again.

"I'm on the ground safe and sound, just grabbed a shuttle to the hotel. I'm in Suite 136. We'll be in meetings the rest of the afternoon and tonight I've got a dinner thing, so I won't be back until late. I'll give you a call in the morning. Love you. Bye."

Harry deleted the message, then shuffled out into the kitchen and over to the magnetic pad on the refrigerator where Kelly had written her hotel information down. Sniffling, he slipped on a pair of reading glasses his optometrist had recently insisted he needed, and dialed the number she'd left. It was answered on the second ring.

"Good evening, Great Night Suites."

The voice was male and monotone, but whispery and soft to the point of sounding nearly mocking.

"Suite 136, please." Harry pulled the glasses off. He didn't know which he hated more, the damn glasses or the fact that for the first time in his life he truly needed them. "*It happens to everyone sooner or later,*" the optometrist had told him. "*The eyes degenerate the older one gets. But otherwise yours are quite healthy at this point.*"

At this point...meaning at some future point they'll get worse. My eyes are slowly weakening and dying along with the rest of me. Even five years ago I didn't need reading glasses. Now I do. What about five years from now? Will I need them all the time? Life begins at forty my ass.

The room phone rang several times but wasn't answered. Could she already be asleep? Unlikely. Besides, wouldn't the ringing wake her?

Suddenly Harry was reconnected with the man at the front desk. "I'm sorry, that suite isn't answering. I can put you through to voicemail if you'd like."

"No, I'll try again in the morning," Harry said. "Thank you."

He hit disconnect. Her business dinner must've been long over by midnight. Where the hell was she at this hour? As if in answer, another coughing spell hit, concluding when a ball of phlegm leapt into his throat. Gagging, Harry made his way to the sink, spat it out, then flipped on the light to study it a moment. Brown. Not good. He washed it away, then dialed Kelly's cell.

Amidst background noise that sounded curiously like the rumble of large machinery, a computer-generated voice said, "We're sorry, the provider for the mobile service you are attempting to reach is temporarily unavailable. Please try your call again later."

Weird, he thought, *never got that message before.* Assuming there was probably trouble with the towers or the satellites due to the storm, Harry hung up, dropped the cordless into his robe pocket and trudged back to the dark den. He stood dejectedly before the French doors and watched the small patio area and backyard. With the outdoor furniture stored in the cellar for the winter, but for the gas grill the patio was barren, slick and wet. Reminding him of the strange dreams he had last time he'd slept, the moon hung high in the night sky, blurred by what looked like a blanket of fog. But despite the moonlight, the night was so thick he couldn't make out much of the yard beyond the patio. At the edge of the property, yard became forest, but that too was shrouded in darkness and rain.

Their house, a modest two-bedroom Cape, was located at the end of a quiet cul-de-sac in Schooner Bluffs, a small coastal town on the southern shores of Massachusetts not far from Boston. When they'd first bought the house back in 1989, just two years after they'd been married, Schooner Bluffs had a population of about five thousand, but in the last few years the town had exploded with new homes and an influx of businesses previously not allowed in town. There was an enormous Wal-Mart now, a Shaw's Supermarket, and in recent months more commercial development followed, but when the financial crisis hit and the real estate market tanked, everything other than commercial growth came to an almost immediate halt, leaving much of the town in financial ruin. There were five houses on their cul-de-sac. Two had already been foreclosed on and had sat empty and for sale by the banks for months, until a huge developer swooped in and bought up an enormous chunk of property, including the entire cul-de-sac. The following year a vast cinema complex would be built in its place, along with two strip-malls and an Olive Garden restaurant. Initially the residents fought the proposal, but the town, desperate for revenue, got behind it. Eventually everything became a tangled mess of lawyers and potential lawsuits, and as property values continued to plummet, Harry and Kelly, along with their two remaining neighbors, took the deal. Harry and Kelly, and Rose Bassinger—the woman who lived across the street—had been the final holdouts on Revere Place, and though they'd finally come to terms with the buyer as well, theirs were the only two houses still occupied on the cul-de-sac. The rest sat empty and abandoned, awaiting destruction. Like Rose, Harry and Kelly had to be out by the end of January, so right after the holidays they'd begin the move to the new home they'd purchased two towns away. As it was already early November they had less than three months left here.

The new place, though much smaller, was nice enough, but Harry wasn't at all happy about leaving. Except for the first two years of their marriage, this house had been their home. He and Kelly had spent half their twenties, all of their thirties and five years of their forties here. Their son Garret had been conceived and raised in this house. He'd taken his first steps in this very den, spoken his first words while in his highchair in the kitchen. Marlon had lived his entire life here. So many happy memories, he thought, so much history.

But then leaving was just another transition in a recent and stressful string of many. There was Kelly's promotion. Garret left home for the first time to attend his freshman year of college at UNH. Marlon had been diagnosed with cancer and died soon thereafter. And to top it all off, the firm where Harry had worked for more than fifteen years (a company specializing in product and market analysis for manufacturers and advertisers), was purchased by a larger corporation, leaving his status as a department head and his future with the company uncertain. What he'd considered a secure job he'd have until retirement could now very well be pulled right out from under him, and he'd be on the street looking for work at forty-five. He'd already gotten the memo explaining how after the first of the year the new owners planned to send in efficiency consultants to determine which jobs were expendable, and rumor had it middle managers like him would be the first targeted. He could only hope his seniority and exemplary record would be enough to save him.

Another spray of rain hit the French doors, breaking Harry's concentration. For a moment he caught a glimpse of his ghostly reflection in the glass. He had a severe case of bed-head, was dressed in old sweatpants, even older moccasin slippers and a loose-fitting sweatshirt, and his heavy robe was open and hanging on him, the belt ends dangling nearly to the floor. Kelly had gotten him the robe for Christmas the year before. Damn thing had always been too big. As another wave of chills struck he pulled it closed and fastened the belt. He was beginning to feel slightly nauseous.

I'm sorry, sir, that suite isn't answering.

"Where is she?" he asked the moon.

It gave no answer, so he returned to the recliner. His temples throbbed and the pressure behind his eyes felt like something was trying to push its way out through his sinuses. Each time he swallowed more postnasal drip slithered down his throat and his airway constricted and clogged. A fat dollop of mucus lodged near the back of his tongue and cried out for him to clear his throat, but he didn't for fear it might lead to more coughing.

If only he could sleep. Exhausted, he opened the recliner and put his feet up, but the moment he was prone the coughing returned with a vengeance. He spit up into a tissue, moaned at the pain in his chest, then blew his nose.

Outside, the storm raged on.

* * *

The next time Harry looked at his watch it was a little after four-thirty in the morning. Rain continued to assault the house, and though he made several attempts to stretch out on the couch and get some sleep, each time his back hit the cushions the cough returned. After a while he tried sleeping sitting up, but just as he'd begin to drift off he'd suddenly snap back to consciousness like he'd been hit with a cattle prod. And then another round of coughing would take hold and throttle him until his throat was raw, his eyes were blurred with tears and his lungs felt like they were exploding through his chest.

A few minutes later his head began to pound, and before long the pain had spread from his temples to the back of his skull. Fearing another wave of coughing, Harry crept carefully down the hallway and into the bathroom, moving as if traversing a minefield. Once there he popped two Excedrin Extra Strength tablets without bothering to turn on the bathroom light.

He shuffled through the kitchen, wiped his nose with the sleeve of his robe and had just started back for the den when a vague hint of something along the outskirts of his peripheral vision caught his attention.

He hesitated at the French doors. They were spotted with rain.

Sunrise was still a few hours away, but the moon had vanished, leaving everything beyond the doors draped in pitch black. Harry pawed at his tired eyes to make certain he was seeing what his mind had suggested. He took a step closer, leaned forward toward the glass panes and squinted through the rain.

There, just beyond the edge of the patio, in the middle of the backyard, a small pair of red eyes glowed through the downpour.

It wasn't that unusual for an animal—foxes, skunks, possum, raccoons, even the occasional deer or coyote—to wander from the forest behind the house into or through the yard at night, particularly of late. With all the building going on their natural habitat was being increasingly compromised and the boundaries separating Man from wild animal were becoming smaller and smaller. But there was something about these eyes, something unsettling, perhaps because they were fixed and seemed to be looking directly at him.

Harry reached for the switch along the wall next to the French doors, and with a quick flick, a powerful flood lit up the backyard like a baseball stadium.

The eyes remained.

Drenched but unmoved by the rain, a lone coyote sat staring at the house.

Although he'd heard the distant ungodly howls from these animals now and then late at night, and occasionally found tracks in the yard, he'd never actually seen a coyote on the property. Their impact had been felt in town however, as much of the smaller wildlife, like rabbits for example, had all but vanished in recent years, the victims of these devastating predators. Few people let their cats outside anymore, particularly at night, because so many had been snatched away, and roughly a year before the local Animal Control Department had found an abandoned den about a mile back in these very woods, littered with bloody collars. The more Man squeezed them out and devoured the woodlands, the more brazen the coyotes became, motivated by hunger and the instinctual drive to survive. In one small town about ten minutes away and closer to Cape Cod, a toddler playing in his yard had been attacked in broad daylight by a coyote that attempted to drag the tot away. The attack was only stopped when the child's mother assaulted the animal with a broom. Even then, she had to beat the animal mercilessly before it finally released the baby and escaped into the nearby forest.

Many locals wanted to form posses to hunt the animals down and exterminate them, but Harry had always found this preposterous. The coyotes were simply being coyotes, doing what they were designed to do. They had to eat, they had to feed their young, what did people expect? Certainly dragging small children away couldn't be tolerated, and animals that attempted such things needed to be stopped and if necessary even killed, but those were rare occurrences. Normally coyotes stayed hidden and fed off other wild animals in forests that were *their* homes, not Man's.

The closest Harry had come to actually seeing a coyote was one night when he'd brought a bag of garbage out to the barrels along the back of the house and startled something that had been sniffing around the trash. Whatever it was darted off into the woods, and he'd only managed a quick glimpse of its hindquarters. He suspected it was a coyote but it could've been a dog, he'd never been entirely certain.

This time there was no question. It was staring right at him.

Despite the coyote's unusual behavior, there was something surreal and wonderfully mystical about seeing such a magnificent creature in plain view and no more than twenty feet away.

There were no lights on in the house, and suddenly Harry wished there were. He watched the animal awhile from the shadows, his hand still poised on the outside light switch. For some odd reason having the ability to return the yard to darkness at any moment made him feel safer, as if doing so would cause the animal to disappear at his command. It reminded him of when Garret was a toddler, and how he'd cover his eyes with his little hands and assume that because he could no longer see his parents they could also no longer see him. But Harry didn't feel particularly threatened by the animal. There wasn't anything remotely aggressive about its stance or demeanor.

And maybe that was just it. It was *too* still. Unnaturally still.

Mesmerized by the coyote's stare, Harry held its gaze. Eventually he began to realize what he was seeing in those feral eyes. They were imploring, as if for help, as if hoping for refuge, sanctuary. Here, with him.

Let me in, the eyes seemed to say, *please*.

He'd always heard coyotes traveled in packs, why was this one alone? Harry scanned the yard but could see nothing that indicated there were more of them anywhere nearby.

In a deliberately slow move, the coyote turned and looked back at the dark woods. The wind picked up just then, spraying rain against the French doors with a dull drumming sound. As the moisture trickled down and ran off, the coyote came back into focus. It had moved closer and was now standing on the patio, its head bowed but eyes raised and locked on Harry once again. A soft high-pitched whine escaped the animal.

It was terrified.

Harry was far from an expert on coyotes but was relatively certain nothing in these parts hunted them. Although coyotes were not originally indigenous to the area, from the moment they'd been introduced some years before they'd become the top predators and sat pretty much at the summit of the wildlife food chain. Just the same, something was spooking the hell out of this animal, and whatever it was, it obviously wasn't that far away. But what in God's name could frighten a coyote to the point where it abandoned its natural instincts and sought refuge *inside* the nearest house?

Please, its eyes begged, *I won't hurt you, just let me in.*

In that strange moment they didn't seem so different, Harry thought. There was an inexplicable connection, a sudden harmony between two beings caught in a storm beyond their control, bonding out of necessity against something else, some...*other*...a foreign darkness that threatened them both and that neither could hope to survive alone.

As if in a trance, Harry felt his hand drop away from the light switch and move slowly toward the lock on the French doors.

Hurry, the coyote's eyes screamed.

A scratching in his throat broke his concentration, and suddenly Harry was attacked by another coughing fit. Bracing himself against the wall with one hand, he doubled over and hacked for what seemed an eternity.

Heart racing and his flesh now covered in clammy perspiration, he was finally able to draw a breath without coughing. But his nose had filled up again and his headache was worse than ever, slamming his temples in time with the rapid beat of his heart. A series of images fired through his mind, bringing him back to the nightmares he'd had the last time he slept, this time revealing odd flashes of what appeared to be a small, disfigured and heavily bandaged person at the far end of a dark corridor, thrashing about in the throes of seizure.

"What the hell," he mumbled, fear rising. He massaged his temples and concentrated on driving the visions from his head.

The pain and images slowly dissipated, but a residue of indistinct and puzzling dread remained.

Harry looked to the French doors, to the patio.

The coyote was gone.

2

By morning the rain had turned to a slow but steady drizzle. Dull light pushed through and eventually overtook the darkness, but the sun was nowhere to be found, leaving the sky an uninspired and dreary gray. The constant sounds of trickling rainwater and runoff echoed through the house like a bevy of faucets, and it felt markedly colder throughout the downstairs. Unsure if it had truly gotten colder in the house or if he was simply experiencing heightened chills due to a fever, Harry rummaged through the bathroom medicine cabinet until he found a thermometer, rinsed it off, shook it down, then took his temperature. It logged in at just under 102. He checked the thermostat in the den. It was set at sixty-five and the temperature read sixty-eight. He cranked it up to seventy.

Harry had now gone two nights without sleep and his nerves were frayed. Coupled with the flu symptoms, he found himself on the verge of physical collapse, and emotionally he wasn't faring much better. Of course the episode with the coyote hadn't helped either. He'd searched the yard for several minutes, moving from window to window in the hopes of locating it, but hadn't seen the animal again. The whole thing, combined with the disturbing and confusing images from his nightmare, had rattled him. And though the memories of his dream were at best disjointed and indistinct, he still couldn't get the image of that terrified coyote out of his head.

And still no word from Kelly.

Well, since today's Saturday at least I don't have to call in sick, he thought. Of course that also meant getting hold of his doctor might prove more difficult as well. He hesitated, found himself in the kitchen. Apparently he'd been wandering aimlessly about the house. Wait…it *was* Saturday, right? His mind moved in slow-motion, as if in a dream state where nothing was quite certain. *Stop and think a minute.* He squinted at his watch, focusing on the tiny square on the face that revealed the day and date. SAT | 6. *Right, Saturday, November 6th.* He nodded, tapping the watch as if to confirm it once and for all. Harry compared the time with the kitchen wall clock to be certain he'd seen it correctly. *Eight-thirty? Already?* Didn't seem possible. Last time he'd checked it was about four in the morning. Or was it five? *When did the incident with the coyote happen?* He sighed, his mind a blurred and jumbled mess.

Having not had a coughing spell in a while, he was confident he could string a few sentences together without hacking his brains out, so he decided to put a call in to his doctor. After searching the downstairs for several minutes Harry finally remembered the cordless phone was exactly where he'd left it: in his robe pocket. He angrily punched the numbers to his doctor's office, and as expected, got the answering service. A woman on the line promised to forward his message but couldn't guarantee the call would be returned before Monday.

"This is urgent," he explained. "I need some antibiotics or something."

"I'll give Doctor Poole the message," the woman assured him.

"Tell him I'm running a fever and I've got a horrible cough that's keeping me up all night. I haven't slept in two days and I need a call back today, I—"

"I'll let the doctor know you called, Mr. Fremont." The woman's tone shifted from sympathy to irritation. "But I can't force him to call you back."

"I wasn't suggesting you could." *Stay calm. If you blow up you'll start coughing.* "I just want him to understand it's serious, OK?"

"If you don't get a call within an hour or so I suggest you seek treatment at your local emergency room."

Yeah, great idea, I can barely stand. Driving a car should be interesting. "Sure," he said. "Thanks."

He disconnected, made a pot of coffee, then retrieved the number from the pad on the fridge, begrudgingly put his glasses on so he could see it, then called Kelly's hotel. Despite his exhaustion, he could feel his body making subtle adjustments to function as best it could without sleep. Though he remained shaky, something akin to a second wind kicked in just as it had the day before.

"Good morning, Great Night Suites."

That same patronizing voice—did this guy work twenty-four hours a day?

"Suite 136."

The phone rang. And rang.

"I'm sorry, sir, that suite's not answering. Would you like voicemail?"

"Please."

"*The party you're trying to reach is not available at this time,*" an electronic voice explained, "*please leave a message after the tone. When you're finished, hit pound for more options, or simply hang up.*"

An unusually long dead space was finally interrupted by a beep.

"Kel, it's me. Where the hell are you? I've been trying to reach you since last night. Haven't been able to catch you in your room and I can't seem to get through to your cell." Harry hesitated as a tickle in his throat threatened to awaken his cough. He closed his eyes and concentrated until it passed. When he reopened them he saw something resembling the dark silhouette of a person moving along the edge of his peripheral vision. He turned quickly, but it was gone. "I'm starting to get worried and I'm sick as a dog here," he said through a sigh, "I haven't slept since you left. I put a call in to the doctor this morning. Anyway, call me back when you get this so I know you're all right." Harry hit the pound key and listened to the various options offered. He chose to replay and listen to the message he'd just left and was shocked to hear how strange his voice sounded. Much deeper than normal and very scratchy, his breathing pronounced but short.

He delivered the message, hung up, and then just for the hell of it tried her cell again. The same message about the provider being unavailable answered. He disconnected and dropped the cordless back into his robe pocket. *Maybe she's in the shower. Or she could've gone out for breakfast or even had an early morning meeting.* But why wasn't her cell working? Could the provider really be down this long? He could never remember that happening before.

Harry knew a reasonable explanation for all this was probable, but he didn't feel good about any of it. Nothing seemed quite right. Everything was just slightly out of kilter, and it was getting worse.

Maybe I'm just being paranoid.

He poured himself a mug of coffee and stared at the rising steam as if it were an exotic magic trick.

Sleep. I've got to get some sleep so I can think clearly.

Leaving the mug and his eyeglasses behind, Harry returned to the den.

* * *

Silence, in and of itself, had never frightened Harry, but there was a certain kind of silence he'd always found particularly unsettling. A heavy silence different than its brethren, he'd experienced it only a handful of times in his life, but the moment it descended upon him there was no mistaking it. Otherworldly somehow, it hung in the air as a tangible thing, jarring as the echo of whispers in an otherwise empty room. Because unlike other silences, there was something *within* this silence, something hidden, calculated and purposeful.

Draped in such silence, one was not alone.

It was precisely that brand of silence from which Harry emerged. Until then he'd been absorbed by the stillness of it all, and as the stupor of uncertainty lifted there came a realization that he'd been void of conscious thought for some time. The question was: How long? *Was I asleep?* He turned his wrist, held his watch up before his eyes. Barely five minutes had elapsed.

Again, his mind was littered with fleeting glimpses from an old nightmare. Dark hallways…the feeling of being pursued…agonizing pain…a small and horrifyingly disfigured and bandaged figure flailing about—a child, or perhaps a dwarf—he couldn't be sure…the moon in the night sky...

Dejected, he clicked the TV remote, but all he got was a blue screen with a series of yellow lines scrawling across the bottom and the words: SEARCHING FOR SIGNAL. *Satellite's down. Perfect.* Harry shut the television off, tossed the remote aside and reached for a tissue from the box on the coffee table. Sitting on the edge of the recliner, he braced himself for the cough that was sure to follow, and blew his nose. To his surprise and delight, his cough remained dormant, so he carefully sat back, got comfortable in the recliner and took in the view through the large bay window on the wall to his right. *If I concentrate on something long enough*, he told himself, *my eyes are bound to get heavy and I'll have to sleep.*

Through the drizzling rain a slight breeze rustled leaves in the front yard, skipping them across the pavement before they tumbled out of sight, beyond the scope of the window. The remaining cluster were swept up and swirled to form a small funnel, whirling about and suspended above the street like a mini tornado. *Something almost magical about that*, he thought. Yet there was nothing whimsical about watching these yellow and brown leaves that still littered the area, remnants of the preceding October that would in a matter of days cease to exist entirely. Instead there seemed something menacing about it, because it went deeper than dead leaves provoked to dance by a chilly November wind. The whole world out there struck him as abnormally ominous. *Out there*, he thought, as if these walls and windows separating *out there* from *in here* might protect him if someone or something really wanted in. It was all little more than an illusion, wasn't it? A deceit people told themselves so they'd believe they were safe and sound in their own homes when they were really anything but.

What peculiar thoughts to have…

The funnel dissipated and the leaves fell harmlessly to the ground.

Harry tried to remember happier times here. Like when Garret was little and together they'd rake leaves into giant piles, then dive into them and begin the process all over again. Funny how something so silly and cliché could be that powerful and moving in memory, so special. Their son was such a carefree and good-natured child then, full of life and always so happy—laughing and smiling—and never more contented than when spending an afternoon with his parents. Then Garret hit his teens and it all changed. He was still a good kid, and Harry and Garret remained relatively close, but it wasn't the same and never would be again. His little boy had become a young man and moved on to things far more important than lighthearted afternoons spent jumping into leaves with his old man.

Kelly was happier in those days too, he thought. Back then her job was important to her but didn't consume her life the way it did now. She was closer to the woman he'd married, and he supposed he was closer to the man she'd married, but overall she'd changed far more than he had. If nothing else, Harry was steady and consistent. Perhaps at times infuriatingly so, but nevertheless, Kelly was the one who had become someone else in the last few years, not him. *No, wait. That's wrong. That's unfair. Not someone else, just…*he thought about it awhile, eyes heavy and his mind so hindered he wasn't quite able to find the words and meanings it was searching for.

It's working. I think I'm falling asleep.

His eyes slowly slid shut, but just as he thought he might finally drift off, a tickle deep in his throat signaled another round of coughing was on its way.

He opened his eyes and tried to draw a slow, deliberate breath. Halfway through he lurched forward and began coughing uncontrollably. With each barking cough his head pounded and his chest seared with pain, and by the time he'd brought some more phlegm up and spat it into a tissue he felt like someone had worked him over with a baseball bat. He wanted—needed—so desperately to sleep, but couldn't slip away without the damn cough noticing. Chest still wheezing but the scratch in his throat gone for the time being, he sat back, blinked his eyes until he'd regained some focus and tried his best to relax and remain calm. *Don't get upset. Keep concentrating. Sooner or later you'll sleep.*

He returned his gaze to the bay window.

Beyond his front yard and the narrow paved street separating them, Rose Bassinger's house sat on a lot directly across from his own. A small colonial, it was impeccably maintained, as was her yard. Rose was the second owner of the property and had lived there for the last seven years, but Harry and Kelly had never really gotten to know her that well. They knew her enough to say hello and to visit occasionally, their conversations usually small talk exchanges about the weather or, more recently, town politics and issues facing them both. But while their relationship over the years had been friendly and cordial, for the most part, it remained superficial. In her middle forties, Rose stood about 5'3", had long blonde hair, hazel eyes and wore glasses. Though she had occasional visitors she mostly kept to herself and was a good neighbor, quiet but friendly, kind, and always available if you needed anything. She commuted to Boston, where she worked in the Medieval History Department at a small college, but had recently told Kelly she'd taken a new position in her native Baltimore City, Maryland and would be moving back there once she'd vacated the house. The only other resident still living on the cul-de-sac, her house appeared unoccupied at the moment. Harry's eyes shifted to the driveway. Her car was gone.

He dabbed his nose with a fresh tissue and gazed at Rose's house awhile. Just as his eyes again grew heavy, he noticed something strange. There, on the roof, a large black smudge. He couldn't tell exactly what he was seeing, but whatever it was looked wildly out of place, perched there just above the gutter on the sloped side of roof facing his house. Harry sat forward, rubbed his eyes. *What the hell is that?* Considerably darker than the gray shingles, it stood out against the lighter backdrop of roof and sky, and looked almost like a big garbage bag sitting there. But that didn't make any sense, why would Rose have a bag of trash on her roof?

Harry struggled to his feet and went to the bay window for a better look. The rain was appreciably lighter than the night before, but coupled with his bleary vision it still made discerning detail far more of a challenge than it should've been. He leaned closer to the window, squinting to see through the blurry, rain-spotted glass. The distance between his house and Rose's was quite limited, but he still couldn't determine what the black smudge was.

Until it moved.

A man squatting at the edge of the roof had just then adjusted his position. Dressed entirely in black—black pants, a black sweater, black shoes or boots and what was most likely a black knit hat—he crept slightly higher on the roof, limbs set and moving now at awkward angles, like a crabwalk. Then he again went still and returned to his squatted position. He appeared to be facing in Harry's direction, but the rain and distance conspired to keep his facial features out-of-focus.

Harry backed a few steps away from the window and moved a little to the side in the hopes of better concealing himself. Odds were the man couldn't see him anyway, but Harry wanted to be sure. As his heart took off like a shot, he searched his mind for answers. Rose had satellite television just like he did. Maybe it was a repairman up there, disconnecting the dish before her move. But there was no truck in the driveway or anywhere in sight, and the man's clothes looked nothing like the uniforms the satellite guys usually wore. Then there was the unusual stance, the peculiar squat, and why was the man at the edge of the slope? There was nothing else there, no wires or any reason for someone to be crouched on that particular stretch of roof. Even if the man was doing something wrong, it seemed a ridiculous place to hide or lie in wait, he was in plain view. If his plan was to break into the house, there were far easier methods than climbing across the roof, and since there were no windows or points of entry anywhere near his position, that made no sense either. Harry quickly scanned the periphery of the house. No ladders, no ropes. How had he even gotten up there? Maybe he'd propped a ladder against the back of the house, gotten onto the roof that way, then climbed up and over the peak and down to the edge of the slope. But even if that explained how he'd gotten there, it still didn't explain *why.*

What are you doing up there?

The phone rang, startling the hell out of him. He'd begun to cough even before he pulled the cordless from his robe pocket. Pacing about, he coughed his way through the assault and answered the phone the instant it weakened. "Hello?"

"Harry? Tim Poole."

"Doc, thanks for calling me back."

"Answering service said you were having some trouble. You don't sound anywhere near the top of your game, chief."

"I feel awful."

"There's some nasty stuff out there right now. Give me a quick rundown."

"I don't know if it's just a bad cold, the flu or what." Harry carefully cleared his throat, moved back to the edge of the bay window and peered out. The man was still there, he hadn't moved. "One minute I'm freezing and the next I'm sweating. I've got chills, my nose is running, I've got this horrible postnasal drip, a cough that just won't quit and—"

"Bringing anything up with the cough?"

"Yes, some phlegm now and then."

"Clear or colored?"

"Mostly brown."

"Any blood?"

"No."

"And the discharge from your nose?"

"Mostly clear but yellow now and then."

"Any fever?"

"One hundred and two, last time I checked."

"Which was when?"

His mind froze. Had he taken his temperature this morning, or was that last night? He couldn't be sure. "Sorry, I—I think it was this morning but I— Doc, I haven't slept in two days. The cough's kept me up. The minute I lay back or even try to lay down it kicks in and feels like my chest is coming apart."

"Any trouble breathing?"

"Not really no, but my chest is wheezing quite a bit."

"Any chest pain when you're not coughing?"

"No."

"OK, I'm going to phone in a few prescriptions for you," the doctor said. "I want to get you on a round of antibiotics right away, and I'm also going to call in some cough syrup with codeine. Couple shots of that should be enough to suppress the cough for several hours, and with the codeine, trust me, you'll sleep. Also, I think it's a good idea to get you an inhaler. Nothing serious, but it'll help keep your lungs open. Otherwise get as much rest as you can. Drink plenty of fluids but try to stay away from anything that might produce more phlegm, and make sure you keep an eye on that fever. If it gets any higher, I want you to call me right away, OK? I'll call these scripts in pronto, so they should be ready for you later this morning. Now listen, even if you begin to feel better, I want you to give my office a call first thing Monday morning. Tell them I spoke to you over the weekend and want to see you immediately and they'll get you in. We'll get a listen to your lungs, and if need be, a quick x-ray to make sure we're not dealing with pneumonia. Now get some rest. We'll talk Monday."

"OK, thanks for getting back to me," Harry said; eyes still trained on the man across the street. "I really appreciate it."

"You bet."

The line disconnected. Harry continued watching the man on the roof. Why was he just squatting there in the rain? If he was up there for some purpose why hadn't he gotten to it?

He called Kenny Pak. They worked together and had been friends for years, and although he and Kelly had other friends, Harry was closer to Kenny than any of the others and knew he could count on him.

Just before the call connected, a chill shot through him and an odd spike of pressure-like pain blossomed across his forehead, spread out like a spider web over the bridge of his nose and down beneath his eyes. "Hey, it's me."

"Holy cow, you sound awful, no wonder you called in sick Friday."

"Got hit with the flu or something, haven't slept in two days and Kelly's in San Diego on a business trip all weekend."

"That sucks."

"I'll be fine, but could you do me a favor? I just talked to my doctor and he's calling in some prescriptions. Could you pick them up for me this morning? I'm too sick to drive, Ken."

"Of course, sure, uh…" A rustling sound, like he'd quickly put his hand over the receiver, then just as quickly removed it. "Give me about half an hour?"

"Sure, that'd be great."

"OK, where am I going?"

"The CVS on Main Street."

"Do you need anything else while I'm out?"

"I don't think so, I…" Harry focused on the man on the roof again. He'd never taken his eyes off him, he hadn't thought, yet it was as if he'd vanished and just then appeared again. "I ah…"

"Harry, are you all right?"

"Just exhausted, I literally haven't had any sleep in two days, and I—Kenny it's the weirdest thing— there's a guy on the roof across the street."

"A guy on the roof?"

"I'm watching him right now. He's dressed all in black and he's sitting on Rose's roof."

"OK."

"He's just...*sitting* there...in the rain."

"Maybe he's working on something."

"That's just it, he's not. He's been up there awhile. Doesn't move, doesn't do anything. I'm not sure but it looks like he's staring at my house."

"Call over there and ask Rose about it."

"She's not home."

"And he's just sitting there, huh?"

"Yeah, I'm going to call the cops, have them check it out."

"I would, better safe than sorry."

"Right," Harry said softly. His chest rose, fell, wheezed.

"OK, well let me go, I've got a few things I have to get done and then I'll pick up your prescriptions and be right over."

"Thanks, Kenny, I owe you one."

The moment Harry hung up a blanket of fear fell about him. Being on the telephone—hearing someone else's voice through the line and knowing they could hear his—made him feel safer, connected to someone who could help if need be. Now he was alone with the sounds of trickling rain, an otherwise silent house...and the man in black across the street.

Another gust of wind hit, rolling in from the forest behind the house and spraying rainwater about. The house creaked and moaned from unseen corners as the wind reached the other side of the street and shook the bushes in Rose's front yard. Harry raised his eyes to the roof and the man still squatting there.

As if irritated by the wind, the figure in black rapidly ascended the slope and vanished over the summit to the far side of the roof, scurrying like an insect on all fours.

Harry swallowed, coughed slightly but was spared another fit. A wave of chills throttled him, but he was relatively certain they had nothing to do with his flu. Mesmerized by what he'd just seen, he stared out the bay window, phone in hand and mouth dangling open in surprise. The way the man moved up that roof, it seemed...*inhuman.* People didn't move like that, not in that crablike position, and certainly not with that amount of agility and speed.

He dialed 911.

"Nine-one-one," a female voice responded, "what is your emergency?"

"Yes, I—ah—OK, I know this is going to sound strange but there's a man on my neighbor's roof." Harry stopped, clenched shut his eyes. The tickle in his throat was threatening again. "And I'm not sure what he's doing up there but it looks very suspicious."

"Is your neighbor at home?"

"I don't believe so, no." He did his best to steady his voice, to control the horrible scratching deep in his throat by speaking slowly and cautiously, but each word threatened to release the next wave of coughing. "And there aren't any repair vehicles in the driveway or on the street. I'm sure there could be a reasonable explanation but it seems odd. He's been up there awhile now."

"Is he attempting to break in or cause damage to the property?"

"I'm not—I don't know—I'm not sure. He's just sort of sitting there."

"You're on 5 Revere Place, correct?"

"Yes." *All that information must come up automatically when you call*, he thought. "My name's Harry Fremont. The man's on the roof of the house directly across from mine, number four. Rose Bassinger's the property owner."

"Can you spell that for me?"

Harry did.

"Is the man alone, Mr. Fremont?"

"Yes, far as I can tell."

"Can you give me a description?"

No longer able to hold it at bay, the cough took over and savaged him. "I'm sorry," he gasped once it was over.

"You sound good and sick," the operator said.

"I've got the flu."

"I'm sorry to hear that." The sounds of fingers tapping a keyboard filtered through the phone. "Mr. Fremont, I'm dispatching a car to your location. Can you provide me with a description to pass on to the officer en route?"

"Definitely looks male, and he's dressed completely in black. It's hard to tell height or weight because he's squatting. He never stood up, but he looks average size. Not huge but not tiny either. Just a minute ago he was on the sloped side of the roof facing my house, now he's gone to the other side, the back side of Rose's house."

"So you're no longer able to see him at this time?"

"Correct."

"I'll advise the officer the man has gone to the back side of the roof." More sounds of typing followed before she spoke again. "Were you able to see if the man was carrying anything?"

"I don't think he was, not that I could see anyway."

"Did he appear to be armed in any way?"

"He didn't appear to be—I didn't see any weapons— but I can't be sure."

"Any other specific description you can provide? Hair color?"

Harry angled his view so he could see down the street. No sign of a car yet. "I couldn't tell. He's wearing what looks like a knit hat."

"Race?"

"I couldn't make out any specific facial features but he's white."

"Approximate age?"

"No way for me to know but this is an adult, not a kid."

"All right, Mr. Fremont, an officer will be there momentarily. Stay by your phone. There's a good chance one or more officers will want to talk with you further. Do you feel in danger at this time, would you like me to stay on the line with you until the officer arrives on the scene?"

"No, I'm fine, but thank you."

He had just hung up when he saw a police cruiser turn onto the cul-de-sac and begin a slow creep toward the end of the street. The man was still on the other side of the roof and out of sight, so Harry dropped the phone back into his robe pocket, folded his arms over his chest and waited to see what was going to happen next. In all the years he'd lived there this was the first time he'd seen a police car on his street, and he couldn't help but find it a little exciting.

Bad boys, bad boys, whacha gonna do?

The cruiser pulled across the mouth of Rose's driveway, the roof lights kicked on and a burly thirtysomething officer in a police-issue raincoat stepped out. He considered the house a moment, said something into a unit clipped to his shoulder, then moved cautiously up the driveway, one hand resting on the butt of his weapon as the other pulled a nightstick free of his belt. Moving slowly but deliberately, the policeman strode up the driveway to the side of the house, then disappeared around back.

Heart racing, Harry watched, waited and rifled through several possible scenarios to come. He fully expected the cop to return with the man in black in handcuffs, a burglar or maybe worse waiting for Rose to come home, his hideous plans foiled. But several minutes came and went with no sign of the officer or anyone else. What if the two were in the midst of a scuffle? For all Harry knew they could be rolling around in the backyard, fighting for the policeman's gun or—

Wait, there he is.

The officer emerged from the opposite side of Rose's house, head cocked and studying the roof as he went. Once he'd made a full circle back to the head of the driveway, he spoke again into his shoulder unit, then approached the front door and rang the bell. When no one answered, he returned his nightstick to its position on his utility belt and started toward Harry's house.

Wrapping his robe tightly around him, Harry cinched the belt best he could and hurried to the door, opening it before the policeman had reached it.

There wasn't much left of the rain, the drizzle had become even lighter than earlier, but the world was still drenched. The houses, the trees, the street, his car, everything glistened and dripped with rainwater. Set beneath a pale sky, everything had a curiously synthetic aura, coated in its luminous sheen much the way plastic fruit looks authentic at first glance, but upon close inspection is too clean and shiny, too perfect to be real. It was also colder out than Harry had suspected, the air thinner and sharper than typical early November.

"Mr. Fremont?" the officer asked while still several feet away.

"Yes." Harry gave a tentative wave. "Hello."

The policeman continued up the driveway, acknowledging him with a quick and rather officious nod. The closer he got the more familiar he looked. Schooner Bluffs was still a relatively small town, and while Harry didn't know anyone on the force personally, many of the cops had been with the department for decades. This officer was no exception; Harry remembered seeing him countless times around town over the years. About six feet tall, with a large square head, small dark eyes and black hair styled in a flattop right out of the 1950s, he was a beefy man with arms like a power lifter and the tree-stump legs of an NFL fullback. Once he reached the door he extended an enormous hand concealed in a black leather glove.

"I'm Officer Nicoletto."

Harry watched his hand vanish into the glove.

"Harry Fremont."

"You put the call in to 911 about the man on the roof?"

"Yes sir."

Nicoletto hesitated at the doorway, noticing for the first time how sick Harry appeared. He released his hand and casually wiped the glove on the outside of his thigh. "Looks like you've got the flu."

Now there's some astounding investigative work. "Yeah, looks like."

"I had a bout with it last year myself. Not fun. Not fun at all." Nicoletto swept some rainwater from his flattop and motioned over his shoulder to Rose's house. "At any rate, I've conducted a thorough search of the property and I've observed nothing out of the ordinary."

Harry sniffled. He'd always found police-speak humorous. No one talked like cops did. No matter what they said it always came out sounding like they were reading from an official report. "No sign of him, huh?"

"None." He removed a small pad and pen from one of his pockets. "The description dispatch gave me was a bit sketchy, can you describe this person?"

"I didn't get a very good look at his face." Harry shivered against the cold. "Listen, would you mind coming inside? I'm freezing."

Nicoletto stepped into the short foyer just inside the front door, remaining on the small rug there as Harry closed the door, then stepped around and back in front of him. "I was a little surprised when the call came in," he said with the air of caution policemen always have. "I didn't realize anyone still lived out here."

"We're the last ones left, Rose and us."

Nicoletto raised a thick eyebrow. "Us?"

"My wife Kelly and I."

He wrote something on his pad. "Did your wife observe this man as well?"

"No, she's out of town on business."

His pen kept moving. "Are you home alone?"

"I am."

"You're the only one who observed the man then?"

"Yes."

"And you and," he glanced at his pad, "*Ms. Bassinger* are the only people still living on the street at this time? The other residences have been vacated?"

"That's correct. By January we'll be gone too."

"I see."

"Commercial development wins again."

The officer finally looked up from his pad, his expression shifted like he'd just then realized he was in the presence of a fanatical anarchist. "Sometimes these things happen in a free country with a free market."

"You don't say?" Harry nervously wiped his nose with the back of his sleeve. He was in no mood for a lecture.

"Well I assume you sold your home and it wasn't stolen from you."

Harry forced a smile. "Anyway, about the man I reported…"

Nicoletto watched him a few seconds before responding, as if gauging whether Harry was going to be a problem. "You saw this man on the roof?"

"Yes, he was there just before you got here." Harry again described the man as best he could and relayed to the officer exactly what he'd seen, from the moment he'd first noticed him until he'd scurried away over the summit of the roof.

Nicoletto took notes and listened intently, speaking again only once Harry had finished. "Did he attempt to burglarize the premises?"

"Not that I saw. He just sat there." Harry took a few steps back, coughed, pulled a tissue from his sweatpants and spit up into it. "Jesus. Sorry."

The cop offered a dramatic sigh. "All through now?"

Embarrassed but too exhausted to worry about it, Harry stuffed the tissue into his robe pocket. "Yeah, I—sorry, this cough just—"

"Mr. Fremont, are you certain it was a person you saw on the roof?"

"Yes sir, I am."

"You couldn't be mistaken?"

"It was definitely a person."

"Do you wear eyeglasses or contact lenses?"

"Glasses, but they're only for reading."

"Uh-huh. Do you know the whereabouts of Ms. Bassinger at this time?"

"No. She works in Boston, but far as I know she doesn't go in weekends. She's probably shopping or running errands or something, I have no idea."

Nicoletto turned to the bay window. "Does she live alone?"

"Yes."

"Could someone be visiting?"

"Her *roof?*"

The cop glared at him.

"It's possible," Harry conceded, "but I don't think anyone's staying with her at the moment."

"But you're not certain?"

"Well it's not like she alerts us whenever she has a houseguest."

Nicoletto was back to jotting notes. "As I mentioned, I made a thorough search of the premises. There's no sign of an intruder or trespasser. All windows and doors appear intact and undamaged. The cellar bulkhead is locked and intact as well. I looked through a few windows and observed no sign of anyone inside. I also observed stickers on the front and rear doors indicating the house is equipped with an alarm, so I had dispatch contact the alarm company. They report no calls from the house or any disturbances to doors or windows. Nothing's been compromised, far as they're concerned, and my investigation supports that."

"Right, but I never saw the man inside the house."

Nicoletto flashed a condescending smile. "Only on the roof."

"That's right."

After another lengthy sigh he said, "The problem I'm having with someone on the roof, Mr. Fremont, is that first of all there's no ladder or any means for a person to gain access. Secondly, due to the rain the ground is extremely wet and soft out there. I found no tracks or any disturbances that might indicate someone jumped from the roof to the lawn or at any point had the feet of a ladder or something similar pressed into the earth." He flipped closed his pad and returned it along with the pen to his pocket. "The only other way someone could get on the roof was if they were already inside the house and crawled out a window. Because there's no evidence to indicate someone jumped off, it's safe to assume that if in fact someone was on that roof, then they'd have to vacate it in the same manner they gained access to it in the first place, and that's through a window. Were someone inside the premises unauthorized, the alarm would've been tripped. That hasn't happened. You follow?"

"I'm telling you what I saw, officer."

"Maybe it was something else. A large bird maybe, and at a quick glance you mistook it for a person."

"How do you mistake a bird for a person?"

Nicoletto assumed the smug posture of a man unaccustomed to being argued with, and was about to respond when a burst of static sounded from his shoulder unit. He gripped the unit, quickly mumbled into it, then returned his attention to Harry. "Are you on any medications?"

"Medications?"

"With the flu and all."

"My doctor just called in some prescriptions, but no, I'm not on anything at the moment, unless you want to count aspirin."

Nicoletto drifted toward the front door, various keys and items on his belt jingling and clacking. "You look awfully tired, when's the last time you slept?"

"Couple days," he admitted softly.

"Well there you go. Mr. Fremont, sleep deprivation can cause all sorts of side-effects, it often results in—"

"Listen to me," Harry snapped, this time ignoring the warning scratch in his throat, "I'm sick and I'm exhausted. I have better things to do than to waste your time or mine, do you understand me? I saw a man on the roof and I called it in because I thought that was the right thing to do under the circumstances. I don't know who he was or what the hell he was doing up there, but I do know I wasn't hallucinating, I didn't dream it, and I didn't see it through some haze of narcotics. I saw a man. A man on the roof dressed in black. *You* follow?"

"I'll make a full report, sir, and I'll have dispatch get in touch with Ms. Bassinger to let her know we were here, and why. Maybe she can shed some light on this. Either way, the property is secure at this time. Should you see this *man* again, give us a call and we'll check it out." The cop opened the door, letting in a gust of cold air. "If there's nothing else…"

"No, nothing else, thank you for stopping by, Officer."

"For what it's worth, I see people suffering from lack of sleep all the time, and I can tell you it's a real killer. You'd be surprised how many vehicular accidents are the results of operator exhaustion. Without sufficient sleep the mind and body weaken, and both can play some nasty tricks on you." He looked back over his broad shoulder. "Try to get some sleep."

Harry nodded, holding in his cough as best he could. "Thanks, I'll do that."

The minute he had the door closed Harry doubled-over, the cough exploded from him and he hacked until his throat was raw and his head was pounding. When it was over he staggered back to the den for another tissue and collapsed into the recliner, exhausted. Through the bay window he saw that the cruiser was still parked at the end of Rose's driveway. Nicoletto was behind the wheel holding a metal clipboard and writing up what Harry assumed was his report. After a few minutes the police car made a U-turn and was gone.

Harry blew his nose, careful not to further irritate the raw skin beneath his nostrils with the tissue. He rested awhile, then went to the kitchen and grabbed a bottle of water from the refrigerator. The cold liquid felt good on his sore throat but did little to make him feel better as he was still annoyed with the conversation he'd had with Officer Nicoletto. He returned to the den, stood before the bay window and watched Rose's house awhile. No man on the roof, no coyote in the yard, nothing out of the ordinary.

An empty street, a quiet house. A gentle rain.

3

“When you’re sick nothing does the trick like chicken soup. ”Kenny popped the plastic lid from the Styrofoam container and slid it across the countertop to Harry. “Here, it’ll make you feel better.”

Harry struggled up onto one of the stools at the island in the center of the kitchen and leaned over the steaming container. “Thanks, looks really good,” he sighed, “but you didn’t have to do that.”

“After I picked up your prescriptions I had to drop off a couple suits at the dry cleaner anyway. Scully’s is right there on the corner.” Kenny rested his arms on the island countertop between them. “They’ve got great soups, figured you could use some.”

“My damn nose is so stuffed up I can barely smell it.” He removed a white plastic spoon and a folded paper napkin from the cellophane wrap it had come in. “Here’s hoping I can taste it.”

“When’s the last time you had something to eat?” Harry had to stop and think. When was the last time he’d eaten something? Was it the day before?

“Yesterday, I think. Yesterday morning.”

"Eat," Kenny said, motioning to the soup. "You look horrible."

"Trust me, I feel worse than I look."

"I should get you to the hospital then. You're probably dead."

"If I could just get some sleep." Harry dipped the spoon into the broth. "The doctor said the codeine should help. We'll see."

"Codeine always helps. When's Kelly due home?"

"Not until late Monday night." He took a sip of soup. It was warm and tasty and soothed his sore throat. "Oh wow, that *is* good."

"Enjoy." Kenny pushed his eyeglasses up higher on the bridge of his nose with his index finger. Three years younger than Harry, he was always meticulously groomed and neat, from his short, no-nonsense businessman's haircut to his small but trim physique, when it came to Kenny Pak everything was always in place and looking sharp. Even in his casual weekend attire—freshly pressed chinos, leather tasseled loafers and a crisp oxford beneath a v-neck sweater, he looked hopelessly formal. Oddly, his rather uptight appearance in no way reflected his personality, which was actually quite laid back, relaxed and peppered with a dryly cynical sense of humor. A second-generation grandson of Korean immigrants, Kenny had lived his entire life in Massachusetts, and resided a few towns over from Schooner Bluffs with his wife Rhonda and their two children. He and Harry had worked together for years and been close friends for more than a decade, but because their wives were friendly but not close and because Kenny's children were considerably younger than Garret, they rarely socialized as couples or families. "I can't stay long, though," he said. "We have to drop Sandra at dance class, then take Tommy to the mall for sneakers. You should see these things he wants. They cost more than a decent used car."

"It's best you don't hang around. You don't want to catch this crud."

"I'm not worried about it. You know me, I never get sick."

"I can't remember the last time I was this sick either but it got me. Just hit me out of nowhere. I felt fine and then all of a sudden—bang."

"Probably stress. High levels can compromise the immune system, you know. That's a fact. Seriously, in the long-term it can kill you."

"Speaking of stress, did I miss anything on Friday?"

"Bruce in Accounting threw a tantrum because apparently no one's been filling out those new expense forms correctly. He was storming the hallways yelling at everybody and waving the forms around like a maniac. Then of course Rodney did his Bruce impersonation—you know, the one where he pulls his pants way up under his armpits—and nobody could stop laughing. Let's see, what else. Gretchen wore that white blouse without a bra again. That was cool. Other than that it was quiet." Kenny shrugged. "You know how it is around the office these days. Everybody's waiting for the ax to fall."

Harry nodded and ate more soup.

"Hey, so what happened with the guy on the roof?" he asked as if he'd just remembered.

"A policeman came by but the guy was already gone, couldn't find any trace of him. I'm pretty sure the cop thought I was nuts." A headache still lingered behind his eyes, but the soup was warming him, chasing away the chills, and the broth was at least temporarily easing his cough and cutting the phlegm. "But the weirdest things have been going on. I mean, I know I'm a little out of it from being sick and not sleeping and everything, but I'm telling you, strange stuff's been happening around here."

"Like what?"

Between swallows of soup, Harry told him about the curious behavior of the coyote the night before, relayed the entire story of the man in black across the street, and then explained his inability to reach Kelly either at her hotel or on her cell phone.

Kenny pushed away from the island, stood up straight and slid his hands into his pants pockets. Harry knew this body language well. He saw it at work whenever Kenny had to explain something. The only time he ever put his hands in his pockets was when he was thinking, processing something and attempting to come to some conclusion. "OK," he finally said, "first of all, the coyote could very well be rabid or sick or something. You should probably call Animal Control and let them know."

"Have you ever seen the guys from Animal Control in this town? They're like something out of a Pink Panther cartoon. And that coyote wasn't sick, Ken. He was terrified."

"Sick, scared—whatever—this is a wild animal we're talking about, a wild animal behaving abnormally. You should probably report it. If it is rabid it could hurt somebody." He paced about the kitchen. "As for the guy on the roof across the street, you said it looked like he was watching your house, right? So maybe he planned to rob the place and realized you'd seen him."

"But the cop said—"

"OK what's the explanation then? The guy appeared and disappeared on the roof magically? He can fly? Schooner Bluffs cops aren't exactly Scotland Yard material, man. The guy just took off. Either that or you hallucinated the whole thing, your choice."

Harry finished up the soup, wiped his mouth. "It wasn't a hallucination."

"Then there was a guy on the roof. He either saw you and realized he'd been spotted and took off, or maybe he just changed his mind. Who knows? Look, I'd be freaked out if there were somebody climbing around on houses in my neighborhood too, but I really don't think it warrants notifying *Unsolved Mysteries*, do you? If you see him again, call the cops."

"What about Kelly?"

"Her cell phone being down is a bit unusual, but providers do experience technical difficulties from time to time, it's not unheard of. I'm sure whatever the problem is it'll be resolved quickly if it hasn't been already. And from the sounds, Kelly hasn't been in her hotel room much. She's there on business, right? So she's obviously busy and you've just missed her the two times you called. I'm not trying to be a tool, but am I missing something here or is this just not that complicated?"

Harry shrugged helplessly, pushing the empty container aside. "Maybe I'm overreacting to things.

I guess I'm not thinking all that clearly."

"Harry you haven't slept in two days and you're sick with the flu and a fever. Of course you're not thinking clearly."

"Yeah, you—you're right."

"I'm going to get out of here and let you get some rest. Take some of that cough syrup. The codeine will knock you out so you can get some sleep. You'll feel better once you've slept some, nothing better for you at this point, trust me."

"OK." He slid down off the stool, feeling slightly lightheaded. "Thanks for everything, I really appreciate it."

The hands came out of the pockets and Kenny moved closer, brow knit with concern. "Besides the obvious, are you all right?"

"I don't know," Harry answered softly. "I guess."

"Is everything all right with you and Kelly?"

His question caught Harry off-guard. "Why would you ask that?"

"No reason. You just seem like you're upset about something a little deeper than not feeling well and seeing coyotes in your yard."

Harry pulled a tissue from his robe pocket and blew his nose. "Everything's fine."

"You're sure?"

"Yeah, Kenny, I'm sure."

"I know you said you weren't too thrilled with all the traveling Kelly's been doing lately, can't blame you on that one."

Harry shrugged, unsure of what to say.

"Did you guys have an argument before she left?"

"Sort of, I guess, a—yeah, a little one."

"Maybe that's why she hasn't been in a rush to call you back or check in." He started toward the doorway and out of the kitchen. "Give her another call, tell her you're sorry. Even if you just get her voicemail. She'll call back."

"Of all the things that could've been bothering me, why did you go right to Kelly first?"

"Well obviously I'm part of a vast conspiracy designed to destroy you and your marriage." Kenny laughed lightly. "Jesus, you're starting to worry me. Do you have any idea how paranoid you sound?"

"Just tell me."

"It seemed a logical choice."

"Why? Why are marital problems a logical choice?"

"I don't know, maybe because you're *married*?"

He reached out, put a hand on Harry's shoulder and gave it a reassuring squeeze. "I didn't mean anything by it, OK? You just looked troubled that's all."

Harry looked at the floor, embarrassed. "Sorry, I guess I'm just feeling like the whole world's changing all around me and I can't do a damn thing to stop it."

"There's a lot happening right now, it's natural to feel that way."

"It's like I'm losing everything, like it's all being taken away and the whole world is in flames." The warmth the soup had wrought was shattered by a streak of chills dancing across the back of his shoulders. "And without it, I...Kenny, I'm not sure who I am."

His expression darkened. "It's that bad?"

Harry knew it was difficult for his friend to see him like this, it was anything but commonplace. In all the years they'd been friends, through all the ups and downs, triumphs and disappointments, Harry held it together and had always been the steady and consistent one. Even at work he was known as a management professional who rarely lost his cool or needed direction. In fact it was Harry other management people sought out when faced with daunting tasks or difficult situations. Now, in his own home, he felt defeated and pathetic. But he'd taken it this far and there was something wonderfully liberating about exposing such raw nerves, so he shrugged off his inhibitions and let it play out. "I'm losing this house, moving to another town, and I'm not even sure I'll still have a job next year," he said. "Garret's off at college, Kelly's so wrapped up in her job I never see her anymore and, hell, even Marlon's gone. I miss that dog."

"No doubt," Kenny said. "Marlon was the balls."

"Now I'm sick and feeling old and useless and—"

"Sorry for yourself?"

Like a punch to the gut. And one he had coming. "That too."

Kenny started back through the house to the front door. Harry followed. "Don't worry about it. Everybody gets a pass to feel like that now and then. But you're forty-five not eighty-five. We're all getting older, and sometimes it sucks, but what can we do? Things are changing, that's all. Just remember this. Change isn't the same thing as loss. At least it doesn't have to be. It's all perspective, right? You're in a state of flux right now. That's life, my friend. Nothing stays the same, you know that. It's clearly hitting closer to home than usual and it's got you a little off balance right now, but why shouldn't it? Cut yourself some slack. Even the great Harry Fremont can't always be ahead of every curve. It's OK to be human." He put a hand on the doorknob. "And if it's any consolation, far as work goes I seriously doubt you've got anything to worry about. You're senior guy, like they'd get rid of you."

"I'm not so sure."

"Either way, you've got a charmed life next to most people. You've got your health—maybe not today, but generally—a wife who loves you, a son you can be proud of, a nice new home you're moving to, couple nice cars, lots of nice things, and an *amazing* best friend, if I say so myself—and I do—my point being—and I know I have one somewhere in all this—lame as it may sound, it happens to be the best advice I can give you. Focus on the blessings, on all the positive things in your life, not the negative. I may not know much, but I do know this. Wallowing in the crap never did anybody any good." He cracked the front door but stood in front of the opening to block the cold air as best he could. "OK, that's all I got or I have to start charging you."

"Thanks, I—I'm sorry I got all heavy, I just needed to vent a little."

"Listen to me, drink the Kool-Aid and get some sleep, all right?"

An odd sensation suddenly came over Harry; a shaky feeling that seemed to threaten something more powerful was following close behind it, something ominous. He nonchalantly braced himself against the wall. Part of him wanted Kenny to stay, as the idea of being alone again had quickly become terrifying for some reason. "I will. I'll be fine."

Rather abruptly Kenny asked, "Does the address 14 Beach Street mean anything to you?"

"Doesn't ring a bell, no."

Kenny grinned; face beaming like a demonic Cheshire cat. "It should."

The look on his friend's face was terrifying. He stepped back. "Why?"

Kenny stared at him, the grin gone. "Huh?"

"Why should it mean something to me?"

"Why should what mean something to you?"

"You just said that address should mean something to me."

"What the hell are you talking about?" Kenny laughed lightly. "Out of the blue you just said 'why'."

Harry felt a sharp pain arc across his abdomen, like something deep inside him had broken. "I..."

"Dude, are you all right?"

"Yeah, I—it's OK, sorry."

He nodded but seemed uncertain. "You're sure?"

"I just can't think straight and..."

"And?"

"Never mind it's not important, I'm just exhausted."

Kenny shrugged. "OK, feel better then."

"Thanks."

"You need anything, call."

Harry stood at the bay window and watched Kenny return to his car then pull out of the driveway. The wind had picked up but the rain was still light and misty. Rose's house looked quiet. He closed his eyes and concentrated. Gradually, his nerves settled, but for the first time since he'd had the soup, a tickle skipped across his throat.

As he headed back to the kitchen to find his antibiotics, the cough medicine and the precious sleep they promised, the cordless phone in his robe pocket began to ring.

* * *

He'd hoped to see Kelly's cell on the caller ID but instead it simply read: *Incoming Call.*

"Hello?" A soft static answered, white noise crackling through the line. "*Hello?*" More static, louder this time and accompanied by a muffled thumping similar to the sound a blown speaker makes. "Is someone there?" From deep within the static came a faint high-pitched tone which, as it fought its way through the crackling hiss, gradually grew louder.

Harry listened as the tone morphed into something resembling a slurred human voice. It rolled through the line in repetitive waves, an electronically distorted attempt at speech that slowly built to a screeching crescendo of agony and desperation.

He held the phone away from his ear but could still hear the wail bellowing through the handset as it became a single decipherable word, screamed again and again like a horrific plea, or perhaps a warning.

"*Harry!*"

Male—he—he was sure it was a male voice but— not quite right, it—he'd never heard anyone sound quite like that. Even sans distortion and static, it would've sounded fraudulent, as if it were a machine attempting to sound human rather than someone speaking naturally.

"Who is this?" he demanded.

He was answered by a burst of static so deafening, he nearly dropped the phone. Holding the handset out in front of him and staring at it helplessly, Harry listened as the static quieted and was replaced by an odd series of loud clicks. And then the line went dead and all he could hear was the annoying buzz of a standard dial tone.

Hands shaking, he hung up, then checked the ID again. *Incoming Call* scrolled across the phone's small digital screen.

He'd seen *Private Call* or *Blocked Call*, but never just *Incoming Call* with no further information. He quickly punched in *69 in an attempt to call back the number.

"We're sorry," a recorded voice told him, "the number of your last incoming call is no longer in service. The call-back feature is not an option at this time."

Harry hung up and dropped the phone on the coffee table. He didn't even want to touch the damn thing. *How the hell could the number no longer be in service if I just got a call from it? What the hell's going on?*

He crept slowly toward the bay window and peered out at the street. Everything looked the same as before, nothing unusual or out of place, but could it possibly be a coincidence that the phone rang right after Kenny left? Why not while he was still there? Was someone watching him?

Maybe the man on the roof saw the police coming and hid. Maybe he knows I'm the one who called them and he's watching me right now and was somehow able to tap into my phone line. I don't care how sick I am or how little sleep I've had, I know I didn't imagine or confuse what I just heard. It's real, there's—there's something happening, I—

"Stop," Harry said aloud, his voice flat and emotionless in the otherwise empty house. He turned his back on the window, snatched up the phone and dialed the operator. A woman with a pleasant but businesslike voice answered, and he explained what had just taken place.

"Hmm," she said. "It's possible the number was disconnected right after the call was placed. Can you verify your name, number and address please?"

Harry did.

"Thank you, one moment."

Suddenly he was listening to ABBA singing *Dancing Queen*, which was ultimately more disturbing than the phone call. Mercifully the operator returned quickly. "Thank you for holding. This call just came in a moment ago?"

"Yes ma'am. It was distorted at first but—"

"I don't find any calls placed to your number in the last few minutes," she interrupted, her tone indicating she wasn't terribly interested in specifics. "The last incoming call was a while ago." She recited a time and number that coincided with Doctor Poole's callback. "But nothing since that time. If it happens again call Repair and report it to them. They'll be better able to assist you."

Whoever the caller was, he'd screeched Harry's name, so he knew damn well it hadn't been any crossed line, technical glitch or other anomaly. But there seemed little sense in belaboring the issue. "All right," he sighed. "Thank you."

He hung up but kept the phone in his hand, gripping it tightly. Angry, frustrated and shaken, his eyes panned along the walls, the baseboards, across the floors and carpeting, taking in each piece of furniture, every knickknack and bit of clutter, every empty space and dark corner, each shadow, all of it there before him like some foreign landscape he'd never before seen. Suddenly all the nostalgia, warm memories and even the sense of coming loss in leaving this place seemed irrelevant. What had previously been a barrier of protection now felt more like a prison, as these walls that once kept out the bad now seemed to serve no greater purpose than to keep him *in.* Until that moment, Harry had lived for years in the house without ever once feeling uncomfortable, afraid or unsafe, but even that had changed in a matter of hours.

Something's happening...

Panic rose from the deepest parts of his being, mounting like a gigantic wave growing stronger and stronger then curling under and into itself, dragging anything in its path under, down to dark bottomless places where no one is ever meant to go.

Hold it together. Stay calm. Breathe, just...breathe.

He did his best to breathe steadily and slowly without coughing, and soon, the panic attack began to recede. A moment later it left him entirely.

Harry had never wanted to sleep so desperately in all his life, and now that he had the medication to make it a reality he was too frightened to take it.

I can't sleep, not now.

Surely sleep would help clear his head and sharpen his mind, but he'd be far too vulnerable in such a state. He couldn't take the chance, not after all that had happened. He couldn't trust...*what* exactly... himself, the house, the phone, the yard, the street, the entire cul-de-sac, the wind, the rain, the noise, the silence—what?

An overbearing sense of dread draped the air like a ghost, leaving him uneasy and self-conscious; a stranger in his own house. The only time he'd ever felt anything like it was years before when his childhood home had been burglarized while he and his sister and parents were away on vacation. They'd returned home from a trip to Disney World to find someone had broken in a day or two before. They'd stolen the television, some small kitchen appliances, a bit of cash his father kept in a desk upstairs and most of his mother's jewelry. From Harry, who was only seven at the time, they'd stolen change he'd been saving for months. Someone smashed open his piggybank (which was a puppy sitting on the roof of a small doghouse rather than an actual pig), and even years later he could still remember standing in his bedroom, looking at what the intruders had left in their wake. They'd rifled through his things—*his* things—emptying drawers and his desk and strewing everything all over the floor. Apparently just to be nasty, they'd pulled model airplanes he'd spent hours building with his father, from their place on his bookshelf and stomped them to pieces. He found the ceramic bank smashed to smithereens just inside the doorway. It was such an odd feeling he couldn't even bring himself to cry. The idea that someone had come into the house—*their* house, *their* domain, the sanctuary he and his family had always relied on to shelter them from harm, the one place they could truly relax and live without fear—and breached the security of that, wandering the hallways, the bedrooms and beyond, resulted in a feeling of personal violation so severe it was more than unsettling or disturbing, it was deeply traumatic. His mother once described the feeling as something she imagined must be akin to having been raped. But all Harry knew was that he'd never again feel safe in a setting where it was natural and necessary to do so. It was a realization that burrowed so deep it left scars that never quite healed, and in the end, it made the world a colder, more brutal place. He resented that most of all, because stealing his basic sense of security was the worst thing the burglars could have done. Once one was robbed of that, like all innocence, it could never be reclaimed.

He'd never gotten a decent night of sleep in that house again.

A sudden surge of wind shot rain against the bay window, spattering it with what sounded like countless tiny fingers tapping the panes. Harry headed for the kitchen. *The antibiotics*, he thought. *I can still take those. They won't make me sleep but the sooner I start taking them the sooner I'll start to feel better.*

Once he'd reached the kitchen counter he snatched the bag from the drugstore and tore it open. A bottle of antibiotics rolled out onto the countertop along with the cough syrup and a box containing a small inhaler. He went for the antibiotics, put his glasses on and read the label. amoxicillin, 500mg capsules: take 1 capsule 3 times a day for 10 days. Once he'd managed to pry the childproof cap free he dropped one of the large cream-colored capsules into the palm of his hand and stared at it a moment. Goop trickled down the back of his throat, his nose was full again and the chills were back in full force. *So much for the wonders of chicken soup.* He downed the pill with a small glass of water, then inspected the other items. After setting the cough syrup aside he opened the inhaler. The directions and warnings were printed on a tiny paper evidently designed by and for woodland elves. Holding it up to his nose, he followed the steps to set up the inhaler, and then checked the warnings. Basically everything from dizziness to one's head exploding was covered, but if whatever was in this thing could clear his lungs and allow him to breathe better and less painfully, it was worth whatever side-effects might arise. He closed his lips around the inhaler, took a deep breath and depressed the plunger. Counting to ten as the directions instructed, he then removed the inhaler, exhaled and repeated the process again. The second time, while holding his breath, he felt a strange sensation deep in his throat, a tickling mixed with a medicinal taste, and for a moment he couldn't be sure if he was going to cough or vomit. Neither happened, but his lungs burned a bit and his head began to spin. By the time he'd counted to ten and exhaled, an odd tingling feeling had spread through his entire torso and he was so dizzy he could barely stand. Bright purple sunburst splotches appeared before his eyes with each blink and drifted slowly across his line of sight, which had taken to pitching and rolling like the deck of a boat on a decidedly choppy sea.

OK, he thought, staggering back toward the den, *my lungs are clearer but I'm having a stroke. Perfect.*

Though the cape had an open floor plan downstairs—the kitchen flowed into the den and a staircase which led to the bathroom and two bedrooms upstairs—the house felt unusually claustrophobic, the ceilings lower than normal, the walls closer. Harry stopped to look at a row of photographs on the wall. Kelly had hung them over the years, adding one or two now and then, but most had been there for quite some time. Odd how he walked by them numerous times each day and rarely noticed them. Yet they chronicled their lives together, and the lives that had come before them, those who had led them here, to this day, this moment. There was something so profoundly significant about that, how could it be ignored?

The lightheadedness lessened, and the purple psychedelic flowers had all but dissipated. Slump-shouldered, he studied the photographs arranged into neat rows, and was confronted by a feeling of such overwhelming sorrow he thought he might cry.

The wedding picture caught his eye first, he and Kelly striding down a church aisle, beaming on the happiest day of their lives. Then he locked on a picture of his parents, both gone now but so alive in the photograph, sitting posed and holding hands, smiling for the camera. Next to it, a baby picture of Garret followed by a first or second grade school picture.

How tiny that boy had been when he'd first held him. So delicate and beautiful, Harry could still remember the feeling of wanting—needing—to protect this child, his son. And from that moment forward he knew little of his own life or happiness mattered. It was all about that little man. Everything he'd do from that point forward would be about being the best father he could be, the best husband, and providing the best life for his family he could. He hadn't always succeeded, but more often than not he had, and no one could fairly accuse him of not trying.

He moved past a picture of Kelly's parents—both still alive—and he smiled, remembering how differently they'd behaved on the day he'd married their daughter. Kelly's father was thrilled—Harry and his father-in-law had always gotten along famously—but her mother was sullen and behaved as if attending a funeral, heartbroken that her daughter was being taken from her by a man apparently not quite up to her standards, whatever those were. Harry had never understood why his mother-in-law disapproved of him so, and to this day it remained something of a mystery. He was a loving husband and father, a good provider, a steady and reliable presence in her daughter and grandson's lives, what exactly was there to disapprove of? On the rare occasions when he mentioned it to Kelly she dismissed it as "just her mother's way." They were very different people, she'd say, as if that explanation should suffice.

Harry reached out and gently touched a small frame, this one housing an old black and white photograph of himself as a six-year-old boy playing outside the house where he'd been raised. He carefully pulled it from the wall and stared at it awhile. His eyes filled, though he wasn't sure why.

So many memories, he thought. *So many—*

Lies.

Harry spun round, heart leaping into the bottom of his throat as his eyes frantically searched the kitchen behind him. He clutched the photograph and stumbled back into the wall, the silver frame cool against the clammy flesh of his palms. He'd heard it. He'd *heard* someone say "*lies.*" He was certain. It wasn't in his head, disguised as a renegade thought, but a voice, a man's voice, deep and guttural and clear as day, spoken as if not more than ten feet from him.

But there was no one there.

Trembling, he moved back into the kitchen, fully expecting someone to jump out at him. "Who's there?" The moment the words left him it felt like someone was choking him. He dropped the photograph and began to cough, his chest rattling as sharp pains shot through his throat. Still trying to keep the kitchen in focus, he staggered about, coughing as he lumbered into the den.

It too was empty.

When the coughing fit finally subsided, Harry was left breathless, back in the kitchen and collapsed over the sink, spitting up phlegm into the drain. He wiped his mouth with a paper towel, then splashed some water on his face. The cold snapped him to attention, shocking him awake. Chest heaving, he looked to the small photograph he'd dropped to the counter. Evidently it hit harder than he'd realized, as the glass was cracked. A perfect lightning bolt fracture ran the length of the frame, splitting the little boy he'd once been in two. He gently touched it with a fingertip to be sure it was real. The rough and uneven edge of broken glass scraped his flesh. *This isn't a dream, I'm awake.*

He knew he had to sleep, but he couldn't. Something well beyond his comprehension was taking place here. *Something bad...something—*

Another sound distracted him, faint but unmistakable.

He held his breath and listened. A repetitive vibrating sound came from the far side of the kitchen, a dull buzz he recognized. Harry hurried to the back door and the coat rack on the wall next to it. His trench coat hung on the last hook, and in the side pocket was his Blackberry. He'd never heard it ring but it was vibrating in quick double intervals, signaling someone had left a message.

Fumbling it from the deep coat pocket, he looked to the screen and saw the identity of the caller displayed in bold black letters.

1 NEW MESSAGE FROM: KELLY.

The voicemail had come in at nine thirty-seven a.m. his time. According to the wall clock it was now 12:08. After verifying the time on his watch, he stabbed the key to retrieve his message and listened.

"It's going to voicemail," a man said, voice bored with indifference. "Do you want to leave him a message?"

From a distance of what sounded like several feet away, just before the call ended with an abrupt click, Harry heard his wife answer.

"No."

4

When Garret was a little boy, eight to be exact Harry took him to a local park for the afternoon. I was a Saturday, and Kelly had stayed home to work around the house so Harry and Garret could have some exclusive father-son time. Harry planned an entire day. They were up early, had breakfast ou as a treat, then drove over to the park, which was only a few miles from the house. They took along a couple baseball mitts, a ball, a bat and a small coole filled with sandwiches, a six-pack of Coke and some juice boxes for Garret. It was a beautiful late summer morning, and once they parked and began walking across the dirt lot, Harry realized there was some sort of antique show taking place at the beginning of the park. Tables were set up to display various dealer goods, and a fairly large crowd was milling about. He and Garret went to another section of the park where there were only a few people sitting on blankets or playing with their dogs and settled in there.

The first half hour or so was great. He and his son talked while throwing the baseball back and forth awhile, enjoying the day and more importantly, each other. It was times like these where all of Harry's fears of not measuring up as a parent vanished. These were situations he'd once fantasized about, days he'd spend with his son, imparting words of wisdom and sharing special moments both would remember for years.

Unfortunately, while that particular day was certainly memorable, the memories associated with it were anything but pleasant. Things turned when Harry went to the restroom, which was located along with a snack bar in a large cement block building about fifty yards from where he and Garret had been playing catch. Garret came with him but didn't have to go, so he remained just outside the door. Harry told him to wait right there and that he'd be out in a minute.

When he emerged from the men's room Garret was gone.

At first he assumed he'd wandered back over to the field, distracted by a dog or perhaps another child. But he could clearly see nearly the entire park from his position, and Garret was nowhere to be found.

Suddenly Harry was running, frantically calling his son's name as he bolted along the walkway, eyes bouncing rapidly back and forth, trying to cover as much ground as he could, his heart smashing his chest and his mind racing. *No, please, no—where is he, where—God help me, where is he?* Every newscast or story he'd ever heard about children being abducted and vanishing came to him in a frenzied rush as his baby's face blinked across his mind's eye. *Not my boy. Please God, not Garret.*

A young woman walking her dog asked him if everything was all right, and Harry explained he couldn't find his son and gave her a quick description. She smiled, then pointed toward the parking lot, which was not visible from where they were located, said she'd just seen him walking in that direction by himself and that he looked perfectly fine.

Thanking her profusely, Harry took off for the parking lot.

He found Garret standing next to the car drinking a juice box. The moment he saw him and realized he was all right, all he could focus on through the sea of relief was how deeply and desperately he loved his son, and how grateful he was that he was safe. He scooped the boy up, peppered him with kisses, then hugged him so hard Garret spilled his juice. With sincere confusion his son asked what was wrong, but by then relief had again turned to fear, this time manifested as anger. Harry put him on the ground none-too-gently, grabbed hold of his wrist and spun him around. "If I tell you to stay somewhere then that's where you stay! You scared the hell out of me! Don't you ever, *ever* wander off like that again, do you understand me?" He spanked him three times. Hard. It was the first time he'd ever hit his son. It was also the last. Heartbroken, Garret nodded, his bottom lip quivering as his bright blue eyes filled with tears. And then Harry's heart broke too, and he was hugging him again, attempting to explain how frightened he'd been that something had happened to him.

"It's over now," Harry assured him. "Let's go back and play catch and have a nice day, OK?"

But at that point Garret only wanted to go home and see his mother, and Harry really couldn't blame him.

"He's not a moron," Kelly had scolded later. "You could've just explained it to him and been stern about it. Wasn't yelling at him enough? You had to hit him too?"

"Oh for God's sake, I gave him a spanking."

"You're a lot bigger than he is. How could you hit someone so small?"

"I panicked, OK? I lost it, I admit it, but I thought someone had taken him, I—look, with all the crazies and perverts out there he needs to do what the hell he's told! He can't just go wandering off whenever he feels like it."

"Absolutely, I agree. All I'm saying is hitting him wasn't necessary."

"If he'd done as I'd told him it wouldn't have come to that."

"Is that the message you want to send Garret? That when someone does something wrong, makes a mistake or doesn't listen properly that the appropriate response is to physically assault them?"

"It was a spanking, not an assault. I didn't hurt him. I'm his father."

"And he's your son, what's your point? It was an innocent mistake. He wasn't intentionally defying you, Harry. You could've just reprimanded him and explained things intelligently."

"He's old enough to know better."

"He's a little boy. And in case you haven't noticed, he worships you."

Though he was too stubborn to admit it that day, Harry knew she was right. Even years later, whenever he thought about that afternoon, he was gripped with the same relief he'd felt when he realized some maniac hadn't kidnapped his child, but also a sense of deep sorrow for how all the emotions he'd felt had culminated in him humiliating his son. A good talking to would've sufficed, as Kelly contended. Right or wrong, sometimes love ran so deep it hurt, but when it turned to anger or even violence it became something else entirely.

Didn't it?

Faced with that memory he attempted to hold his emotions in check and sort through the voicemail message logically. His first impulse was to behave as if wounded, with anger and suspicion, but he distracted himself by playing it again and listening more closely to the man's voice. He couldn't be certain, but the man sounded a lot like Aaron Searcy, Kelly's boss and someone Harry knew had gone on the trip as well. He'd met Searcy and his wife Gloria at a few Christmas parties over the years, and Kelly mentioned him in conversation quite often, but Harry had only spoken to him over the phone perhaps half a dozen times. Still, even if it *was* Searcy, why had he called the Blackberry rather than the home phone, and why wasn't Kelly making the call herself? It had come in at nine thirty-seven Harry's time, which meant the call was placed from San Diego at six thirty- seven in the morning. What was Aaron Searcy, or anyone for that matter, doing in his wife's suite at such an early hour?

Using his Blackberry, Harry tried her cell rather than calling the hotel again. Apparently whatever problems her provider had been experiencing were solved, as this time the call went through and the line began to ring.

"Kelly Fremont."

"Kel," he said, stunned he'd actually gotten her.

"Harry?" Her professional voice relaxed into her non-work version.

"Yeah, it's me, I—"

"You sound awful, are you all right?"

"No, I'm not. I've got the flu."

"You looked tired when I left, I had a feeling you might be coming down with something. Did you call the doctor?"

"Yes, I—look, where are you?"

"In a cab heading back to the hotel, just got out of a meeting. Turned out to be quite productive, actually."

"Didn't you get my message? I left one on your voicemail at the hotel."

"I left really early this morning. I'll look for it when I get back."

"I've been trying to reach you since you left."

"Well I tried calling you this morning but you didn't answer."

"Yeah, that's because you called my Blackberry instead of the home phone and I had the ringer off. I got your voicemail, though, nine-thirty my time."

A few seconds of silence came and went before she answered. "But I didn't leave a message."

"Why would you call my Blackberry and not the home line, Kel?"

"You're listed in my cell under your name and the home phone is listed as *Home*, it was just a mistake."

"I guess that's what happens when someone not entirely familiar with your cell phone uses it to call me, huh?"

"What do you mean?"

"What do you think I mean?"

"Harry, *what* are you talking about?"

"I heard some guy ask if you wanted to leave a message and you said no. Who was that?"

"Oh, that was just Aaron," she said, as if his question was the silliest thing she'd ever heard. "Sorry, I didn't understand what you meant."

"What was Searcy doing in your hotel suite at sixthirty in the morning?"

Dead air answered again. "What's with the accusatory tone?"

"Just answer the question, Kelly."

"Well, Mr. Prosecutor, we met in my suite before heading out for a meeting this morning. I was in the bathroom straightening my hair and I asked him to do me a favor and dial your number for me.

He must've seen your name on the list and hit that number instead of the one marked *Home*, which explains why it went to your Blackberry rather than the house. He said it was going to voicemail so I figured you'd gone out or were in the shower or something. Rather than leave a message I just thought I'd catch up with you later."

Her nonchalance irritated him even more than the tone of faux persecution. "I asked why Searcy was in your suite at six-thirty in the morning."

"I just told you, we had a meeting and—"

"Nobody has a business meeting at six-thirty on a Saturday morning."

"They don't, huh?" She laughed, but it was clear she found nothing humorous about their conversation. "How about someone who owns a chain of pastry shops here in the city that wanted to host us for breakfast at his largest location? Think maybe someone like me, you know, working for a *coffee* company and all, might be interested in attending something like that? What do you think I'm doing here, Harry, sightseeing? And the meeting wasn't at six-thirty, it was scheduled for seven-thirty, but it's on the other side of town so we wanted to head out early. OK? Are we all set with the interrogation now? What is this, high school? God, I'm *so* glad you called. What a treat."

He blew his nose but didn't respond. Everything she said made perfect sense. He had no reason to doubt any of it.

"Harry?"

"I'm here," he said softly. He felt like a jerk. "I'm sorry, I don't feel well and I couldn't get a hold of you and then when I got that message and—"

"You said you called the doctor," she interrupted. "How'd that go?"

Just like Kelly, he thought. *Like a shark, constantly on the move.* Sometimes that quirk came in handy. He explained about the prescriptions and how Kenny had picked up the medications for him.

"Are you running a temp?"

"102."

"Yikes. Take some aspirin, Hot Stuff. How long since you've slept?"

"Haven't been able to sleep since you left, this damn cough makes it impossible."

"Not good. Have you tried the cough syrup?"

"Not yet."

"Don't wait. Take some and go to bed. Sleep's the best thing right now."

"I…yeah, I know it's just…"

"Just what?"

"Some weird things are going on. I—"

"Hold on a sec." There was a muffled sound like she was covering the phone, then another like she'd taken her hand away. "Sorry, had to pay the driver. What kind of weird things?"

Harry wondered if it was even worth going into at that point. He already knew she'd say his mind was playing tricks on him because he was sick and exhausted and he needed to get some sleep pronto. "Nothing, I should just get some sleep."

"Sounds like a plan sweetie, but listen, let me hustle. The thing this morning was kind of informal and our meetings this afternoon aren't, so I have to change real quick, fire off a couple emails, then head right back out. I don't want to wake you so I won't call later, but once you've gotten some rest give me a buzz, OK? Call my cell rather than the hotel, that way you'll be sure to get me."

He looked at the small mudroom through the panel of tiny windows on the interior back door. It looked as it should, the exterior door closed, secure. "OK."

"Get some sleep. I love you."

"Love you too."

"Bye."

"Kelly?"

"Yes?"

"I'm sorry about before, I…"

"Don't worry about it, just feel better."

Harry told her he loved her again, but she'd already hung up.

* * *

Although occasional bursts of wind still rocked the house now and then, the rain had finally stopped. Harry sat on a stool at the island in the kitchen, staring at the bottle of cough syrup. He couldn't remember exactly how long he'd been sitting there, but his lower back was aching, he was becoming increasingly weaker and he knew he couldn't stay on the stool much longer. Part of him wanted to take the two tablespoons of cough syrup called for and be done with it. To just go to bed, lie down on the welcoming mattress and feel the cool sheets against his flushed skin, to let his head sink down into the pillows and finally be able to fall away into a deep sleep uninterrupted by incessant coughing was so appealing he wouldn't be able to ignore it much longer. But another part of him still worried about what might happen if he let sleep take him.

Since his conversation with Kelly he'd begun to question things again, including his concerns, but try as he might, he couldn't dismiss everything he'd experienced as simple figments of a sleep-deprived imagination. The fact that he'd so quickly suspected Kelly of infidelity bothered him as well. Maybe he was naïve when it came to his wife and such things, but in all their years of marriage he tended to overlook her shortcomings and sometimes inconsistent behavior because he loved her so desperately and felt that in the end they didn't amount to much anyway.

For his part, he'd never cheated. There had been temptations a few times over the years, but he never pursued them. Kelly was the love of his life, the mother of his child, his wife—they were happy— why look elsewhere? And he believed Kelly felt the same. She didn't give any indication she wanted a relationship beyond or outside their marriage, and knowing her as he did, he couldn't picture her running around behind his back anyway, it wasn't her style at all. If Kelly had a problem she tackled it head-on. That's how she operated in business and at home, always had been. Besides, they'd always had a strong marriage. Hadn't they? While many of their friends had divorced or separated over the years they remained together and true to each other. Like any other couple they had their ups and downs, and of course they'd fallen into familiar routines and patterns that maybe weren't quite as exciting or romantic as things had been years ago, but they were a happily married couple. Surely being together and in love for twenty-one years had to count for something.

Now he felt like an idiot for suspecting her, and with Aaron Searcy no less, the CEO of the company she'd worked with for years. Harry knew workplace romances happened all the time, he'd seen them blossom in his company several times over the years, and often among unlikely couples who, had they met in any other environment, probably wouldn't look twice at each other.

Aaron Searcy had married his wife Gloria (a hairdresser and one-time prom queen), while she was still in her early twenties and he was nearly fifty. They'd never had children. The few times Harry had met them at company functions or holiday parties, Searcy struck him as a laughable sort, while Gloria, an attractive though rundown redhead, came off as a tired woman who drank too much and whose better days, like her husband's, were well behind her. The only difference between them was Gloria seemed aware of this fact while Searcy remained clueless. Darkhaired with thick eyebrows and the body of an aging weekend athlete, he was well into his sixties, with decidedly turtle-like facial features that had probably served him better in his teens. Despite the fact that he was pushing seventy, he still carried himself like a big-man-on-campus type, but it was forced and embarrassing, and clearly no one else seemed to be on board with the concept.

Take the damn cough syrup. You're so exhausted you actually thought Kelly was having an affair with that moron, what more do you need? Sleep. When you wake up you'll feel better and your mind will be clear.

He reached for the bottle, but something stopped him. His hand hung there, suspended in midair. But what if...

What? But what if what?

The vision of the man in black scurrying over Rose's roof came back to him. *What was he up to? Why was he watching the house, and what if he's still out there?* Harry looked at the ceiling. If the man were on his roof he'd be able to hear him moving around up there...wouldn't he? *And what about the coyote, what about the phone call? I heard my name.* He'd obviously made a mistake about Kelly and let his mind run wild with that, and he was even willing to concede that perhaps he'd misinterpreted some other sound when it came to the voice whispering "lies." But he hadn't imagined the rest and refused to continue entertaining the notion he had.

You can't sleep until you figure this out. Something is *happening.*

He looked to the coffee pot on the counter. *If I'm going to stay awake I need to be alert as possible.* The pot he made that morning was still full. He'd poured himself a mug earlier but never drank it. Sliding off the stool, he turned the coffeemaker back on, set it to Warm, then put the mug in the microwave.

When it was done he grabbed the mug and headed upstairs. If he was going to ride this out he felt he needed to change his clothes. He hadn't bathed in a couple days and that concerned him too, but the last thing he needed was a chill on top of those already coursing through his body, so he nixed that idea and followed the hallway to the bedroom. At the very end of the hallway, just beyond their room, Garret's bedroom door stood closed. Harry was still getting used to his son not living there on a permanent basis, and knew it would be quite a while before he warmed to the idea. He remembered the many nights during Garret's later high school years when he'd be out with friends or off on a date or at some party. Harry would nervously lie awake or wait up for him to come home, so relieved each time he finally saw car headlights pierce the darkness and pull into the driveway, or whenever he heard the front door open, then close, followed by Garret's footfalls, signaling his son was home safely. He never thought he'd miss that, but he did. Like so many other segments of his son's life, he'd never know them again. They were gone. Just gone.

He stood in the hallway a moment, sipped his coffee and considered the wall to his right. More framed photographs met his gaze, more memories in neat little rows imprisoned beneath glass, wood and metal.

For someone constantly on the move, Kelly had always been a demon when it came to photography, snapping pictures of everything throughout their lives, always there with a camera, afraid she might miss something. It was a leftover interest from her youth, when she'd toyed with the idea of becoming a professional photographer. But like many dreams, it was never quite realized. She never got there, but then she'd never fully pursued it in any real sense either, opting to work her way up the corporate ladder instead. Her constant need to take endless rolls of film of everything over the years had sometimes annoyed him, but now he was glad she'd done it. In some instances those photographs were all they had, the only evidence that remained to prove their lives had been what they'd all believed them to be.

His eyes gravitated to an old Halloween photo of Garret when he was five or six and dressed like a bunny. Cutest damn thing he'd ever seen. Now his boy was taller than he was, a strapping young man who found such reminiscences clichéd and awkward. But when Harry looked at the photograph he remembered that little boy in the bunny suit carrying a plastic pumpkin full of candy, how his little hand felt in his as he walked him around the neighborhood that windswept October night and something else.

Garret ran into Kelly's arms the moment they'd gotten home, excitedly showing her the spoils of his outing. Why hadn't she taken him that year? Why hadn't she come with them? In his memory Kelly was still dressed for work. Maybe she'd worked late. Yes, that must've been it.

Her career almost always took center stage but that didn't mean she was a bad or absent parent. His career had driven him as well, was she supposed to be held to different standards simply because she was a woman? He thought about how weepy and clingy she'd been after Garret was born, a proud and painstakingly attentive mother. And yet, it had only been a few months before she returned to work and Garret was sent to daycare, something they both disliked and had never wanted for their son.

We needed both incomes. That's the only reason she went back to work so soon. It was my fault if anyone's.

Had I made more money, been more successful then she could've stayed home with Garret longer.

"But I was always there for you," he said to the photograph. "Wasn't I?"

Was Kelly?

Of course, she's a wonderful mother, always has been. Stop.

He sniffled, cleared his throat against a new dribble of nasal drip, then took another swallow of coffee. Pulling himself away from the photo gallery, he moved into their bedroom and searched his bureau for a change of clothes. He threw off his robe, undressed, then slipped into a fresh pair of sweatpants and a heavy sweatshirt. His reflection in the mirror over Kelly's dresser caught his attention. He turned and looked. *Yeah, that worked wonders. I'm a total man of action now that I'm out of that robe and into my nifty new outfit. I look like I've been run over by a stampeding herd of water buffalo. Twice.*

Without warning he began to cough. He shuffled into the adjacent master bathroom, spit up into the toilet, then took a drink of water from the sink. Hopeful he might be able to find some regular cough syrup that might help suppress his cough without making him sleepy, he rummaged through both sides of the medicine cabinet. At the very back, hidden behind an old tin of Band-Aids, he found a sticky brown bottle of Robitussin that looked like it had been purchased before the advent of indoor plumbing. He twisted off the cap, sniffed at the syrup, remembered his nose was too clogged to smell anything, then took a long swig. Certain he now knew what unwashed feet dipped in turpentine tasted like, he gagged and put the bottle aside.

He returned to the bedroom, retrieved his coffee and stood before one of the two windows facing the street. From this higher position he had an even better view of Rose's roof. No one there. Her house looked quiet, as did the rest of the cul-de-sac. All the other houses sat dark and empty, making the street look like a mysteriously forsaken colony. The buildings were perfectly good, functional and relatively new, yet deserted and lifeless, victims of a hasty exodus, their frightened inhabitants abandoning the homes under threat of some powerful malevolent presence, victims themselves of a greater unseen evil.

And now he was alone with whatever had taken the rest.

Harry was reminded of a book he'd read several years before concerning the legend of the "Lost Colony" of Roanoke, and the late 16th Century settlers who inexplicably vanished there without a trace in a mystery that remains unsolved to this day. Like the author of that book, he'd believed there had to be a reasonable, non-supernatural explanation for what had taken place. Now he couldn't be so sure. What if something unnatural *was* responsible for what happened to those people? If they'd become prey to an unthinkable horror beyond anything imaginable then or now, had it taken them all at once, or slowly…one by one, until there were only a handful left, and then… finally…just one? Had it been that final survivor who carved the enigmatic word "Croatoan" in a tree as a last-ditch effort to leave those who would eventually find it some clue as to what had happened?

What if something happened to him while he was here all alone? Would anyone ever know? Would he too have time to leave clues?

He thought about the people who had once lived on the cul-de-sac, remembered a time when the street was vibrant and alive. It wasn't so long ago, why did it already seem like a lifetime had passed since those days?

The wind blew, disturbing the branches of several trees and causing them to sway back and forth in unison. There was nothing unusual about that, of course, yet there seemed something ominous about it just then, as if there might be something more behind it than the wind. Harry worked his way through an enormous yawn, then chased it with more coffee. In the distance, he heard the familiar rumbling sound of an empty plastic garbage can rolling along pavement. He scanned the street but saw nothing out of the ordinary. After listening more closely he surmised it was coming from the side of the house, which meant one of their cans had probably been knocked over and was rolling back and forth along the portion of driveway closest to the house, trapped between the fence gate leading to the backyard and Kelly's SUV. He craned his neck but could only see his car and the backend of the SUV in the driveway. He'd have to look from the bay window to see the area where the garbage cans were located.

On his way to investigate he stopped and locked on a photograph atop Kelly's dressing table. One of the few in the house she hadn't taken herself, it was from a cruise to the Bahamas they'd gone on three years before. In the picture she and Harry stood near the railing of a cruise ship, both smiling broadly, their arms around each other. He was dressed in shorts and a loose-fitting shirt, a typical everyday guy most wouldn't look twice at or even notice, someone who could easily blend into any crowd. Kelly was far more captivating, with her short blonde hair, big blue eyes, dazzling smile, pretty features and attractive figure. Of course the baby blue bikini helped too. He smiled. She still had an amazing body, one most women half her age would've killed for. Weight had never been a problem for her, she'd always been thin and in shape, and even after Garret was born she was back in the gym within weeks, determined to tighten and get her figure back where she wanted it.

Without realizing it, he'd reached out and touched the photograph, his fingertip resting against her cheek. All the years of marriage, routine and familiarity had done nothing to weaken his love and attraction for her. To Harry, Kelly was still the sexiest woman he'd ever seen. She'd aged somewhat, but more or less looked the same as she had in her twenties. He, on the other hand, had put on a few extra pounds and aged more obviously. He felt the same, but she looked the same. He mulled that over in his tired mind awhile.

They'd had an awful lot of fun over the years, hadn't they? Sure there were some bad times, but didn't the good far outweigh them? Hadn't their lives together been something special, wonderful and blessed? His memories were accurate, weren't they? Or had things changed, slowly, gradually, and without him fully noticing until recently that the patterns they both had fallen into masked a greater truth? Twenty-one years was a long time. Could anything really maintain a consistent level of joy over such a vast amount of time? Was it natural for something to grow and thrive over the decades or to slowly decay and die? Maybe the answer was both. After all, Life and Death walked hand-in-hand in a relationship symbiotic, infinite and profound in its purity.

The incessant rumble of the garbage can rolling in the driveway tore him from his thoughts. He left his robe at the foot of the bed, gathered up his old clothes and tossed them in the hamper. As he headed back downstairs, his legs were shaky and riddled with fluinduced aches and pains. He descended the stairs carefully, then crossed back into the den and looked out the bay window. The wind had picked up considerably, but strangely enough, the rumbling sound had ceased.

Now able to see the small section of fence next to the gate where they kept their three plastic garbage cans, he realized all three were intact, exactly where they were supposed to be and secured with a large bungee cord per usual. From this position he could see the entire driveway. No renegade trash cans.

Maybe one of Rose's got loose and that's what I heard.

He looked across the street. Nothing.

Tension rose in him again, and the muscles in his neck and across the tops of his shoulders tightened and quickly turned stiff and sore. He angrily yanked open the front door. Frigid air rushed in. He nearly coughed but somehow managed to suppress it. *Maybe the cough syrup from 1902 is actually working*, he thought, the awful taste still coating his tongue. He stepped out onto the stoop and looked around cautiously, as if he'd never set foot outside the house before. The wind was stronger, cold and harsh and bending the trees more violently than before, but he couldn't see trash cans or anything else that could've made the loud rumbling sound. Frustrated, he searched the street again, eyes slowly panning up, then down, across then back, covering every yard, every driveway, each stretch of paved street along the cul-de-sac he could make out.

Again, nothing.

Shivering from the cold, his flu or perhaps something else, Harry turned to go back inside when he saw a small mail truck turn the corner and make its way up the street. It rolled to a stop in front of his mailbox, which was located just to the left of the foot of his driveway, and the man inside, an older guy in full postal uniform, tossed a banded stack of mail into the box. Their usual mail carrier was a young woman. *Must be a weekend fill-in*, he thought. Harry offered him a halfhearted wave. The mailman stared at him for several seconds, as if not quite certain what it was he was looking at, then gave a lackadaisical wave of his own.

As the mailman swung the truck around, dropped some mail in Rose's box, then took off, something on the mailbox caught Harry's attention. Their mailbox was a large tan plastic model Harry had purchased a few years back after some local kids had vandalized all the metal boxes in town, including theirs. A large number five decal decorated the side of the box. He remembered putting that on there himself, but beneath it, in matching black decal letters it read: FREEMONT. For some reason he had no memory of that being there before. He swallowed hard, blinked his eyes until he focused better, and hugged himself against the cold wind. He studied the name a moment. FREEMONT. He knew it was spelled correctly and yet...it didn't *look* right. Had Kelly added the name to the mailbox at some point? Wouldn't he have noticed it sooner if it had been there any amount of time? How had he missed it? Or was he mistaken? *Did* he know about it? Had it always been there? *Yeah, it—of course it's been there all along.*

But just below the name he noticed something else, a series of strange symbols etched in black across the mailbox. Quite small, they resembled Egyptian hieroglyphics but were unlike anything he'd seen before. He rubbed his eyes and squinted, hoping for a better look.

The strange symbols were gone.

More confused nonsense from an exhausted mind. Relax... breathe...

But what about the rumbling sound? He couldn't write that off as mere confusion, he'd heard it. Though rattled, he forced himself down the driveway to the mailbox, slippers shuffling on damp pavement. It felt strange to be outdoors. The air, the light, everything was different there, and even more so on this day.

The mail delivery consisted of a few bills, a flyer for a local department store and a card reminding him his car was due for an oil change. The last piece in the stack was a small postcard with no name, only an address scribbled across the front: *14 Beach Street.* The same address he thought he'd heard Kenny mention. But there was no Beach Street in town that he knew of, and yet the address struck him like an anvil. Why did that look so familiar?

14 Beach Street...I know it means something...why can't I remember?

He pawed at his eyes and looked again. This time the address was correct and printed professionally, an advertisement for a local furniture store that was going out of business. He looked closely where he thought he'd seen the other address, and then to the section of mailbox where he'd seen the symbols. No sign of either.

The wind whipped down the street. Something felt wrong, out of synch. He looked around. Though he was alone, he felt anything but. Someone was watching him, he was sure of it. He could feel a presence not just nearby but all around him. In the air, the trees, the houses, the ground beneath his feet, taunting him with barely audible whispers disguised as an angry wind.

As he started back up the driveway he had the sensation someone was coming up behind him quickly. In his head he saw a vision of the man in black running toward him as a tingling fear crashed his back, crackling up along his spine and over the backs of his shoulders. Horrified, he spun around, but there was no one there. Shaking, he remained where he was a moment, eyes darting about. "What do you want?" he whispered. "What's happening?"

No answer came, but the house phone began to ring.

Harry hurried inside, slammed the door closed and locked it behind him.

5

He'd left the cordless on the coffee table in the den when he'd gone upstairs to change. It took him a moment to remember that but once he had Harry grabbed it and quickly checked the ID.

Wireless caller...

"Hello?"

Kelly's closest comrade Jasmine was on the line. "Sorry," she said with such astonishment it sounded as if she'd been offended, "did I *wake* you?"

"No," Harry said, glancing behind him at the bay window. Had he seen something dart across the corner of his eye just then, a flash at the very edges of his peripheral vision? "No, I just—I'm not feeling well—I've got the flu."

"Ah. Lots of fluids and plenty of rest, kiddo, that's the ticket." Jasmine, who had been friends with Kelly since not long after high school, was the branch manager of a local bank. Like Kelly, she'd walked through the door at the bottom rung and clawed her way up. Beginning as a teller, she returned to college on the bank's dime and had done quite well for herself. She and her ex-husband Dennis, a morose, balding, slump-shouldered man, had divorced two years ago.

When they were still together Harry and Kelly had sometimes socialized with them as couples, but Jasmine was essentially Kelly's friend. Harry had little in common with Dennis and whenever they got together he felt like a child on a forced play-date. It was one of the more unusual aspects of their relationship, Harry supposed. He and Kelly had few friends that were *theirs*. While neither had large numbers of them, for the most part, he had his friends and she had hers. When it came to Jasmine specifically, Harry didn't harbor any particular dislike of her, he'd just never been crazy about her either, and the feeling was mutual. Still, they'd been interacting with each other for so many years they'd learned to play the game and pretend they were a lot friendlier than they actually were. "So…is Kel around?" she asked when Harry offered no response. "I tried her cell earlier but there was something wrong with her service or something."

"She's out of town on business." He found it odd Jasmine didn't know this, as she and Kelly tended to tell each other everything. "She didn't tell you?"

A few seconds of silence and then: "She probably did but I've been so busy lately I've been absolutely comatose. Where in the world is she this time?"

"San Diego." Harry gnawed his bottom lip. Unlike most of her business trips, Kelly had announced this one only two days before she left. He hadn't thought it strange at the time but now it made him wonder. "It was kind of a last minute thing."

"You know, I *do* think I remember her saying something about that now that you mention it."

Yeah, sure you do.

Jasmine sounded like someone who had just accidentally stepped in a steaming pile of excrement and was now suggesting she'd done so purposely. "She and Aaron Searcy made the trip," he said, testing the waters and already feeling guilty for doubting his wife again.

"That Aaron's a hoot, isn't he?"

"Yeah a real charmer." *Why are you so nervous Jasmine?*

"Oh well, no big whoop, Giancarlo and I are going to a wine-tasting later in Boston and I thought she might like to come along, that's all."

"Wine tasting?"

"You would've been more than welcome to come too, of course, but I didn't really think that was your kind of thing."

"It's not." Far as he knew it wasn't Kelly's either.

"I'm new to the whole thing myself," she explained. "Giancarlo turned me on to it. He's an absolute *wizard* when it comes to wine."

How exciting for Giancarlo. Whoever the hell that is.

"Among other things," she added, laughing mischievously.

"Uh-huh. Great."

Since her divorce Jasmine had dated a string of men and seemed to be going through a midlife crisis that involved sleeping with as many of them as possible. Ridiculous as it seemed, could her behavior be influencing Kelly? Was Jasmine plotting to turn her against him so she could have a partner in crime on the open market like when she and Kelly were single? "Well just let her know I called, would you? And tell her we'll catch up when she gets back."

"Will do."

"When *is* she back anyway?"

"Monday night. But if you need to reach her the cell's working again. I just spoke to her a few minutes ago."

"Fabulous! I'll give her a jingle."

The tone signaling call-waiting sounded in Harry's ear. "Jasmine, I've got another call."

"No problem," she said, sounding relieved to be on the verge of escape. "Hope you feel better, kiddo. Hugs and smooches."

"OK, thank you," he said awkwardly. "Bye." He pressed the *flash* button, banishing Jasmine and her spurious warmth into telephone oblivion as the line clicked over to the new caller. "Hello?"

Silence.

"Hello!"

The soft static he'd heard previously returned, crackling through the line along with the muffled thumping sound. As before, they were joined by a high-pitched tone which gradually grew louder.

"Who the hell is this?"

Like last time, the tone slowly became an electronically distorted attempt at something similar to a badly slurred human voice. Again, the voice was male, and although it wasn't screaming in agony like its predecessor, it was even more disturbing because it sounded so eerily familiar. As it dawned on him exactly what he was hearing, Harry realized that whatever *thing* was endeavoring to sound human wasn't imitating a stranger's voice this time, but his own.

"Who the hell is this?" he heard the voice say back to him.

He gritted his teeth and quickly wiped his runny nose with the back of his sleeve. "If this is a joke I don't find it the least bit funny."

"If this is a joke..." The voice was swallowed by the hissing sound only to return a second or two later, the words coming slower now, like whatever was parroting him was trying to better enunciate the words. "If...this...is...a...joke..."

The voice sounded clearer now, more human, more like him.

"How are you doing this?" Harry asked. "*Why* are you doing this?"

"...I don't find it the least bit funny."

Cold fear scurried through him. The last line was nearly a perfect imitation of his voice. "Who are you?

What do you want?"

Static...thumping...odd electronic noises, pulses and clicks and squeals...

"Answer me goddamn it! What do you want?"

The volume and anger of his outburst caused a tickle in his throat that quickly escalated into a coughing fit. Short of breath, head spinning, chest rattling and vision slightly blurred, once it was over he sank down into the recliner, then returned the phone to his ear. The caller had vanished. A dial tone was all that remained. Ignoring the desire to throw the phone down or fire it at the wall, he placed it on the coffee table, blew his nose, then stood there without a clue as to what was happening or what he should do next. If nothing else at least there could now be no doubt that someone was screwing with him. But who? And why?

He knew the front door was locked but checked it again anyway. Even though the deadbolt was already over as far as it could go, he tried turning it harder, as if that might somehow lock the door tighter. As he ventured back into the den he looked at his hands. They were shaking uncontrollably.

Calm down, it's probably just kids with electronic equipment or some jerk that gets his kicks harassing people over the telephone.

There was no point in lying to oneself. Why then did it feel so natural to do so?

He still couldn't shake the feeling that someone was watching him. And the fear associated with it was getting worse…stronger…more palpable.

He turned to the bay window. It hadn't rained in a while but was still overcast and dreary out. He took a long sip of coffee. It had turned lukewarm. *If only I could clear my mind enough to think just a bit more clearly, maybe I could make some sense of all this, I—*

A shadow darted across the window, a dark blur flying past so quickly he didn't have time to discern exactly what it was, but for just an instant it blocked out the light before disappearing as rapidly as it appeared.

Harry didn't realize he'd dropped the mug until it hit his foot and spilled coffee all over the floor. He stepped back, away from the window, and lied to himself again.

Maybe it was a bird, a—a blackbird—or a piece of debris riding the wind. That has to be it, what—what else could it be?

The wind blew. The house creaked. His heart beat faster.

Though fearful whatever had gone by might lunge out and shoot past again at any second, Harry forced himself back to the window regardless. Warily pressing the side of his face to the pane, he cocked his head in an attempt to better see the sky.

An empty gray canvas. Nothing more.

He wondered now if he'd made a mistake not telling Kelly he'd phoned the police about the man on the roof. He looked across the street to Rose's place. No man in black. No man at all.

But you're there, aren't you. Somewhere close. Watching...

He hurried to the kitchen, pulled a couple paper towels from the roll and returned to the den to clean up the coffee spill. The mug had broken, the handle severed, so he scooped up the entire mess and threw it away. After checking to make sure the coffeemaker had sufficiently warmed the coffee still in the pot, he poured himself a fresh mug.

He checked the back door. It too was locked, just as before.

Back in the den he tried the French doors. They were locked, but there was something just beyond them. There, on the patio.

The coyote was back.

* * *

As it had the night before, the sudden appearance of the animal froze Harry in his tracks. In daylight it still looked wildly out of place in the backyard, but not nearly as mysterious. Like a midsize dog or perhaps a small wolf, the coyote was thin but clearly powerful and fast, its coat a blend of short tan and black fur. The ears were pointed, its snout long and tapered, nose wet and black, and its tail a bit bushy. Its golden eyes gave a slow blink, acknowledging Harry and meeting his gaze with one of even greater intensity.

His entire body trembled.

Christ, buck-up and stop being such a pussy.

But fear wasn't entirely to blame. Perhaps it was physical exhaustion, the coffee-jitters or a combination of the two mixed with the relentless chills and shivering brought on by his flu—he couldn't be sure—but a curious tremor shook him from head to toe like a subtle current of electricity.

The coyote watched him, silently imploring once again. *Help me. Please help me.*

It seemed the perfect metaphor, this exotic and rarely seen animal so clearly and unapologetically in his presence, this living creature that occupied many of the same or nearby spaces he did, a being that was without question real and literal—flesh, bone, blood and spirit—yet almost always disguised as a vague feeling, a whisper of sound, a dark blur in the corner of one's eye. It lived among them but went largely unnoticed, almost completely hidden, there and yet not there, leaving behind only scraps of evidence that they even existed at all. Shadows in the night, noises in the darkness, howls in the distance, it was a phantom not of fantasies, nightmares or relegated to legend, but the genuine article, indisputably alive, *actual.*

Were there others…*could* there be others that lived among them as well? Existing in secrecy, using the impossibility of it all to their advantage, undetected and noticed only in the most extreme or unusual circumstances, and even then denied or dismissed as something else? And if so, were these others predators too? Predators of such savagery that even an animal as fearless as a coyote cowered in their presence?

Normally Harry would've laughed at such a concept, considered it asinine and reserved for people who liked to indulge in silly theories best left to UFO nuts and conspiracy loons. But after nearly three full days without sleep, his mind was opening, perhaps even expanding, and though the fear was rising, there was something unexpectedly cleansing about it as well. He was exhausted, yes, and he wasn't thinking clearly in a traditional sense, but it wasn't as simple as all that, and the longer he stayed awake the clearer that became. Maybe they weren't nuts and loons after all. Maybe some were, but surely not all. To completely disbelieve something was just as ignorant and implausible as completely believing something, wasn't it? Using UFOs or ghosts as an example, to suggest that every sighting was completely and rationally explainable was just as moronic as suggesting every sighting was without question a flying saucer from a distant planet or a spirit from another dimension. At the end of the day no one really *knew* a whole lot of anything for sure. Like it or not, there truly were mysteries in life. There were those who believed in life after death and those who scoffed at the idea. But neither really knew for sure.

That was the reality. Of course there were the true believers who thought everything was real and often refused to acknowledge facts to the contrary, and the totally closed-minded (who often falsely labeled themselves “skeptics”) who refused to accept anything as real and approached everything from a point of disproving it rather than having an even remotely open mind. The truth, as in most things, Harry felt, was more than likely somewhere in the middle.

Maybe a lot of people denied the reality of most things outside their realm of understanding because it was easier to do so. Certainly the world was a far less frightening place if one had all the answers. But there were always things that went bump in the night, and there always would be. They might be the wind, or a branch brushing a window, or the settling of the house, or a car’s headlight distorted and slinking along the wall. Or they might not be. Either way, surely it was safer to believe the former. Perhaps it was why many never investigated a strange noise in the night, not because they were sure of what it was, but because they were unsure of what they might find instead.

There had been times in the past when Harry had heard something strange, seen something from the corner of his eye he couldn’t account for, felt something he couldn’t explain, and had ignored it. Not this time. Something was happening here, something unusual but something real. Harry knew it.

And the coyote on the other side of the glass knew it too.

The animal moved a bit closer to the French doors then crouched lower, bowing its head but keeping its eyes trained on Harry. *Open the door. Please.*

Harry looked past the animal to the yard and forest beyond. The trees moved with the wind but otherwise the area appeared ordinary. Could there be someone, some*thing* deeper in the woods, just out of sight but watching this whole thing play out? It seemed not only possible, but probable. The curtains between everything Harry believed real and unreal were billowing, disintegrating slowly as each side bled into the other.

"You've seen them too," Harry whispered to the coyote. "Haven't you."

He remembered how when Marlon was alive he'd sometimes suddenly spring to attention, his face turned to a window or door, his eyes filled with intensity— fear?—and his body rigid with anticipation. Like he'd heard or seen something he hadn't expected to or that didn't quite belong. Harry remembered how sometimes the dog would stare at a corner of the room or at a wall, eyes moving as if following something, seeing something, head cocked in amazement or perhaps confusion. *Had* he seen something Harry and other humans, under normal circumstances, could not?

Please, the coyote's eyes begged, *let me in.*

On any other day Harry would've called Animal Control as Kenny suggested. But he felt a bond with this animal, one he couldn't ignore.

I can't let him in the house. I can't. No way, don't be absurd, it's not some stray dog it's a frigging coyote.

Kelly would kill me, and besides, there's no telling what he might do or how he might react. He could attack me or trash the place and he could be sick or rabid or—no, it's ridiculous, I can't do this.

The coyote was so low to the ground its belly was practically touching the patio, but its eyes remained locked on Harry. *Please, I won't make it another night out here.*

He didn't know what, but he had to do something, he couldn't turn his back on the animal, he just couldn't. There was something so pure about the coyote's eyes. In a way they reminded him of Marlon and—*Marlon*, he thought. *That's it.*

"Wait," Harry said, holding a finger up at the glass as if the coyote might somehow understand what that meant. "I have an idea. I'll be right back, OK?"

Grabbing a tissue on the way by, he headed for the kitchen, blowing his nose as he went. At the back door he stopped and looked through the windows at the mudroom and outer door. Everything looked as it should, so he opened the door and stepped out into the mudroom, a small pantry-like area with a cement floor and a storage closet along one wall. The area had once housed Marlon's food and water dishes, as it's where they'd always fed him at night. Near the bottom of the back door leading outside was a pet door that had been locked since Marlon's death. *The coyote could definitely fit through that*, he thought. *The question is will I be able to get him to use it?*

He opened the closet. A pair of shoes he'd worn a few days before sat on the floor, covered in sand and what appeared to be dark mud. *Odd*, he thought, *where would I have gone to get them that filthy? And why did I put them in here?* A sharp pain fired through his temple. He gasped, rubbed the spot and it slowly faded. Head clearing, he looked to the shelves.

Two metal dishes, a couple cans of dog food and a half-empty bag of dry food were still there these few months later. A lump the size of a golf ball formed in Harry's throat as his eyes filled with tears. His emotions were so raw, so close to the surface he seemed powerless to combat them. Wiping his eyes and nose with the back of his sleeve, he cleared his throat, coughed awhile then pulled the dishes down, setting them against the wall. He filled one with dry food, emptied a can of wet food on top and filled the second bowl with tap water. In the linen closet he found an old blanket they rarely used and put it down on the mudroom floor.

After making sure the outer door was locked, he looked out the windows to the backyard. The coyote had evidently heard him moving around in the mudroom and had left the patio and was now sitting just a few feet away. Harry crouched down, slid the pinlock over on the pet door, pulled it open, then let it slap back into position. He peered out the windows again to see if the coyote had noticed. He had, and was inching closer to the flap, sniffing at it cautiously.

Harry turned and hurried back into the kitchen through the interior door, closing it behind him. He watched as the pet door lifted and a little black nose appeared. It was followed by the snout and finally the coyote's head. His eyes darted about suspiciously before finally looking up and noticing Harry on the other side of the door.

"That's the best I can do," he told him. "It's OK, come on, that door will let you come and go as you please. Come on."

The head backed out, the flap closed.

Harry returned to the French doors but the coyote had not done the same. Perplexed, he checked the mudroom again. This time he found the coyote fully inside the room, moving slowly, nose working furiously as it sniffed every inch of wall and floor it could reach. At least for the time being it seemed uninterested in the food, opting instead to sit on the blanket and stare at the outside door as if expecting something to come knocking at any moment.

"It's all right," Harry said through the door.

"You're safe."

The coyote glanced at him.

Maybe, the eyes answered, *but not for long*.

He watched the coyote awhile, still unable to believe what he was witnessing. *What in God's name could cause a coyote to behave this way?*

Before he could fully ponder the question, the strange scraping sound he'd heard earlier and suspected was a runaway trashcan returned. Echoing along the street, this time it sounded like it was coming from out in front of the house. Less consistent and methodical than before, it came in periodic bursts, then fell silent, only to return several seconds later.

The coyote's ears reacted. He'd heard it too. The animal quietly backed as far into the corner of the mudroom as possible and lay still.

Harry went fast as he could to the bay window and its view of the street. The wind had let up some what but the sky threatened more rain. The cars in the driveway were undisturbed, and again, there were no loose trash barrels or—

There!

A man stood in the middle of the street dressed entirely in black, his back to the house. Hunched over, he was wrestling with some sort of large pipe that looked to be about five feet in length and at least three feet in diameter. An odd shade of metallic dark gray Harry had never quite seen before, it appeared similar to the kind of stovepipes used on freestanding fireplaces and woodstoves, but not exactly, as this particular length of piping—or whatever it was—appeared quite heavy, awkward to maneuver and much bigger around. One end of the pipe was touching the street, the other held in the crooks of the man's arms as he struggled to drag it along the pavement to wherever he was headed. With each effort the pipe scraped the ground, making the sound Harry had heard.

At first he thought it might be the same man he'd seen scuttling across Rose's roof, but as more detail came into view he became convinced it was not. The roof-squatter wore pants, a sweater and a knit hat. This man was dressed in black overalls, a black turtleneck, black boots and a black conductor-style cap. Harry couldn't make out his face as it was turned away, but black hair stuck out in tufts from the back of the hat.

Unsure of what the man was doing or exactly what he was dragging, Harry watched from the window, peeking but careful to remain partially concealed. Despite the coffee his fever made it difficult to function or concentrate for anything other than very short intervals. His eyes were heavy, he'd again begun to feel terribly weak and he couldn't be sure of his legs just then. He leaned most of his weight against the wall as he watched the strange man outside continue to lug the pipe up the street in the direction of the abandoned houses. It was obviously this man the coyote was reacting to, so whoever he was, his mere presence and proximity managed to elicit crippling fear in the animal the likes of which Harry hadn't previously believed possible. *Odd*, he thought. There didn't seem to be anything intrinsically terrifying about him.

The man bent his knees, put his back into the lift, then dragged the pipe another few feet, but it slipped from the cradle of his arms and down into his hands, which he now held cupped beneath the underside. With his chest heaving and his shoulders slumped, it looked like he might drop the pipe at any second. But despite the precarious grip, he managed to hang on, and then his posture slowly straightened and the man stood very still.

Harry blinked rapidly, keeping him in focus, but the man still had his back to him, concealing any facial expressions that might offer a clue as to who he was or what was happening. The shift in body language seemed to indicate something had changed, though, like something had just then occurred to the man, or as if perhaps he'd heard something unexpected and was reacting to that.

Very slowly, the man's head pivoted, turning to look back over his shoulder.

Harry leaned out of sight, fell against the wall and hid along the side of the window. The man was still essentially in line with the property, so once he looked behind him he'd be looking right at the house, and more precisely, right at the bay window. But Harry had moved out of the way well before the man had turned, so he waited, trying to breathe in short little inhales and exhales so as not to incite his cough. He knew that at that distance, and with a wall and window between them, the odds that the man could have somehow heard him were nearly nonexistent. So why then had he looked back at the house? Had he *sensed* Harry behind him, watching? Had this strange man experienced the same feeling Harry had been grappling with for hours now—the sensation of being watched—and was simply reacting to that, checking to see if it was coming from behind him? With his back flat against the wall next to the window, Harry silently counted off the seconds, waiting for an appropriate amount of time to pass before he could safely take another peek. He'd hoped the sound of the man dragging the pipe might resume but it didn't.

Harry waited.

He could hear his chest wheeze with each inhale and exhale of breath, threatening to unleash another coughing fit, and he'd begun to perspire again, a good sign, perhaps, in terms of his fever. His head was filled, his nose running, and he desperately needed a tissue, but he didn't want to leave his position just yet, so he wiped at his runny nostrils with his sleeve and continued to count off the seconds.

After a minute, he figured it was more than likely safe to take another look.

Moving stealthily, Harry peeled his back from the wall, turned to the edge of the bay window, then slowly leaned his head out for a better view.

And looked directly into the face of the man.

He was right there, just inches away, his impossibly pale face pressed against the window, hands up on either side of him and touching the glass.

Harry let out a horrifying scream and staggered back as if punched in the chest and knocked off-balance. The room spun, ceiling becoming floor, floor becoming ceiling, everything a blur of speed and motion as he felt himself falling, coughing, trying desperately to draw breath through lungs clogged and swollen. Even once he'd toppled over and crashed to the floor, sprawled there and flopping about like a beached fish, he continued to scream—or at least tried to—because he'd finally gotten a good look at the man's face.

Only it wasn't the normal face of a man at all. The eyes were abnormally large, bright and moist, unblinking and set an unnatural distance apart. There were no discernable lips around a mouth that barely contained freakishly large teeth stained brown with decay and rot, and the nose was thick, hooked and flattened like a boxer's.

Get up, you—you have to get up and get to the phone!

He struggled back to his feet, but fear slashed at him again and again, cutting him clean to the bone with each arcing strike. A relentlessly primal fear, it was unlike anything he'd ever felt before, a hysterical terror that left him feeling insignificant and weak, prey caught alone on an open plane, already marked, already chosen, already doomed, already dead.

Head spinning, he coughed and gagged and fell again, this time pitching forward. His forehead just missed the edge of the coffee table, and though he managed to break most of the fall with his hands he still ended up face-first on the floor. Rolling, he forced himself to his knees. Spittle dangled from his lips as he continued to cough, unable to stop now, his lungs rattling, his throat raw and his eyes teary and burning.

The phone—where's the phone, I—the coffee table, I left it on the coffee table!

He rose to his feet, legs quivering as he lunged for the cordless, then spun back around to check the window.

No one was there.

The cough finally subsided and Harry stood there a moment, swaying and trying to catch his breath, mouth agape, bottom lip sporting long drools of spit and phlegm that hung from him like strands of spaghetti. He wiped them away with his free hand, his other clutching the phone. His chest continued to wheeze, but otherwise the house was quiet. With his thumb he hit 9-1, then waited, slowly inching back to the bay window, neck craned for a better view out to the street.

No man. No pipe. Just an empty cul-de-sac.

Harry wiped his eyes but soon realized they hadn't simply been tearing due to the cough. He was crying. Tears streamed his cheeks and his head filled up even worse than before, but he couldn't help it. Again, emotions were running through him unchecked and he could no longer control them. Like a frightened and abandoned child, he stood before the bay window and wept for some time.

After a while he realized there seemed little point in calling the police. They'd think he was crazy—he wouldn't blame them—and he had no desire to go through another episode like he had with Officer Nicoletto. Without looking, his thumb slid to the disconnect button and hung up the phone.

Once he'd regained some control of himself, Harry shuffled back into the kitchen to check on the coyote. He was still lying on the blanket, and when he looked up at Harry his eyes remained filled with terror. Only this time the terror was in Harry's eyes too.

What should I do? What—what am I supposed to do? I don't know, I—I don't know what the hell to do, I'm not equipped for this, I don't know anymore, I can't think straight and I don't understand any of this!

Suddenly he was confronted with an overwhelming desire to laugh. He caught it just in time and reined it in, knowing that if he let it loose he might never be able to stop it. Like a tiny crack in his defenses, it would spread and grow, fracturing him deeper until he crumbled to pieces, broken beyond repair.

Madness was right there, so close he could feel its breath against the back of his neck. All he had to do was let it swallow him. It seemed so easy, really, so much easier than fighting it. But fighting was all he had left.

The flu, the lack of sleep, the madness, the stress and all the other things that were going on had stripped him of everything. His physical and emotional strength, his clarity of mind, his sense of safety and security and comfort, his health, his ability to sleep and heal himself—all of it—they'd taken all of it. His desire to fight, to never succumb to the everclosing darkness was all that remained. His will. It was weakened, badly wounded even, but it hadn't yet been broken. In the end, nothing could rob him or anyone else of that. It could only be given away, and in that strange and wondrous moment, standing in his kitchen alone and afraid, confused and exhausted and riddled with sickness, Harry promised himself he would never let that happen.

But I can't keep going on like this, not with...those eyes, my God, they...

He checked his watch. Just a little before three. In another hour or so it would start to get dark.

Kelly. I have to call Kelly. I can trust her, I can—I can tell her what's going on and she'll know what to do, she'll—

A sudden and violent knocking shook the house.

6

Harry grabbed a baseball bat from the back corner of the hallway closet next to the stairs. He'd kept it there for ages along with two old mitts that hadn't been used since Garret was a little boy, yet it was battered and scarred with several nicks and smears of what looked like some black substance. He remembered the two of them using it sparingly at best but apparently it had gotten a lot more use than he'd thought. The old Louisville Slugger was also a lot heavier than he remembered, or he'd become even weaker than he realized. The damn thing felt like it was made of granite rather than wood. Holding it with both hands, he pointed it toward the floor, then kicked the closet door closed with his heel. Already out of breath and sweating profusely, he inched toward the front door. When he got to within a foot or two of it he stopped and waited for a break in the knocking.

"Who is it?" he called out.

A muffled voice answered. It sounded female.

He moved closer, this time taking a step to the side so he could get a peek out the windows on either side of the door. Someone was standing on the front stoop in a light pink raincoat but he couldn't see a face. Harry looked to the street.

A pink Volkswagen Bug was parked directly in front of the house.

"Hello?" the voice said, louder this time and obviously annoyed.

Cautiously, he reached for the knob, turned it and opened the door just a crack, leaning close so all anyone would be able to see of him was the left side of his face. A middle-aged woman stood before him.

"Harry, we need to talk, right now." Her voice was laced with a mixture of barely contained rage and tears. "Right goddamn now."

He knew the woman but couldn't place her. "I'm sorry…I don't…"

"It's *me*." She sighed and leaned closer. Her hair was a tad long for a woman her age but worked, particularly since she wore it up and had wrapped an attractive silk scarf around her forehead. Her brown eyes had probably been quite striking when she was younger, though they had since turned glassy and bloodshot. She wore quite a bit of makeup, including generous amounts around her eyes and a pink glossy lipstick that matched her waist-length belted raincoat.

Finally, it clicked. He hadn't seen her in months (had only met her a few times, in fact), and she looked a lot different than the last time he'd seen her. She'd changed her hair color from its natural red to a softer auburn, and the style itself was longer and had a purposely mussed look.

What the hell is Aaron Searcy's wife doing here?

"Gloria," he mumbled. "I'm so sorry. I didn't recognize you."

"You're awfully pale," she said as if she'd only just then noticed him there.

His nose clogged. "I…uh…I have the flu. I'm a little hazy, sorry."

"There's some terrible stuff going around, a lot of people are sick." She wet her lips with her tongue and her expression softened. "I know I probably shouldn't have just appeared like this, all emotional and everything, but we need to talk. It's time we talked."

"Is everything all right?"

"Do you think I'd be here if it was?"

Still mostly hidden behind the door, Harry let the baseball bat rest in the corner between the windows and the wall, then revealed a bit more of himself. The fresh air felt colder than it had just moments before. "What's this all about?"

"Can I come in? I don't want to talk about it on your front step."

"This isn't the best time, Gloria, I really don't feel well."

"Yeah," she said, "me either. How could either of us feel well with this going on?"

"With *what* going on?"

"You don't have to play stupid with me, Harry."

She brushed a renegade strand of hair from her eyes.

She'd had a recent manicure, her fingernails painted a light pink. If nothing else she was color-coordinated. "Are you going to let me in or not?"

"You didn't happen to see somebody out there just now when you pulled up, did you? Like a workman type, a really pale guy in black overalls dragging what looked like a big piece of pipe?"

Gloria stared at him as if he'd spoken in tongues.

"No. Why?"

"I thought I—nothing, I—I thought somebody was out there earlier."

"He must've left before I got here," she said, folding her arms over her chest. "Let me in, Harry. You know as well as I do we need to talk about this."

With a defeated nod he stepped back and opened the door so she could enter. As she swept past a scent of sweet perfume and liquor wafted about in her wake, pungent enough for him to detect even with such limited breathing capability.

Gloria hovered around the beginnings of the den, pacing around like a madwoman uncomfortable in her own skin and unsure of what to do about it. "I'm so pissed off, I—I'm trying to figure out which emotions to hang on to and which ones to throw away, you know? I mean, what are *we* supposed to do anyway? How are *we* supposed to act?"

Harry followed her deeper into the house, albeit reluctantly, feeling grotesque and repellant and weak. "Can I get you something? Coffee or…"

"Is it OK if I smoke?" she asked, rummaging through a large pink leather handbag slung over her shoulder.

"I wish you wouldn't. I can barely breathe as it is."

She looked over at him and nodded, releasing the purse. "Yeah, sure—of course, sorry—I wasn't thinking." She stepped closer and reached out for him without warning, placing her palm flat against his forehead. "You're burning up. When's the last time you took your temperature?"

"While ago," he answered, standing there like a schoolboy at the nurse's office. "It was around 102."

Gloria's hand dropped away. "Do you have any Tylenol?"

"Probably somewhere."

"Take a couple every four hours or so, it'll bring the fever down."

"Yeah, I'll do that." Harry's legs ached so badly he knew he couldn't remain standing much longer.

He also knew it was best to keep Gloria in the den.

The kitchen had to remain off-limits. If she were to look in the mudroom he'd have to explain the coyote.

He motioned to the couch. "Have a seat."

As Gloria put her purse on the floor and undid her raincoat, he shuffled over to the recliner and sat on the edge of the chair. She tossed her coat over the arm of the couch without much care, then flopped down onto the cushions and crossed her legs at the knee. She was wearing a pretty but basic pink sleeveless dress cut low enough to show off an ample amount of cleavage, matching plastic hoop earrings and a pair of pink pumps with spike heels. She wore no nylons but her legs were smooth, silky and in good shape. A delicate gold bracelet adorned her left ankle. Sandwiched between a thick gold wedding ring and a second band sporting a row of diamonds, her engagement ring was larger than Kelly's and sparkled like she was planning to land planes with it. Though overdressed for a typical Saturday afternoon, Harry assumed she'd come from work at her salon. She struck him as one of those women who were constantly coiffed, a throwback to some 1950s-housewife-type whose husband never saw her without her hair done and her makeup in place.

"I gotta tell you," she said. "You look rough."

"I feel rough."

"You haven't slept in a while, have you?"

"Not in three days. What can I do for you, Gloria?"

"I'm sorry to barge in like this." She broke eye contact, looked instead to the floor. "But I didn't know what else to do."

Harry knew what was coming, but had no idea what to say or do until she came out with it, until she gave him something concrete to react to. "You said we need to talk. Go ahead."

"You know what's happening too, I know you do.

How could you not?"

His chest wheezing, Harry somehow managed to will away the looming threat of another coughing fit. "Lay it out for me. That's why you're here, isn't it?"

"I know you're sick, but I can tell by your eyes you've been crying. I don't say that to embarrass you, OK? I've done nothing but cry over the last few days either."

Harry self-consciously wiped at his eyes. "I'm just exhausted, that's all."

"Look at you," she said softly. "Look at me. And where are they? Where are they, huh? Our loving spouses, where are they? Are they here? Are they here caring for us, supporting us, helping us? Not a chance. They're too busy with each other."

"How much have you had to drink?"

"I've had a few. And I'm going to have a few more, and then a few more after that." Again she rummaged through her purse, this time coming back with a little silver flask. "You wanna see my ID? Don't I look twenty-one to you?"

Harry snagged a tissue, blew his nose and waited. Time bled through the room, falling in slow agonizing drops as the silence of the afternoon closed in around them.

"I've suspected since forever," she finally told him, unscrewing the top of the flask. "All the signs were there. But

Aaron and I've been together for so long I guess I just didn't want to believe it. It didn't seem real. It still doesn't. Thing is there comes a point where you have to see the truth, Harry, you have to see it even though you don't want to, even though it's disgusting and awful and hurtful. And the truth of the matter is that your wife and my husband are having an affair."

There they were. He'd heard the words somewhere other than in his own head. "That's a pretty serious accusation."

"Oh please, spare me." She rolled her eyes and threw back some of whatever was in her flask. "They've been running around for years. I always knew something was there I just never wanted to see it, so I pretended not to."

Harry forced a swallow. It caught in his throat, amidst the mucus. "How do you know for sure?"

"The same way you do."

"I never said—"

"You don't have to. You don't understand yet, but you will." She drew a deep breath and fell silent a moment, as if the hesitation might help her consider her words more carefully. "I know we don't know each other that well, but you're not a moron, are you? It's right in front of your eyes. Maybe you don't want to know, don't want to face it. That I understand. I didn't either. I haven't wanted to for a long while now, but after a while it starts to gnaw at you. It breaks you down and you can't ignore it or make excuses anymore. Maybe you're just not ready." She bobbed her leg up and down nervously, the pump slipping off her heel and dangling from her toes. "But I am."

Harry rubbed his eyes, stifled a yawn. "Look, you show up at my door unannounced, ranting and raving like a lunatic, drinking in the middle of the afternoon and talking about an affair, but I haven't heard one scrap of evidence or anything that would lead me to believe your suspicions are warranted."

"Here, have some." She held the flask out for him. "It'll help relax you. Then maybe you can get that board out of your ass. It's obviously wedged so far up there it's pushing on your brain."

"I can't drink, I'm on antibiotics." He waved her off. "Now I know the situation with Kelly and Aaron can be frustrating because they've worked so closely together for so long and they're out of town together a lot and all that, but Kelly and I have a solid marriage, do you understand? I know my wife. I know Kelly, Gloria, I know—"

"Do you *know* they're probably not even in San Diego?" She arched a heavily made-up eyebrow. "How about that, do you *know* that?"

"What are you talking about? Of course they're in San Diego. I have the hotel information, and Kelly called me once she'd landed there."

"Aaron gave me some hotel information too. Only it didn't check out. When I called there looking for him they told me they couldn't divulge the names of guests so I told them I was his wife and there was a family emergency and I needed to speak with him immediately. A manager came on the line and told me they had no such person registered there. No Kelly Fremont either. Aaron probably didn't think it would be a big deal because I always use his cell anyway. But this time I called his bluff, and the hotel had no idea who the hell I was talking about. Think about it, did you actually reach Kelly through the hotel phone, or was it her cell? When she called you once she'd supposedly landed in San Diego, did she call you from the hotel or from her cell?"

Harry's mind struggled to remember. Had he ever actually gotten through to her at the hotel? Had he ever asked for her by name or simply for the suite number she'd given him?

Call my cell rather than the hotel, that way you'll be sure to get me.

"I've known they were up to something for a long time," Gloria said, taking another swallow from her flask. "And this time when all of a sudden a last minute trip popped up, I knew something was wrong with it. I could feel it, you know? You know how when you know someone so well you can sometimes just *feel* it? So this time I decided enough was enough. I don't know what it was about this time that made me act but I decided to check up on him and make sure what he was telling me was true. And just like I knew all along deep down, he was lying. Aaron's been lying for a long time now Harry, and if you're honest with yourself Kelly's been lying to you too."

"All right then," he said, doing his best to mask his mounting concern. "If they're not in San Diego where are they?"

"I have my suspicions but I'm not sure." She reached for her purse, found a tissue and dabbed her eyes. "I only know they aren't on a business trip. When the hotel had no record of them I thought maybe I'd gotten the wrong information, so I called Brody."

Harry knew she was referring to Brody Fay; the senior V.P. of the company Kelly worked for. "You called him at home?"

"I told him I had a slight emergency and needed to reach Aaron and did he have the right hotel information for him in San Diego? He had no idea what the hell I was talking about. So I told him how Aaron said he and Kelly were on a business trip to San Diego for the company. Brody got real quiet and then real nervous. He tried backpedaling and saying he didn't know for sure if they were on a business trip or not, but I could tell he was full of crap. He said he'd try to reach Aaron and find out but I told him not to bother, that I'd handle it. He didn't argue, I could tell he just wanted to get off the phone as fast as he could. Can't really blame him, I guess."

Harry subtly adjusted his position. It felt like he'd been sucker-punched in the gut and the resulting agony was growing worse, spreading across his torso and out into his extremities with each stabbing pain, limiting his breathing and sending his heart into a panic. *What if this is true? Would Gloria lie? Would she go to all this trouble just on suspicion alone and make up all the rest?* It didn't seem believable that she would, and yet the very real possibility that Kelly was having an affair didn't seem believable either. He'd had his brief suspicions but those had been based on anger and poor judgment, a lack of sleep and—

"I know it's a lot to deal with," Gloria said. "Believe me, I know it is. I've looked the other way for a while now and I'm not doing it anymore. I can't, I just can't. I don't know what…" She dabbed at her eyes again. "I don't know what I've done to…"

Harry wanted to cry. For her. For him. For all of them. He bit his lip, thought of Garret. *How could Kelly do this? Why would she do it?* "I know it doesn't look good, but maybe there's a reasonable explanation."

"Yeah, and what would that be? Ever lied to your wife and gone on a trip with another woman? And if you did, what do you think you'd be doing on that trip, Harry? Any guesses? I'll give you three and the first two don't count."

"I'm just saying I think we ought to talk to them directly before we decide to condemn them. Don't we owe them that much?"

She leaned forward and raised her voice, as if he were hard of hearing. "My husband is *fucking* your wife."

"You don't know that. There could be a—"

"I've spent my whole life trying to make that dickhead happy and this is how he repays me. I'm not perfect, God knows, but I've been a good wife, Harry, a damn good wife. All these years wiping his ass and being there for him. We never even had children. Know why? Aaron never wanted any. I did but who cares about what Gloria wants? Just get your ass to the shop and cut some more hair, bitch, leave me alone to chase secretaries and waitresses and God knows what else." Her eyes glistened. "I always wanted kids, from the time I was a little girl I dreamed about being a mother one day. But I chose him instead. I thought if it meant being without him then having children wasn't worth it. Can you imagine? Turns out the only thing not worth it was him." She relaxed her posture and sat back, deflated, and took another drink. "Piece of shit, that's what he is, a lowlife piece of shit."

Harry closed his eyes, felt his head spin. He couldn't take much more.

"What have we done?" she asked. "What have we done to make them hurt us like this, Harry?" When he offered no response she said, "Want to know the truth? I always thought you guys were an odd couple. You're so different. You seem like a sweet guy, predictable and kind of boring to be honest, but steady and dependable and decent. The kind of guy who goes to work every day, stays out of trouble, doesn't drink too much or do drugs, pays his taxes, obeys the law, doesn't beat his wife or run around with other women, the type who gets his ass home every night, a good man, a good husband and father. Maybe not the most exciting guy on the block, but somebody a girl can count on. And Kelly, she always came off like she totally took you for granted, like her job was everything and you were kind of an afterthought, this base she knew would always be there because where the hell else would you be? Hey, I'm a career woman myself, OK? I know the score. The first few years we were married Aaron's company was still struggling, so I rented a chair at a place in Boston, an upscale joint. I made a bunch of money and we socked it away for a couple years until I had enough for a down payment on my own shop. Once I took the plunge I never looked back.

Now I'm the one renting chairs to other girls. I built a solid clientele and worked my fingers to the bone to make that place a success. You try spending half your life on your feet, twelve hours a day, washing and styling hair. But as dedicated as I was, as hard as I worked, it never took priority over my husband, our marriage or our life together. Everything I did was for us, OK? Aaron makes a fortune. I haven't had to work in years. Now I do it for my own sanity, OK?" Gloria fired back another gulp from the flask, then sat forward with such ferocity she nearly toppled off the couch as even more cleavage spilled from her dress. "*OK?*"

Harry nodded. "OK."

They sat in silence awhile. Countless thoughts fired through his mind but he couldn't transform even one of them into anything coherent. So he said nothing, just sat there, remembering how Kenny had immediately suspected marital problems. Was it that obvious? Had it really been right in front of him for a long time like Gloria suggested, and he'd simply missed it, not seen it, or not wanted to? Had he been sleepwalking all this time?

"Was this your dream, Harry?" she asked, still leaned forward but more relaxed now, less intense. "We all have dreams, was this yours?"

"Yes," he heard himself say. "I never wanted an extravagant life. I wanted a wife, a family, a good job, nice place to live, security, happiness."

"Shouldn't be too much to ask, huh? You think this was Kelly's dream too?"

"I thought so."

She looked at the flask as if trying to remember something. "I wanted to be a hairdresser from the time I was a little kid. Something about it seemed so glamorous, you know? Silly, but when I was a little girl it seemed that way. I wanted to work in the movies, to be a hairstylist for movie stars. So I went to hairdressing school right out of high school, it was a year-and-a-half thing but I came out licensed and ready to work. A week after graduation I packed a suitcase and moved to New York City. All alone, can you imagine? Twenty-years-old and ready to take on the Big Apple. I thought anything was possible back then, and I think maybe it was. Maybe it's just all in how the cards fall." She took a sip from the flask. "I didn't even last a year in New York. Tough town, I was way out of my league. I got a job cutting hair but it wasn't anywhere near the movies or TV or even theater. I came home about seven months after I left. Aaron came into the place I was working and I styled his hair. He asked me out and we started dating. He was older, sure, but so dashing and worldly and... well anyway, long-story-short, we ended up falling in love and getting married. All those feelings of failure and loss went away. I felt alive again. He made me feel special, like anything was possible just like before, like I could do anything as long as we had each other. Maybe my dreams weren't going to come true exactly as I dreamed them, but they were coming true and that's what mattered. That's the power of love, Harry, it makes you feel alive again, makes you feel invincible and successful, unstoppable. It makes you believe things even when they're not true, and you don't care, because it's such a powerful feeling you can't let go. You don't ever want to be without it again. So I held on tight to Aaron and I loved him with everything I had. The rest, as they say, is history. Isn't that a magical story?" She let out a contemptible bark of laughter, then took another drink. "We built a life together for what, *this*? What a waste. What a horrible waste." She raised the flask as if preparing for a toast. "Here's to our lives, Harry, yours, mine and ours. Ashes, ashes, we all fall down."

"You better take it easy with that stuff. You won't be able to drive."

"I could stay the night." She gave a naughty wink. "That'd fix their asses."

The nausea was back, and all he knew at that point was that he had to get Gloria out of there. Ignoring the sudden urge to run for the bathroom, Harry cleared his throat and said, "Look, I'm sick as hell, I haven't slept in days and the *weirdest* things have been happening around here. I'm so out of it I can't make much sense of anything. Now I don't know for sure what's going on with Kelly and Aaron, but you getting drunk while the two of us sit here being suspicious and upset about it isn't going to help the situation any. I think it'd be best if you went on home, got a hold of your husband and talked to him directly. I'll do the same with Kelly. We need to know what is or isn't happening here, I agree, but the only way to do that is for you to handle your business and for me to handle mine. Does that sound reasonable to you?"

She slapped the top back on the flask and slowly turned it tight. "You still don't believe it, do you?"

"I don't know what to believe at this point."

She tossed the flask back into her purse. "You think I'm lying, is that it?"

"That's not what I said."

She slowly ran her index finger along her cleavage, purposely pushing the tip between her breasts as she went. "Why don't we hurt them back, Harry?"

"Gloria—"

"Nobody needs to know. *We'll* know. That'll be enough."

"Even if I wanted to," he said through a cough, "and I don't, I'm in no shape to—"

She rose from the couch and teetered before him. "I'll take care of you."

He put his hands up with the hope of warding her off. "OK, we need to stop this right now. You need to get your coat and—"

"Don't you think I'm pretty?"

"Yes," he sighed. "You're very attractive, but—"

"Then let me suck your cock."

"Jesus." He got to his feet and started for the door. "Come on, you—"

"You know you want it." She reached out, took his wrist and held on tight.

"No," he said, removing her hand. "I don't."

She offered a drunkenly seductive smile. "You can cum in my mouth if you want."

"Well aren't you a trooper." Laughing nervously he motioned to the door. "Let's go. Don't say anything else. You're upset and you've had too much to drink. Let's just forget any of this ever happened and—"

"They're doing it, why shouldn't we?"

He draped her raincoat over her shoulders. "We don't know that."

"Yes we do." She moved closer. So close he could smell the chemical stench of her hairspray. "My husband's a dog, and you're wife's a whore."

"Come on, you need to get home." He took her by the shoulder and gently pushed her toward the door. "And don't drink anymore between here and there."

"Do you know none of the other employees like her? They complain about her all the time, call her an ice-cold bitch and say all she cares about is getting ahead and one day being CEO. They badmouth her all the time, say she does whatever Aaron wants. It's pissed a lot of people in the company off."

Harry reached for the doorknob. "Go home and have some coffee, Gloria, I don't want to hear anymore, all right?"

"You need to hear this," she said, purposely blocking him from opening the door. "Aaron was fucking Kelly within a few weeks of her starting work there. He's been bending her over his desk for a long time, and word is she goes down on him whenever he wants her to. She's been my husband's sex toy for years, a good little office slut always right there to tend to his needs. Bet you didn't know that, did you? Well it's common knowledge, Harry. It used to drive me crazy. He'd come home and go on and on about how wonderful Kelly is, how smart she is and how dedicated she is and how *fond* of her he is. It makes me sick. Didn't you ever wonder how a receptionist shot up through the ranks so fast? How do you think she got all those promotions? You think she was the most qualified?"

"Yes, actually, I do," he said through gritted teeth.

He'd expected his nausea to worsen but it had actually subsided. "Kelly's worked her ass off and earned everything she has, and as a successful woman yourself I'd expect you of all people to be offended when a woman's accused of only being able to make it by using sex instead of her brains, determination and talent."

Gloria leaned in close, sneering at him now. "The only thing that offends me is women like your wife. She gives us all a bad name and makes it tougher for everyone. Sad thing is Aaron always says how bright she is, so she didn't have to do it that way, she could've made it on smarts. I guess she just likes it."

"Please," Harry said. "I'm asking you to leave."

"Last chance, sick-boy." She stuck her tongue out and wiggled it at him. "Wanna make some revenge?"

"I want you out of my house, that's what I want." He reached around her roughly and pulled the door open, brushing it against her shoulder as it swung fully open. "Just go home, all right? I'm sorry about all this, but please, go."

As she straightened her hair her fingers brushed the silk scarf around her head. She flinched as if it had pained her and then looked away, confused. "I just wanted you to know," she said softly. "I know it's my fault for telling you, but I wanted you to know why."

"Your fault?"

A small dark bead appeared at the bottom edge of the scarf near her temple, slowly fattening until it broke free and became a trickle along the side of her face. A trickle of blood.

"Jesus, Gloria, you're bleeding." He reached for her but she leaned away. "Did you hear me? You're *bleeding*."

"It's all right."

"It's not all right, you—Christ—you're bleeding from the head. What happened?"

She pushed her way by, purposely shielding the side of her face as she hurried past. "It doesn't matter now."

Harry stood in the open doorway, watching as Gloria stopped halfway to her car, pulled off her heels, then padded the rest of the way to her car. With a violent slam of the driver's side door she made a quick U-turn, then screeched away. The Volkswagen disappeared around the corner at the end of the street.

Feeling as if someone had just hit him in the head with a shovel, he inhaled the fresh air while trying to absorb everything that had just happened. But none of it wanted to compute. His mind was on overload and slowly crashing like a doomed hard-drive. The situation with Kelly had sent his emotions on a rollercoaster ride, leaving him shell-shocked and beyond confused. One moment he'd suspected her of infidelity, and then convinced himself that was ridiculous and the things he'd suspected were simple coincidences Kelly had been able to easily and innocently explain. And now, just when he thought he was beyond such concerns and had determined the truth, the uncertainty and suspicions were back and stronger than ever, leaving everything he thought was true in jeopardy. How could it not be after everything Gloria had just said and done?

As if her obvious but unexplained head wound wasn't enough, the accusations about Kelly and Aaron Searcy were even more disturbing, not just due to the content but because in years past, on more than one occasion, he'd questioned her relationship with him. Never to Kelly, just to himself now and then, but they were fleeting and he'd always dismissed it and scolded himself for feeling even slightly suspicious when there was no cause to be. The relationship Kelly had with Searcy always seemed a bit too close to him though. Why then hadn't he questioned it more? Why did he dismiss it unless it seemed the right thing to do, unless somewhere deep down he knew his concern was unfounded?

But if these accusations *were* true then they'd been happening for a very long time. In all the years she'd worked for the company Harry had never heard a single rumor or innuendo about Kelly and Searcy. He'd never harbored anything other than those vague or passing suspicions, and had never once even considered them seriously. There'd been no reason to. He knew her work and home life were two entirely different worlds—so were his—but the idea that over all these years she'd been servicing her boss and then coming home to him and going about her life as if none of that was happening or mattered seemed beyond belief. He couldn't imagine

Kelly being able to maintain such a situation for so long without cracking, without giving some indication, without slipping up even once. And even if she hadn't, if it were common knowledge as Gloria had told him, wouldn't someone else somewhere along the line try to expose her? Wouldn't there have been rumors or talk? How could she have kept something like that completely quiet year after year after year? And even if she'd been able to pull it off, *why* would she do such a thing? The woman he knew wouldn't, it just didn't add up.

Kelly and Searcy were close, though, he knew that much was true. She'd always described him as a mentor who had helped her come into her own as an executive. But far as he knew Searcy had been happily married to Gloria for decades, and while Harry knew they shared a basic fondness, a friendship, the-old-master-and-his-young-apprentice kind of thing, never in a million years had he honestly suspected anything sexual might have happened between them. Even now it seemed almost laughable. And yet, he could no longer simply dismiss it. He had to rethink some things. He needed to go back, to discard his usual blasé and sentimental approach and try to remember the past more clearly and objectively. Thunder rumbled in the distance, rolling closer and closer and bringing the rain with it. Hissing from the heavens, it fell with even more ferocity than before.

Night was getting closer. Perhaps the truth was as well.

Something on the couch where Gloria had been sitting caught his attention. He moved closer, retrieved a small scrap of lined paper that looked as if it had been scribbled on, then hastily torn from a small notepad.

14 Beach Street.

Had she left it behind purposely, or had it fallen from her purse?

14 Beach Street.

He crumpled it up and threw it across the room.

I need to know what's real, Harry thought.

The Kelly mystery wasn't going to unravel easily, but maybe there was one thing he *could* figure out right then and there, once and for all.

Earlier he'd seen the man lugging the pipe just outside the window with his face pressed to the glass. If that wasn't a hallucination and had truly happened, then there would more than likely be some sort of physical evidence left behind.

I need to grab hold of something—anything—that's real, that I can prove and know for sure.

Harry stepped far enough out the doorway to see around the bushes in front of and below the bay window. The dark mulch there was still wet from the previous rains.

Just below the window were two indentations, side by side.

Like footprints.

7

Although the topic had only been of moderate interest, over the years Harry had seen documentaries and read a book or two about haunted houses and people who claimed to have had paranormal experiences. Hoaxers and the mentally deficient aside, he neither believed everyone who alleged such things were lying, nor was he pompous enough to think he had all the answers, but he'd never been comfortable with supernatural explanations either. After all, people made mistakes. They honestly misidentified and misinterpreted things all the time, but the concept wasn't something Harry spent much time thinking about. He'd always felt safe, comfortable. *Maybe too comfortable...so comfortable I didn't realize what was happening right under my nose.*

Could that be it? If there truly were beings beyond the pale of everyday existence, wouldn't it stand to reason they'd prefer to move among those who didn't believe in them? Wouldn't it be easier to operate undetected amidst those who don't believe you exist rather than trying to hide among people looking for you at the edge of every shadow, behind every gravestone or in every photograph marred with distortion?

Is that what he was dealing with, ghosts?

Ghosts don't leave footprints.

Then again, wasn't this all an enormous and completely unfounded leap? He'd seen some strange men, but they *were* men. Wasn't it far more likely that they were human beings than otherworldly creatures beyond his comprehension? After all, there was no proof of any such thing.

But the man's face, he—it was distorted and—no, I have to be wrong about what I saw—of course it wasn't as bad as I'm remembering. I'm wrong. The man was there, the footprints prove it, but I was wrong about his features.

Harry snatched the baseball bat from the corner and held on tight. Silly as he felt, the weapon afforded him at least a limited sense of security (however flimsy), in an otherwise frightening maelstrom of confusion and uncertainty. He knew he needed to focus and deal with everything that had been placed before him, he just couldn't figure out where to begin. Was his wife really someone he didn't even know? Had their lives together been little more than an ongoing series of lies? There was still a possibility, however remote, that Kelly was innocent. As for the strange phone calls, they *had* happened, there was no question about it, and while they were unsettling and difficult to understand, again, there was at least a small chance he might yet uncover a reasonable explanation for them. But the men fell into another category altogether. The man in the window left behind evidence, irrefutable *proof* he'd been standing there.

His purpose remained a mystery, his existence did not.

I was wrong about his face.

He repeated that like a mantra until it sounded irrefutable.

Glancing out the windows as he went, Harry made his way to the kitchen and checked on the coyote.

He was curled up on the blanket but awake and still watching the back door.

Harry leaned against the island and tried to think. He could call the police and report the man with the pipe, but by the time the cops got there the footprints would be distorted beyond recognition or obliterated altogether by this latest rainfall. Without proof they'd write him off as the same sick and exhausted guy on meds seeing strange things in his neighborhood who'd called last time, a nuisance dialing 911 over nothing.

But if the men were real, and Harry no longer had any doubt they were, didn't he have to report it? Wasn't doing so his civic duty and ultimately a means of protecting himself in the long run as well? While he was certain he'd seen two different men, they were obviously connected somehow and definitely up to something. He had no idea what, but it sure as hell wasn't anything good. The chills returned, followed by a coughing spell that left his throat raw and his chest aching.

The men must be working together...but on what? And how do the phone calls figure into this? Then the Kelly thing, it—it can't be connected too, can it? No, how could—no—can't be.

He tried desperately to sort through it all but his mind simply couldn't keep up. The exhaustion was too much, the fever and the confusion too great.

All of a sudden my wife's a stranger, there's a coyote *hiding in my mudroom, I'm getting phantom phone calls and I'm seeing bizarre symbols and strange men all over the neighborhood.*

Even the most nebulous sense that everything would eventually be all right eluded him. All he felt was fear, and it was getting stronger.

Such a delicate thread between control and hysteria...

Maybe the rest was just wishful thinking; fairytales recited to children so they could sleep at night believing mayhem and madness and all the demons festering within could never touch their souls because that was all so very far away, a horror that crippled other people in other places they didn't need to be concerned with. After all, they were protected by love, by walls and doors, nightlights and trusting assurances that there really wasn't anything under the bed, hiding in closet shadows or lurking just beyond the windows.

Lies.

With the bat clutched to his chest, Harry staggered back into the den. Afraid to look out the bay window for fear of what might be looking back, he kept his head down until he'd reached the recliner, then forced a peek.

Rain sprayed the pane, dripping and sluicing along the window. As the water beaded and rolled it left something behind. Forming on the glass in its wake, the same strange hieroglyphic-like symbols he'd seen on the mailbox appeared, as if a film had previously concealed them but had now been washed away by the rain. They faded as quickly as they appeared, gone before he could make any sense of them or even be sure they'd been there in the first place.

Grimacing, Harry turned away as shockwaves of nerves, disbelief and fear throttled him from head to toe. *Goddamn it, this is* real.

Night was coming, rolling in with the thunder, and the only other thing Harry could rely on, the one constant that would calm and center him, was his son and the love they shared. He unceremoniously hacked up a ball of phlegm, then grabbed the cordless phone and scrolled through the numbers programmed into speed-dial until he found Garret's dorm.

The call was answered by Hank, Garret's exceptionally grating roommate.

"It's Mr. Fremont, Hank, is Garret in?"

"Yo, Mr. Free, what up with that rumble, playah?"

"Pardon?" He watched the other windows, eyes bouncing from pane to pane in a search for additional signs or symbols. They revealed nothing more.

"You all raspy, dude."

"I'm a little under the weather. Can I speak to Garret please?"

"Aw-ight, hoed-up." The phone clunked down. "G-dog! Phone!"

After what seemed like forever Garret finally came on the line. "Hello?"

Just the sound of his son's voice somehow made everything seem a little better. But it was no longer the voice of a child. Garret had become a man. "Hey, it's Dad."

"Whoa, are you all right?"

"I've got the flu, *G-Dog*."

Garret laughed, and it was the most comforting sound Harry had ever heard. "Hank has no idea he's a white boy from Ohio with red hair and freckles."

Though it took effort, Harry laughed too. "Somebody should probably break it to him."

After an awkward silence Garret said, "So is everything OK?"

"Everything's fine, I just wanted to check in."

"Is Mom sick too?"

That's one way to put it. Could be she isn't even close to the person you and I have always believed she was. Maybe she's lost her mind...

"No she's in San Diego on a business trip."

Or maybe I've lost mine.

"So you're sick and all alone?"

Harry felt himself smile. "Yeah but I'll be fine. How are things there? How are classes going?"

"It's all good, but actually I'm sort of heading out, we're going to a party on campus. You know, being Saturday night and all."

"Sure—right—I understand, I—"

"It's just, you know, we're already running a little late."

"No problem. You and Vanilla Ice have fun."

Rather than laugh he said, "Dad, are you sure everything's OK?"

Nothing's OK. I'm lost in the dark and I can't find my way out.

"Everything's fine, pal, relax."

"You don't usually call just to say hi."

"Well shame on me then." Harry swallowed back the emotion. How did he know for sure this wasn't the last time he'd ever speak to his child? *I don't. That's the reality. I don't.* "I was just thinking about you, that's all. Wanted to see how you were doing."

"OK," Garret said, though it didn't sound like he'd quite bought it. "I hope you feel better."

"Thanks."

"Anyway, I should go."

"I love you, son." Though he often told Garret he loved him, he knew this time he'd said it with unusual intensity, and he could almost see the confusion drifting across his son's face. "I love you very much. No matter what, I want you to know that."

"Yeah, I love you too, Dad."

"Night, pal."

"Bye."

The line clicked and Garret was gone. Harry disconnected, put the phone down and tried to picture his son up in New Hampshire hurrying around his dorm room getting ready for a party. He could scarcely remember what those carefree days of youth were like. But he had experienced them…hadn't he? Or was his past a lie too? Was he chasing real memories or simply tracking wishes and fantasies honed to memory?

Harry checked his watch. Had enough time passed for him to pop another Amoxicillin? *Whatever, close enough.* He shuttled back to the kitchen and downed the antibiotic with a glass of orange juice, somehow managing to do so without coughing. He eyed the cough syrup with the codeine a moment. One quick swallow of a couple tablespoons and all he'd have to do is lie down and drift off. Appealing as it was he couldn't risk it. Turning his attention to the inhaler, he took another blast from that, and once the dizziness had gone and he was able to breathe better, he paced around the kitchen awhile, rehearsing what he was going to say to Kelly. If at all possible, he'd approach the situation with her first, because at least he had some idea where and how to begin. And if he didn't get these things under control soon he knew the entirety of this madness would engulf and shut him down completely.

Line them up and knock them down one at a time.

That's how he always tackled challenges in his life, in an organized and efficient manner.

But this is different. This isn't a minor problem around the house or some stupid situation at work that needs to be resolved. My entire life's unraveling, coming apart at the seams. Nothing's right. It's all confused and wrong and—

"How could you do this?" he said aloud, staring at the tile patterns on the kitchen floor. "*Why* would you do this?"

Hurt, angry and still not quite able to believe the things Gloria had told him, he grabbed the wall phone and dialed Kelly's hotel.

"Good afternoon, Great Night Suites."

A female this time, but with the same condescending monotone delivery.

"Can you tell me if you have a Kelly Fremont staying there?"

"I'm sorry, sir, but security and privacy reasons prevent us from divulging any information regarding our guests."

Harry bit his lip. "She's my wife."

"If you have a suite number I'd be more than happy to—"

"136."

The phone rang endlessly. Finally, the woman at the desk returned.

"I'm sorry, sir, that suite's not—"

"Yeah, not answering, I got it." He slammed the phone down, wiped perspiration from his forehead, then resumed his pacing. In the tug-of-war between anger and fear, anger was winning. With his wife's face filling his mind's eye, Harry yanked the phone free again and dialed Kelly's cell.

It rang once, then went to voicemail.

"You've reached Kelly Fremont. I'm unable to take your call at this time. Please leave a message and I'll get back to you soon as I can. Thank you."

"It's me," Harry said after the tone sounded. "I don't care what time it is when you get this, call me back. I need to talk to you." He hit the pound key and listened to his message. If his incensed tone wasn't enough, his voice sounded like he'd spent the afternoon swallowing rusty nails.

He hung up and waited, listening to wind and rain crash the house.

Now what? Do I try to find evidence of an affair?

Where the hell would I find that? I don't even know where to look.

Her computer seemed as good a place to start as any, but she'd taken her laptop with her, and as she never used his there was no sense in even searching that one. The only other computer in the family was Garret's desktop, but that had taken up residence in a dorm room in New Hampshire.

Far as he knew Kelly didn't keep a diary, blog or anything like that, and even if she'd made incriminating calls, they'd be on her cell not the home phone. And what exactly did incriminating calls look like anyway? Maybe numerous calls to one number at odd times or calls made at times that didn't coincide with where she was supposed to be? What other evidence could there possibly be?

Behavior...

Her behavior had been a bit off of late, but he'd dismissed it as stress over her job and the upcoming move. Had he missed something? Their sex life had always been good. They didn't make love as often as they used to but usually still went to bed two or three times a week unless Kelly was away on business (which recently she had been an inordinate amount of times).

And Aaron Searcy almost always made the trip.

Did everyone else know some alternate Kelly Fremont, a freewheeling party-girl version Harry had no knowledge of, one she only let him see in tiny snippets or if and when it suited their life together?

She's been his sex toy for years.

Surprised his latest wave of nausea hadn't turned into full-scale vomiting, Harry begrudgingly trod back upstairs. Once in their bedroom he slowly took it all in, trying to study everything as if he'd never seen any of it before. It proved more difficult than he imagined. He wasn't even sure what he was searching for.

What did you expect to find?

He couldn't help but feel he was the one betraying her. Considering Gloria's accusations as real possibilities seemed disloyal, and yet if *any* of them were true he had every right to...

It's all coming down, he thought, *all of it.*

Balancing a multitude of emotions Harry returned downstairs, and after arming himself with another cup of coffee, decided to hunker down for what was sure to be another long evening. When Kelly called back he'd deal with her then, but there was a bigger picture here he could not ignore. It was time to batten down the hatches and prepare for imminent night. Only this time he'd be in control. He'd remain awake not as a helpless victim but because he chose to, determined to face the darkness and all its mysteries head-on. Exhaustion and illness weakened his body and mind with each passing moment, and the fear in him continued to rise, to inexplicably grow and take shape all around him like the carnivorous organism it was. But Harry refused to be broken.

He checked the mudroom again. The coyote lifted his head from the blanket, troubled eyes locked on Harry's. *It's just us now, you and me.*

"Yeah," Harry replied through a sigh. "And whatever else is out there."

Trees on the edge of the property rocked in the wind like they had all day, branches swaying as if controlled by something greater than the elements, and the notion that he was being watched had evolved from suspicion into certainty. Harry could feel a presence prying deep inside him, someone or something decidedly hostile peering into his soul, and unsettling as it was, he remained powerless against it.

An ancient oak tree near the mouth of the cul-desac stood firm and defiant against the wind, its barren branches decorated with numerous blackbirds weathering the elements as best they could. Like sentries, they watched the house in silent vigil.

Vigil. From the Latin vigilia, *meaning wakefulness, a state of observance, of purposeful sleeplessness.* Harry had no idea where he'd obtained such information, it simply came to him, whispered from the darkest corners of his mind as if to remind that even his thoughts were no longer his own.

Purposeful sleeplessness...yes...

As Harry stood hypnotized by the graceful motion of violently writhing trees, night crept closer.

Off to Never Land.

* * *

With newfound purpose Harry moved through the house, securing everything and double-checking all doors and windows to be sure they were locked. In the downstairs bathroom off the kitchen he took his temperature, and upon learning it was down to 100, popped a couple Tylenol. After splashing cold water on his face he retrieved the cough syrup from upstairs, deciding to keep that, the baseball bat and the cordless phone with him. The satellite signal was still down, so he had no television, and though the phone and his Blackberry were both fully operational, he wanted a backup, a secondary connection to the outside world, so he removed his laptop from his briefcase and set up something of a command center in the den. Positioned in the recliner with the computer on a small folding table, powered up and accessing the wireless signal in the house, he leaned the bat against the side of the chair, and along with a box of tissues, his medicine, the thermometer, and a large travel mug full of steaming hot coffee, had everything he needed for the time being within reach. From where he was sitting he could see out the bay window and was only a few steps from the kitchen and the view through the back door.

The wind howled as if mortally wounded.

I know you're out there, but you're not getting in. Not tonight. Not ever. I won't allow it. This is my house.

Harry heard and felt his chest gurgle as he drew a breath. If there was to be a siege on his home tonight, he'd be ready, provided one could ever truly be prepared for such a thing. This was his fortress—that's how he needed to view it—and along with his body and mind, heart and soul, past and future, his reality and even his dreams, he'd defend it all as best he could.

To the death, if I have to.

As darkness descended, Harry sipped his coffee, put his glasses on and turned his attention to the Internet. His homepage, CNN, showcased mostly bad news and the more recent horrors taking place all over the world. Doom and gloom dominated the headlines, most articles centering on the rapidly declining economy, the worsening recession, the continued drops in the stock market, the housing and mortgage crisis, and government bailout money being spent on bonuses for already bloated and overpaid business executives. The rest covered various genocides and atrocities happening in places few knew anything about or even cared to, the ongoing wars in Iraq and Afghanistan, and some celebrity-flavor-of-the-month's latest arrest. It was all so hopeless and dark, which was why months before Harry had begun limiting his exposure to the news. He'd once been a voracious newspaper reader but now kept up by checking the CNN page or occasionally watching network news on television. Being informed came at an awful price these days. Perhaps it always had.

Convinced there was a connection between his lack of sleep and all these strange occurrences, he manned the laptop and logged onto his favorite search engine. He entered the word: insomnia. A series of website links appeared.

****Natural Remedies for Insomnia****

****Get Relief for Insomnia****

****Insomnia causes, symptoms, diagnosis and treatment****

****Got Insomnia? Horny Sluts in Your Area Need Sex Tonight****

He returned to the search page and tried: SLEEP DEPRIVATION.

****Sleep Deprivation Research****

****Sleep Deprivation Studies and Analysis****

****The Effects of Sleep Deprivation****

****Sleep-Deprived Nude Amateur Wives & Girlfriends****

Certain one could enter literally anything into an Internet search engine and get at least one porn hit, Harry clicked on the third link. A page appeared citing various risks associated with getting insufficient amounts of sleep. Symptoms included the more obvious, like irritability, drowsiness, depression and an inability to focus, but also covered such things as increased risk for cancer, the weakening of the immune system and even hardening of the arteries.

After surfing numerous sites over several minutes, his eyes began to cross. Returning to the main search page, he downed more coffee, then clicked the next page for further results. Amidst numerous sites, some relating to the topic and some not, he noticed one in particular at the bottom of the page that read: *Sleep Deprivation Experiments.*

Inexplicably drawn to the link, he clicked on it and discovered a site that documented and chronicled numerous sleep-related experiments that had been conducted over the years in the United States. The first section covered experiments sponsored and conducted by numerous universities across the country from the late 1950s to the present, and though interesting, the pages that followed promised to be far more provocative. The subsequent section concerned several sleep deprivation experiments conducted by the military and/or government intelligence agencies, and included documents that had only recently been made public through the Freedom of Information Act.

Sleep, a voice in his head whispered, *while you still can.*

Perspiration beaded along his forehead yet he suddenly felt cold, as a chill fell across his shoulders like a shawl of ice. His eyelids grew heavy and his sinuses were running like a faucet, so he sipped more coffee, then blew his nose. After a coughing fit he carefully brought the cursor to rest on the first link. Though shaken, he was convinced he'd been led to this site for a reason. He had to move forward.

Croatoan.

He hesitated. Another shiver left him trembling as earlier memories and worries returned to assault him a second time.

If anything happens, no one will ever know what took place here. No one will ever know for sure what really happened to me.

Harry knew then he had to begin chronicling these events as best he could. As he attempted to explore the various ways he might achieve this, his mind dragged along with infuriating lethargy, unable to keep up with everything he wanted and needed it to process.

I want them to know. I want Garret to know.

A few years before, Kelly had gotten him a digital camera for his birthday. Although he'd never learned the intricacies of it he knew the basics well enough to use it effectively should more visual evidence arise. Along with a nylon case, the battery and some other accessories, the camera was on the shelf in the front closet next to the stairs. He retrieved it and put it next to the recliner.

The video angle covered, he next found a handheld Dictaphone in his laptop briefcase he often used at work for reminders and taking notes. Nervously fumbling with the unit, he yanked the tiny tape free, threw it aside and dug a fresh one from the case. Once he'd liberated it from its plastic wrapping he slapped it into the Dictaphone and snapped shut the cassette door.

90 minutes. 45 minutes each side.

Funny thing, time, how it all fit together despite such arbitrary beginnings and endings, the whole of it played out and calculated down to the very second, each breath, every sunset, dream and waking moment designed, the beat of every heart accounted for, each life a preordained piece of a much larger puzzle, a precisely measured unit in the infinite vacuum of space and time.

Harry cleared his throat, coughed a bit, then hit record and began to speak, relaying everything that had taken place thus far as best he could. He touched on the Kelly situation, but only to the extent that he'd found some of the happenings surrounding his attempts to contact her odd and perhaps somehow loosely related. Otherwise he steered clear of insinuating anything about extramarital affairs and the like. If he needed to include that at some point in his chronicle of what was taking place he'd do so, but not unless it became integral to the bigger picture. As he spoke into the small recorder he struggled to remember each detail and every nuance regarding the bizarre things taking place, and the longer he spoke the more difficult it became to enunciate and speak not only clearly, but coherently. He covered the odd phone calls, the unusual symbols he'd seen, the coyote, and the strangers. With his gurgling baritone he sounded like a disembodied version of himself, his voice alien and riddled with unusual amounts of emotion.

Though coughing fits twice caused him to pause the recording, he pressed on until he'd finished, doing his best to focus on facts and keeping personal asides to a minimum. He checked the Dictaphone counter. The entire rundown had taken about ten minutes. He had neither the strength nor the desire to play it back, and he could only hope no one else would ever have to hear it either. But just in case, Harry switched the unit to voice-activated mode so it would automatically begin recording from where he'd left off whenever he (or anyone else) said anything audible. He set it on the table next to the laptop, then did his best to shake off the fatigue and make another quick inspection of the windows.

"Probably sounded completely insane," he grumbled, eyes moving from rain-blurred window to rain-blurred window, tracing each shadow, studying each dark corner, the stairs and what little he could see of the house beyond.

Satisfied all was quiet at least for now, he refocused on the website.

Head spinning, fever lower but still lingering, and exhaustion attempting to drag him down to sleep, Harry worked by rote, fingers surprisingly deft as he swept through the information on the site, his tired eyes and sluggish brain doing their best to keep pace. After surfing the site awhile, he settled on one group of experiments that had taken place in the late 1960s involving inmates from an array of maximum security prisons that had "volunteered" to be transferred to a government mental health facility where they would become test subjects for advanced sleep deprivation studies.

"*...As expected, when a subject's normal sleep cycle is consistently interrupted or missed entirely, their minds tire and cease performing normally. As the brain does not regenerate properly when deprived of sleep, the parts of the* *brain that manage and manipulate memory, language, the ability to prepare and plan, and the basic sense and understanding of time are all severely affected...This was the case in all tested subjects, as was increased appetite. Test subjects were given whatever they requested to eat and drink, with no limits placed on quantity or reasonable availability. As a result, caloric intake increased exponentially, and insulin and blood sugar levels of the test subjects became elevated to levels mirroring those of typical Type II diabetics...*"

Harry slid the mouse down to the next paragraph.

"*...After subjects were kept in a sustained state of wakefulness for a minimum of 15 hours, the effects on the brain became remarkably similar to the effect of alcohol consumption. By the 20-hour mark the effect on the brain of nearly all subjects was equal to those produced by the consumption of at least three alcoholic beverages. Subjects also experienced great difficulty responding to quickly changing situations and found making generally rational judgments far more difficult than they had only hours before...*"

Harry looked at a series of grainy black and white photos scattered throughout the site that showed various men in an institutional setting. Often strapped to beds, their heads and upper bodies were fitted with various electrodes and wires. One young man in particular looked up at him through the screen, a ghost frozen in time, the uncertainty in his eyes flirting with terror...his expression oddly familiar. So lost...so...hopeless...

"*...Sleep deprivation as torture was also studied in select volunteer subjects. Results varied as to its effectiveness, but all subjects consistently experienced blurred vision, slurred speech, memory lapses, confusion, poor judgment, nausea, heightened levels of agitation, fear and paranoia, unbridled emotion (studies have shown the emotional centers of the brain are 60-70% more reactive in subjects suffering from sleep deprivation), visual and auditory hallucinations, temporary psychosis, and in one case, permanent psychosis. Sustained sleep deprivation beyond the introduction of psychosis has led* *to death in lab animals and would certainly lead to death in human beings. As an interesting sidebar, numerous clinical studies have conclusively shown that some form of consistent sleep interruption and/or disturbance occurs in nearly all psychiatric disorders. These findings, coupled with the results of this and numerous similar studies, illustrate the importance of further investigation into the connections between sleep and mental illness..."*

Although he'd already scrolled well past the photograph, the young man's face refused to leave him.

Harry wondered if the man was still alive. He'd be much older now. Maybe he had children of his own, a life and a partner that loved him. Or maybe he'd died deep in the bowels of some military hospital or government medical center. Maybe he was still there, strapped to a bed or wandering the halls at night, unable to sleep even now, a hopeless shell, medicated and shuffling mindlessly along dark corridors, forgotten and alone.

Or had those thoughts become confused and merged with the memories from his nightmares? Hadn't they involved a labyrinth of dark corridors as well, a series of hallways that very easily could've belonged to an institution or hospital of some kind? In the dreams he remembered the strange disfigured and bandaged figure, being lost in those hallways... and then the moon hanging above him in the black sky, a silent witness to those pursuing him, its pockmarked surface barren and gazing down at him like a cold, long-dead deity.

And pain...there was pain too.

The cordless phone began to ring.

Startled, Harry grabbed it and saw Kenny's number scroll across the ID. For a moment he considered letting it go to voicemail but the idea of connecting with someone just then was comforting. "Kenny?"

"Harry, you need to stop, OK?"

The minute he heard his friend's voice he knew something was wrong. Kenny rarely sounded angry, but there was no mistaking his tone. "What?"

"Come on, you're killing me here. You need to stop."

"Stop what?"

"Why are you doing this?"

"What are you talking about?"

"You've called me six times in the last ten minutes."

Harry hesitated, unsure if he'd heard him correctly. "What?"

"The phone calls need to stop right now. I'm serious."

"Kenny, I haven't called you since this morning."

"You know how pissed Rhonda gets if anything interrupts our family time on Saturdays." He purposely muffled his voice so his wife wouldn't hear. "You can't keep calling or I swear to God she's going to blow a clot. And what's with all the crazy babbling? You weren't making any sense. The last time I'm not even sure you were speaking English."

"You don't understand—"

"I understand it's annoying the hell out of Rhonda and making it really difficult for me to defend you, not to mention it's frigging creepy."

Harry ran a hand through his hair. It came back sticky and damp with perspiration. "Listen to me. I've been getting calls from someone who sounds like me too and—"

"If your goal is to make me seriously concerned about the state of your mental health right now, mission accomplished, OK?"

"Kenny I'm trying to tell you I've been getting the same calls."

"Do I need to come over there and take you to the hospital or what?"

"I don't understand it myself and I know it sounds crazy, but the voice only sounds like mine. I swear to you it's not me."

Kenny let loose a halfhearted laugh. "Right, of course, it's someone who *sounds* like you, I get it. So anyway here's the thing. You're delirious with fever and exhaustion. You must be coming in and out of it and not even realizing half the things you're doing or saying. Please tell me you're not using the stove."

Something drew Harry's attention to the stairs. Had a shadow just moved across them or was it only night drifting through the windows?

"Harry I know you're there. I can hear you breathing."

"Sorry, I…"

"Just go to sleep. Why are you even still up? You haven't slept in three days. Take the damn cough syrup already. Wasn't that the whole point of getting the codeine in the first place? Take it and go to bed. You'll wake up in the morning feeling better and with a much clearer mind, I promise. Come on, this isn't that complicated. What are you, twelve?"

"I can't sleep." Harry checked the bay window. Just rain. "Not now."

"Have you even tried? Take the cough syrup and go lie down. If you still can't sleep call your doctor back and find out if he can do anything else for you. I'll make another drugstore run if need be but otherwise or unless it's an emergency don't call again, all right?"

"I didn't make those calls! That's what I'm trying to tell you! The same thing's happening to me!"

"Hey, thanks for screaming directly into the phone, doesn't make me want to hang up on you at all."

"Kenny…" Frustration strangled Harry to silence. He already knew it was futile but the words left him anyway. "The craziest things are happening and I think I might be on to—"

"Right, the coyote and all that, I know. We already went over this when I was there. Which you'd remember if you'd slept in the last seventy-two hours."

Another rush of cold washed over him, this time deadening his emotions as well. "Yeah," Harry answered softly, "you're right. I'll go to bed now."

"Good." Kenny covered the phone, muttered something unintelligible, then came back on the line. "Get some sleep and I'll check in on you in the morning."

Before Harry could respond Kenny hung up.

The house creaked and shifted, doing its best to ward off the rain.

Harry put the phone aside. Whoever or whatever had made the harassing calls had also made them to Kenny, so now it had gone beyond him and had now touched others. But why? He wondered if it had happened to anyone else he knew. If so it was only a matter of time before other friends and colleagues started calling and complaining about nonsensical calls he hadn't made. If nothing else, there was no longer any reason to question the reality of the strange calls or his interpretation of them. They *had* happened, and exactly as he'd experienced them. But rather than feeling vindicated the knowledge left him more horrified and confused than ever.

Unless...

Could he have made the calls without even realizing it?

No. Bullshit.

The den darkened, the walls absorbing night as a peculiarly long shadow glided across the floor. He followed it to the bay window. Telephone wires along the street and coming off the house were barely discernable in the rain and remnants of dusky light. Yet they were unavoidable—black vines everywhere he looked—alive, ominous and threatening. There were telephone poles and endless networks of wires overhead everywhere, but how often did anyone truly see them? Normally the human mind had a curious way of editing such things out, but apparently Harry no longer possessed those filters.

The world was a very different place once you took the time to notice it.

Harry knew that turning lights on inside the house would make it easier for someone outside to see in and harder for him to see out, so he left them off. The only illumination came from his laptop, which cut a swathe through the increasing darkness.

He returned his attention to the computer screen and scanned several pages until he came across a section dealing with hallucinations in test subjects.

"...as sleep deprivation continued well beyond the 15-hour mark the activity patterns in the brains of test subjects changed more profoundly. The patterns indicated subjects had

regressed to more primitive brain function, and as a result, found it increasingly difficult to control emotions and to experience them in logical context...The amygdala, a mass of gray matter in the temporal lobe containing short-term memories and believed to control emotion, also serves as an alarm for the brain when faced with dangers it needs protection from. In the test subjects' brains, this alarm function became so accelerated the prefrontal cortex ceased activity, making reason irrelevant while prohibiting the brain's ability to logically assess threat levels. This resulted in vast confusion and uncertainty when subjects' brains attempted to interpret the appropriateness of the fight-or-flight response...In most cases, the subjects had a difficult time discerning a difference between real and imagined dangers, more-often-than-not lumping them all into the former category rather than the latter...As one example, when test subjects that had endured more than 24-48 hours of sleep deprivation were shown a slideshow of graphically violent images from several Hollywood films their brains were unable to process the information prop erly. Normally, the Amygdala would alert the brain that the images were not real and therefore nothing to fear. Instead, the test subjects' brains connected with the locus coeruleus, a nucleus in the brain stem concerned with responses to stress and panic, which produces noradrenalin designed to defend against threats to survival. With its release, the subject felt a heightened sense of threat and danger, along with the need to summon the fight-or-flight reflex in situations the brain would normally define, understand and dismiss...Combined with both visual and auditory hallucinations, which began in most of the test subjects at this point, the result was an unpredictable subject running on raw, unrestrained and irrational emotion. Primarily fear..."

Harry looked up from the screen. Something had changed. He listened. The rain, it had stopped. Only the wind remained, and it too was weakening.

The storm was dying.

"...Many subjects began experiencing visual and auditory hallucinations that were quite vivid and detailed... several reported hearing disembodied voices, whispers, voices in their heads, strange sounds they could not identify and sounds that occurred out of synch (such as telephones ringing when they were not, radios playing when they were shut off, etc.)...Nearly all the test subjects reported 'seeing' dark figures or blurs along the edges of their peripheral vision as well. In some cases these mysterious figures (which were consistently described as human or humanlike) were stationary, while in other cases they were moving, drifting past the field of vision, sometimes sluggishly, sometimes rapidly...As the state of wakefulness continued, many subjects began to 'see' these figures beyond their peripheral vision as well, and some believed they were interacting with them in various ways...With few exceptions, all subjects who experienced this were terrified by what they were seeing and hearing, and wanted desperately to get away from these things...To the subjects these hallucinations were appallingly real, and tests revealed that those suffering from massive amounts of sleep deprivation consistently 'saw,' 'heard' and experienced things others did not (or perhaps could not)...Because so many physical changes take place to human beings exposed to extended periods of sleep deprivation, not only in the brain but throughout the entire body, further studies were conducted on a select group of highly volatile subjects to determine if their eyes were functioning abnormally or differently, and to determine if the literal physiology of the eye became altered under such extreme circumstances..."

Night had fallen; Harry could feel it moving through him. He forced a swallow down his dry and scratchy throat, considering the information before him. Prior to reading this material he was so sure he wasn't imagining any of this. Now he had no choice but to at least consider it. Was this all real or just his brain going off the rails, debilitated by sleep deprivation?

"...Further tests were conducted to determine if severely sleep deprived subjects were able to see beyond the usual

spectrum of light human beings are normally capable of perceiving. Results were inconclusive, and stressed subjects to dangerous levels of psychosis and physical fatigue that in several cases nearly resulted in death…While studies indicated the human eye and human vision in general might be affected to the point of altering not only what the subject sees but how *they see and the extent to* which *they see, nothing definitive was established in these areas…Many animals are capable of seeing well beyond the limited range human beings are able to, and it is suspected that humans subjected to extreme cases of sleep deprivation may experience ocular changes capable of allowing them to see a wider range of the spectrum than is normally possible, perhaps including segments of ultraviolet and infrared light…Certainly there are large segments of 'reality' human beings cannot see with the naked eye. But the question remains, does this strictly include such things as radio and microwaves, or living organisms—both known and unknown—as well?"*

Harry rubbed his eyes, blinked until his vision cleared a bit. Was that it? Had the lack of sleep not only altered his consciousness but also the literal physiology of his eyes? Were the things he'd seen not hallucinations at all but rather segments of reality that until then had been concealed beyond the range of normal human vision?

"*The human brain, in an attempt to make sense of the information it is receiving, will often fill in the blanks in the visual plane, substituting similar objects from memory for those it cannot readily identify, particularly in cases of peripheral vision…For example, if an object cannot be seen clearly, a visual substitution of something similar will be used from memory in an attempt to fill in the blank spaces or explain what a blur or undefined field is…These substitutions are normally vivid and appear quite real...The concept of 'seeing' the movement of dark blurs or even dark figures in the peripheral vision (typically described as the corner of one's eye), is a fairly common occurrence in most human beings, even during lucid moments…Most reports indicate that if the subject turns to look at the figure, it moves away rapidly or vanishes by the time one is looking directly at it..."*

"But these didn't vanish," he muttered to himself.

"...An overwhelming majority of studies (including our own) have shown that this phenomenon increases dramatically during periods of extreme duress or exhaustion, as the eyes begin to function less efficiently and therefore the need to substitute visuals becomes more and more necessary...

Those inclined toward occultism believe these visions are glimpses of real entities, perhaps ghosts and the like, but the phenomenon is a simple optical illusion...

However, these visions are so powerful they may result in the manifestation of other 'real' experiences beyond visual occurrences, meaning these events could be 'real,' strictly imagined, or a fusion of both. The greatest difficulty in determining that is the fact that once the subjects have endured sleeplessness for extended periods sufficient to produce these events in vivid detail beyond the norm, they slip into a state of consciousness where it is problematic (and sometimes impossible) to determine if the participant is still awake (in any meaningful way) or if they are in fact asleep. This is a consistent phenomenon in human test subjects in these and other studies, as numerous parallel tests show that without exception, subjects experiencing extreme periods of sleep deprivation all eventually fall into this state, where the person is essentially trapped somewhere between consciousness and sleep, existing in neither but rather in some alternate form of consciousness not yet fully understood..."

Outside, the pipe-scraping noise sounded again, echoing along the street as before but this time sounding much farther away. Harry winced as fear that began in the pit of his stomach crept toward the back of his neck. Like icy fingers it slowly walked up his spine, then fanned out across his shoulders and down into his arms.

Memories of the man at the window returned. Without the wind and rain it had become deathly quiet, and somehow that was worse. He removed his glasses, reached for the baseball bat and slammed shut his eyes, praying for the noise to stop.

Much to his surprise it did.

But his relief was short-lived, as from the ensuing silence came another sound, one far more disturbing.

Harry looked up at the ceiling, listened, and heard it again.

There was someone on the roof.

8

The beginnings of moonlight moved through the windows and fell across the base of the stairs, providing a sliver of visibility. Baseball bat in hand, the Dictaphone in his pocket, the digital camera slung around his neck and the cordless phone stuffed into the waistband of his sweatpants, Harry crept to the staircase and gazed up at the second floor landing.

Shadows...darkness...silence...

He absently reached for the light switch on the wall but caught himself just before flipping it on, remembering that at least for now, it was safer to remain in the dark.

There was movement on the roof again.

His stomach clenched. Gagging back the nausea he continued forward, slowly ascending the staircase. An errant ache shot up his right leg, across his knee, along the thigh and into his groin. Groaning quietly, he slumped against the wall, one hand dragging the bat and the other clutching the railing. He was about halfway up the stairs and already lightheaded, out of breath and sweating profusely. The dizziness left him quickly but his heart continued to race. The fear was getting worse, and his inability to rein it in threatened to shatter what little patience he had left.

Hold it together...

In response a legion of images fired through Harry's brain like a movie reel, and the same dark figure he'd seen earlier emerged, lying back on its hands and feet in that unsettling crablike position. Only this time he was much closer, moving across the roof above him and searching maniacally for avenues into the house.

And Kelly...her image was there too...watching him from the corner of a dark room he didn't recognize. Barefoot and wearing a delicate but full slip, she was backed into a corner draped in shadows and the webs of unseen spiders. Her makeup smudged, eyeliner running down her cheeks like she'd been crying and her hair mussed, she wore an expression of sorrow and despair that looked as if it had been permanently carved into her face, the flesh like newly chiseled stone, a dark vision from some crazed sculptor's nightmares.

From the back of his mind came a whisper: *"Tunnel of love."*

As it all fell away into oblivion, an itch tore at Harry's throat and erupted into a brief coughing spell. He managed to muffle it by holding his forearm to his mouth, and then he hurried to the upstairs landing.

The hallway waited...quiet...empty...dark...the bedroom doors closed.

Sudden footfalls running directly overhead stopped him dead. He looked up at the ceiling, following the sound as whatever it was hurried across the roof toward the front of the house. If he'd tracked the footsteps correctly the person, or whatever it was, had moved to the portion of roof above his and Kelly's bedroom. Harry swung the bat up near his shoulder and cocked it back. It felt awkward and heavy, causing his grip to tremble as if he were struggling to hold aloft a piece of granite. Cautiously, he moved toward the door, then reached out, turned the knob and pushed.

The door swung open, revealing the dark bedroom beyond.

Nothing appeared out of place or disturbed. Harry's nose had filled and clogged again, so he breathed quietly through his mouth and stood in the center of the room and listened. As gunk trickled down the back of his throat he noticed through the window that Rose's house was still empty and quiet, but a nearby streetlight had come on, producing a single pool of light on the otherwise dark cul-de-sac. He lowered the bat and pulled the Dictaphone from his pocket.

"I'm having a harder and harder time thinking straight but I know for sure there's someone on the roof," he whispered into the microphone. "I'm in the bedroom and I can hear whoever or whatever it is moving up there."

Slinking closer to the window, he listened for further movement, but the night had again gone quiet. His eyes stung as another wave of dizziness slammed him, and he could feel his fever rising, burning through him and dragging him toward total exhaustion. Harry tore his eyes from the ceiling and allowed them to sweep the room. Almost immediately he felt something new, a sensation that something was wrong not just outside and on the roof, but inside as well.

Here, in this room. The bed was just as he'd left it, the comforter askew and the sheets kicked aside. It felt like an eternity since he'd curled up in bed, but he fought off his body's pleas for rest and continued surveying the room. The bureaus, Kelly's dressing table—everything was fine—nothing disturbed, nothing in the corners, nothing in the shadows. His eyes slid along the mirror over the dressing table, and he caught a glimpse of himself standing there.

Jesus Christ Almighty.

He looked like a lunatic, a deranged member of the paparazzi, his hair mussed, his face pasty and pale, eyes ablaze with sickness and terror, a camera dangling from his neck, a recorder in one hand and a baseball bat in the other.

But before he could worry too much about it he noticed something else in the mirror...something behind him that chilled his blood...

The closet door was open.

It had been closed when he entered the room, he was sure of it.

I'd have noticed otherwise. I walked right by it.

Inside, beyond the open door, there was only darkness. No longer simply a closet, it had become a pitch-black portal to a place of nightmares and horror. He slowly brought the Dictaphone to his mouth.

"They're inside the house," he whispered. "I think...I think they may be inside the house. The closet, it..." He gripped the bat tighter with his free hand. His heart felt like it was about to explode from his chest, thudding so violently it left him short of breath. "The closet's open—it—someone's opened the closet door."

His throat suddenly constricted.

Not now for Christ's sake!

Breathing through his mouth in short shallow intervals, he dropped the Dictaphone back into his pocket, gripped the bat with both hands and backed away, trying to slide closer to the far wall as he made his way toward the hallway. By the time he'd reached the doorway the need to cough had gone. With one foot in the hallway and one still in the bedroom, he raised the bat and readied for a swing were it to come to that.

"I know you're in there," he said, but it came out as little more than a croak. He cleared his throat, and with all the authority he could summon, said, "Come out. Now goddamn it!"

In answer, deafening silence.

Gritting his teeth, Harry started back toward the closet, taking each step as if it might be his last. The closer he got the deeper the darkness inside the closet became.

He continued toward it. Closer...and closer still...

Pouncing, he threw the switch just inside the doorway and the closet filled with clarifying light. As his eyes adjusted to the sudden intrusion, Harry focused on the clothes hanging on the bar, then the shoes on the floor and finally the very real possibility that someone could very well be hiding in the back of the closet.

Sudden visions of a crazed psychopath vaulting out from between the hanging clothes flashed across his mind's eye, his screams and the maniacal cries of the intruder echoing in his head long after the images had gone.

The inside of the closet door distracted him. The same strange glyphs he'd seen before covered every inch of it. Only this time they appeared to have been painted across the inside of the door in blood, the symbols appearing to have been hastily smeared there by hand.

Harry pushed the clothes aside with a single violent shove. The hangers screeched as they slid in unison along the pole and out of the way to reveal the back wall of the closet. It too was covered with hieroglyphs.

He put the bat aside long enough to steady his hands and take a few pictures, then took up the Dictaphone. "The same odd symbols have been marked on the back wall of the closet and on the back of the closet door," he whispered. "I don't know what they mean or what they say. They could be a form of communication, an attempt to establish contact with me. Or maybe it's a warning—I don't know—but I've taken pictures of them, evidence that *proves* someone's been in the house."

Call the cops—I need to call the cops right now, and—

But what if they didn't believe him? What if they wrote him off as a nut again? Even worse, what if they thought he was responsible for these things himself? The glyphs, the footprints...

Was that possible? Could he have done these things and not realized it?

Harry studied the glyphs more closely. Though a few looked similar to letters most were just odd lines and designs so it was difficult to tell if any of it looked like his handwriting. And what exactly had it been written in? It could've been a red dye or paint of some kind but looked an awful lot like blood. And if it was blood, then whose was it? Could he risk having the police here without knowing for sure if he'd had anything to do with this or what it all meant? He hadn't made the phone calls to Kenny either, but who would believe that?

"I didn't do this," he told the Dictaphone, clinging desperately to the scraps of sanity he had left. "I did *not* do this. Whoever hears this tape, I want you to know that. I did not do these things. I don't know anything more at this point. But someone or some*thing* has been in the house and left this behind."

Just hearing himself say such things was deeply disturbing, but even more so was the realization that if they'd gotten into the house once they could do it again, probably at will. There were no more boundaries, no more walls or safe zones. All bets were off.

He looked up at the section of closet ceiling that housed the pull-down stairs leading to the attic. Gaining entry through attic vents in the roof would be difficult at best, but that was surely how they'd gotten in. He eyed the door in the closet ceiling. There was no way for him to lock it. The only option was to wedge something between it and the floor, preventing anyone on the other side from pushing it open and dropping the stairs down, but he couldn't think of anything tall enough that would do the job properly.

Harry stepped out of the closet, closed the door, then dragged the chair from Kelly's dressing table over to it and propped it up under the knob, fixing it in place as tightly as possible. It wouldn't prevent a determined intruder from gaining entry, but it would certainly slow them down.

Them.

Another shuffling sound scraped the roof.

Whatever was up there was on the move again.

There was no way to see the roof from inside the house, but at least upstairs in the bedroom he could keep tabs on the movement.

What if it's a distraction?

Could others be trying to get in while he waited here, listening intently to the activity on the roof?

Other than through the attic, the only other way into the house from the roof was if one hung onto the gutter and swung down and through a window. All the windows were locked, therefore the pane would have to be broken, and now that the storm had gone and the night had become so quiet he'd hear it shatter from anywhere in the house.

Harry started for the door, stopping just before it to peek out into the dark hallway. Satisfied the area was clear, he hurried to the staircase. Faint gray moonlight touched the last two stairs. The surrounding shadows moved slightly, flickering as if someone had moved by the bay window. A bat or night bird in flight perhaps, or the moonlight disturbed by an unknown presence rustling the bushes.

Legs weak and shaking, he carefully descended the stairs, then waited and listened. All was quiet.

He looked to the den. Even in sparse moonlight, the glow from the room couldn't be ignored. So many little lights everywhere. The lights on the face of the satellite receiver and DVR, the muted but still lit brand name on the front of the television, the digital clock and multicolored lights—reds, blues and greens—on the DVD player and Garret's old XBOX. In the corner, two lights on the base for the cordless phone. Though everything was allegedly off, things still moved in the wires, things still live…*alive*… things that continued to function, receiving and processing information without him, operating on their own in the dark. In today's world, anyone could stand in virtually any room in their house at any time of day or night and see a vast array of lights, tiny windows, clues to the existence of a silent electronic universe operating independently. Or maybe they weren't windows at all, but little eyes watching him, keeping track, missing nothing and cataloguing his every move for whatever was on the other side of those lights, the other end of those wires.

The world never really sleeps. No one's world does.

Harry went to the door and flipped on the front lights. A large pool of light immediately filled the darkness around the door, driveway and even a small portion of the front lawn. He expected to hear more movement overhead as a result, but none came. The lone streetlight allowed him to better assess the road, but from what he could tell there was no one out there at the moment either.

He checked the kitchen. The coyote was standing and staring into space as if it were straining to listen to something far in the distance, which perhaps it was. After a few seconds the animal turned and looked back at Harry, its eyes riddled with concern.

They're here.

Harry nodded to him through the glass.

I know.

He returned to the den, flipped the back lights on to illuminate the patio and beyond. Nothing looked out of the ordinary and yet the backyard didn't look quite right either. Even the mundane seemed menacing, as if it were only a curtain designed to hide that which was hidden beneath. The plastic garden hose caddy, the green hose coiled around it, dirty and kinked in several spots like a dead and decomposing snake…the barbeque grill partially covered with a black tarp ravaged by weather, split and torn in spots as if by some wild animal…the empty patio, the outdoor furniture that normally resided there already packed away in the cellar...it all seemed so…*threatening*. But Harry had no idea why.

He focused on the light. There was no way to know if illuminating the area would in anyway discourage the intruders, but it was worth a try.

At least I'll see them coming.

As he crossed by the bay window, he stopped and crouched. He'd seen something out in the road—something that didn't belong—a quick blur that shouldn't have been there. He leaned back toward the pane and squinted out into the night.

Watching the house from the center of the road was a lone figure. Dressed in black, its flesh was deathly pale like the others, but this stranger was small, like a child. Only it wasn't a child.

Something else…

What he'd originally mistaken for pale flesh was in fact a wrap of some sort around the being's limbs and face. *Bandages, it—it's bandaged…*

He stared in disbelief at the being from his nightmare, the same strange bandaged figure he'd seen flashing in his head, quaking about in seizure.

Apparently disfigured by some sort of birth defect, degenerative disease or injury, the dwarfed figure stood hunched forward, the posture reminiscent of a stroke victim, arms in tight against the chest, wrists protruding from the dirty bandages and curled upward, fingers balled into loose fists. As it took a few steps closer to the house Harry was better able to see the face. It too was wrapped in what appeared to be old and badly worn bandages, but for a slit for the mouth and a pair of jagged eyeholes. Tufts of hair protruded from openings in the bandages wrapped about its head, and although the being appeared to be human, it moved with a strange hobble, as if the legs were not the same length, or perhaps mere stumps. It continued forward nonetheless, and from the angle it took Harry realized the right leg stump was dragging behind along the pavement with a disturbing scraping sound.

His mind told him to reach for the camera but he couldn't move. Horrified, he watched as the being limped into the mouth of the driveway. Slowly, and with what appeared to be great effort, one of the gnarled hands came away from the body, the arm extending out as a single finger uncurled and pointed.

Directly at Harry.

* * *

Don't open the door don't open it please don't please God help me don't open the door no don't—don't open it, help me, I—

"Mr. Fremont?"

Harry blinked away memories and wiped perspiration from his forehead with the back of his hand. "I'm sorry, I…"

"I understand you're not feeling well and under a lot of stress right now, sir, but I need you to stay focused to the best of your ability. Do you think you can do that for me?"

The police officer stood before him, a petite and attractive brunette with her hair pulled back into a ponytail and held in place with a rubber band. She didn't look like a cop. Were she not in uniform he'd have guessed schoolteacher, or maybe a sales or public relations person. The radio on her belt crackled, so she lowered the volume a bit, watching Harry in an obvious attempt to discern precisely what it was she was dealing with. Her eyes were large and deep brown, almost black, and though mired in typical policeperson demeanor she came across less officious than most, her tone patient, nonjudgmental and sprinkled with genuine compassion. Harry guessed she was about twenty-five.

Technically young enough to be my daughter, for God's sake.

"Do you think you can do that for me?" she asked again, eyeing his little command center and the baseball bat he'd left leaned against the wall.

"Yes, I'm sorry. I'm just so tired, I...I'm exhausted." He knew she'd introduced herself when she first arrived but he couldn't remember her name. Ironically the nametag above her right breast read: Guy.

"I take it you play baseball or softball, Mr. Fremont?"

"Not since I was a kid."

"Then what's the bat for?"

"Take a wild guess."

Her expression made it clear she did not find his answer amusing.

"I keep it in the house for protection," he sighed.

"What is that all over it?" she asked.

He glanced at it with disinterest. "Old scuffs and some mud, I guess. There's no law against having a dirty baseball bat is there?"

She didn't seem to completely accept his answer, but for some reason didn't push the issue. "Of course not," she said, clearing her throat, "but this is the second call you've made to

911 today and we've yet to find an emergency here either time. There *are* laws against abusing the 911 system."

"Is that what you think I'm doing?"

She drew a breath, let it out slowly. "No sir, I don't. Not intentionally."

Harry already regretted phoning the police, but he'd been so frightened at the time he couldn't help himself. It seemed the only sensible thing to do.

Once she arrived he removed the camera from around his neck and left it on the table, then closed the laptop so she wouldn't see the sites he'd been researching on sleep deprivation. While she searched the property he waited inside, feeling like a complete ass. *Old enough to be her father and hiding in the house like a coward while she protects me from...from what?*

He'd neither shown her the glyphs in the closet nor asked her to search the house for fear she'd see the coyote in the mudroom. Much as he wanted to take her upstairs and show her the inside of the closet door, he couldn't risk it. Not without knowing it wasn't some kind of setup. Paranoid or not, he had to consider it as a possibility after the phone calls to Kenny. The way things were going, with his luck he'd get her up there and the glyphs would be gone anyway. And besides, all Officer Guy needed to see was the closet door barricaded with a chair and she was likely to go from being suspicious of his mental state, to convinced he needed serious intervention.

"But earlier today you reported a man on the roof across the street," she reminded him as she consulted a small notepad. "Officer Nicoletto responded to the call, and according to his report he was unable to find anything to support your claims. Unfortunately I have to tell you I've come to the same conclusion, and my report will reflect that. There are no indications anyone has been on your property, sir, much less your roof. And I certainly," she licked her lips in a clear attempt to prevent herself from smiling, "saw no signs of a little person."

"I don't know for sure it was a midget, I—"

"You're not supposed to use that word."

"Excuse me?"

"Midget," she said. "They find that word offensive. You're supposed to say 'Little People' now."

"All right then," he said drowsily. "I don't know for sure if it was a *little person*."

"See? It's really not that difficult to be kind and considerate. Cruelty takes effort, not kindness."

Her statement annoyed him. He was sure she meant well but the last thing he needed at that point was lessons in how to conduct himself. Then again, from her perspective that was probably exactly what he needed. "Whoever it was, I found the situation and this…*person*…threatening. I wasn't thinking about being kind. I never said for sure that it was a dwarf or a little person or whatever term we're supposed to use, just that it was someone small. I assumed it was a little person."

"Could it have been a child, a kid playing a prank?"

"I don't think so, I…" He tried to clear his mind, to find the right words and to put them in the correct order, but they eluded him. "I'm not…"

"Mr. Fremont," she said, dropping into a crouch next to the recliner so they were eye-to-eye. "In his report Officer Nicoletto indicated you admitted you hadn't slept in a few days and that you were also under the influence of some prescription medications for your flu. I can tell by your behavior, appearance, and by speaking with you that you're in a severely debilitated condition at this point. You just said yourself you're completely exhausted and having some serious issues here." She wasn't wearing cologne but smelled fresh and clean, like she'd scrubbed with a heady deodorant soap. "We need to address those issues before things get out of hand, do you understand? I'll do whatever I can to help you, but you can't keep dialing 911 and tying up units on false alarms. The shift commander is allowing me to make the call this time. If we have to come back here tonight he won't leave it up to me again. He'll insist I take you into protective custody. I can do that now, Mr. Fremont, but I'd rather not."

Harry listlessly pawed at his eyes. "You're going to arrest me?"

"No, sir, it's not an arrest. It's protective custody, something we do for a person's protection if we determine it's not safe or in their best interest to allow them to remain alone or under their own supervision. We'd put you in a cell for the night so you could sleep in an environment where we could be sure you'd be safe." She smiled ever-so-slightly, almost guiltily, as her thin lips parted to reveal very straight, very white teeth. "But I'm hoping we don't have to do that. I'm hoping you'll agree to take whatever medications you need and go to bed. You obviously need sleep, and I think in your situation you'd do a lot better here in your own bed, don't you?"

"Yes," he said, confused as to why he was having such mixed emotions about this woman. She seemed like a good cop. Was she a good wife too?

Officer Guy stood up, resuming a position of authority. "I don't want to remove you from your home, Mr. Fremont, but if it becomes necessary I will."

I bet you have plenty of opportunities to stray from your marriage.

"Do you understand?" she pressed.

"Yes," he answered. "I won't call again. I promise."

I wonder if you do.

"If you need us, call. That's why we're here. Otherwise—"

"I understand. It won't happen again. I'm sorry, I—I'm just confused. I feel so ridiculous. Here I am a grown man calling you to come and..."

"Don't worry about that." She gave his shoulder a gentle pat. "You're so exhausted you've begun to see things, to confuse reality and fantasy, and if you don't sleep it'll just get worse."

He looked up into her big brown eyes. If eyes were in fact windows to the soul he decided hers was a virtuous one.

"I know these things are frightening, and that they seem very real, but they're just tricks of the mind. Remember back in school, in science class, the first time you learned about microscopic organisms? All those little bugs and mites and whatnot that can only be seen through high-powered microscopes but exist everywhere—on our bed sheets, on our clothes, our skin, in our mouths, our eyes—but we just can't see or feel them because they're so small? For days I was freaked out thinking about these little bugs all over me and everyone else. But then I realized I had to stop. Of course they exist, but whether those organisms were really there or not was immaterial. If I focused on them and allowed those thoughts to be in my head all the time they'd drive me crazy. I'd lose my mind with worry and fear about things on and inside me I couldn't see with the naked eye or even hear or touch. I wouldn't be able to function because I'd be searching for or worried about those things swarming all over me. The point is it's really easy to become obsessed with things like that, and if you're not careful before you know it they've driven you completely out of your mind. Do you see what I'm saying, Mr. Fremont? None of us can control whatever microscopic organisms exist in nature anymore than in your present state you can control the way your mind is reacting to being deprived of sleep for days, but we *can* control how we think about things and how much power we're willing to give them."

He looked to his hands. She was right. They were swarming with hideous organisms neither of them could see. "Can I ask you a question, officer?"

"Sure."

"What's your first name?"

Through a sigh she said, "Donna."

"I see you're married. You wear a wedding band."

"My personal life isn't relevant here, Mr. Fremont," she said, shifting back to a cop that sounded as if she were reading from a script.

"Can't we…" He looked to the floor. "Can't we just talk like two human beings for a minute? Is that so difficult?"

"I'm sorry you're having a tough time, sir, and I'm doing my best to help, but this isn't a social call. I'm on duty and I have other things I need to do. If you're having personal problems and feel you need to talk with someone I can put you in touch with—"

"I didn't mean to pry it's just that I'm married too," he explained, visions of Kelly flooding his mind with equal measures of ecstasy and agony. "I'll bet I've been married almost as long as you've been alive."

"I'm older than I look," she said. "I've always looked a lot younger than I am. The older I get the more I've come to appreciate that."

He tried to force the pictures in his head to stop but they refused to leave him. "I've always enjoyed being married. It's...nice."

"Yes," she replied quietly. "It is."

"To know that...well, that at least you have each other."

"And that someone has your back," she added.

But is that really how it is? Or just the way I want it—need it—to be?

"Is your husband in law enforcement too?" he asked.

"He's in IT. You know, computers."

"Evil."

"Excuse me?"

"Evil," he said again, pretending he'd meant to all along. "You must see a lot of it in your line of work."

"Sometimes I do, yes."

They're watching us right now...I know it...

"Do you ever feel like it's a losing battle?"

"I try not to. I've only been on the force here in town about a year. My husband's company transferred him to Massachusetts but we're originally from Indianapolis. I was a cop there for seven years." She nervously scratched her ear. "I learned early on there are very real, very powerful forces of evil in the world. You come to realize there's no question about the existence of evil, only what forms it takes. And it's not always what we think. In fact it seldom is."

"Yes," Harry said softly, "I think you're right."

"You just have to hang in there, Mr. Fremont. We all do. In the end we have a lot more control and influence over our existences than we think we do.

Life's just a learning curve."

"Are you sure about that?"

"Better hope so."

The gun on her hip caught his attention. It looked impossibly large for her, almost comical hung on a woman so diminutive. Yet he had no doubt she knew how to use the weapon and could wield it with extreme prejudice if need be. There was something about her, something at once wholesome and cunning, like she could go from a fresh-faced girl-nextdoor to a pitiless slayer of evil in a heartbeat. He tried to imagine what she looked like at home with her husband. Did she wear her hair down he wondered? Did she speak differently once the badge and gun came off? Was she someone else entirely or was it a minor transition from cop to wife? Did her husband know both versions of her or only that which she allowed him to see?

"Your husband must worry about you strapping on a gun everyday."

"It's not easy for anyone to be married to a cop."

He nodded as if he understood, but he really didn't. Had Kelly held a job where she needed to be armed and was always in harm's way he never could've endured the stress. "My wife's a business executive, a much safer profession than yours, but I worry about her constantly just the same. Even after all these years, when she's away I still miss her terribly. Isn't that silly?"

"I think it's sweet."

Or is it pathetic? I'm not even sure I know who my wife is. I'm beginning to wonder if I ever have.

"I'm sure your wife worries plenty about you too."

"Be nice to think so." He watched the window.

"Lately, I…I don't know."

"Maybe she's just lost her way."

"Maybe."

"We all do from time to time. But sooner or later we find our way home."

"What if home turns out to be worse than being lost?"

"That's probably a lot like being trapped in a nightmare."

"Yes," he said, "it is."

"You can remedy your situation," she told him. "If you just go to sleep, this will stop. If you've had enough, sleep. Just sleep. That's all you have to do."

Harry smiled at her, mostly in thanks. But he was embarrassed too. Though he was sure she meant well, she looked at him like he was some disarmingly senile old man, a lonely fool bothering the police with nonsense.

"You love her very much, don't you Mr. Fremont?"

Don't cry, don't—don't start crying you stupid bastard, she'll PC you.

"I do."

"You mentioned earlier she's out of town on a business trip?"

He nodded.

"When's she coming home?"

The answer should've been right there at the tip of his tongue, but he couldn't quite remember. His mind sluggishly struggled to find the right answer. "Tomorrow, I think, I…no…wait…is tomorrow Monday?"

"It's Saturday night. Tomorrow's Sunday."

"She's coming back Monday."

Officer Guy considered this a moment. "Would you like me to try to get a hold of her for you and see if maybe she could come back a little sooner?"

A call from the police would scare Kelly to death. Tempting, but…

"No, that's not necessary. I wouldn't want to worry her."

"You're sure?"

He was suddenly struck with a violent coughing fit. "Yes," he finally managed once it was over, "but thank you."

"That's a nasty cough. Do you have anything for it?"

"Yes," he answered, wiping thick globs of saliva from the sides of his mouth. "Guess I need to take some more."

"Tell you what." She removed a business card from her shirt pocket, scribbled something on the back, then handed it to him. "This is my card."

Harry found the concept of cops having cards humorous, but when he realized she'd written an alternate phone number on the back he was touched.

"That's my cell," she told him. "You need to promise me you won't abuse it, but if you're having trouble again call that number instead of 911. You can reach me until seven tomorrow morning, that's when my shift ends. Between now and then if you get scared or confused or—well—if you need me just call that number, OK?"

No one can help me. I understand that now.

"Thanks." He pushed himself to his feet. "That's very nice of you."

"I hope you feel better, I really do." She headed for the door and Harry followed. When they arrived she said, "Go to sleep."

"I will."

"Goodnight then."

"Goodnight." He stood in the doorway as Officer Guy returned to her cruiser.

Even before she'd reached the car he saw them.

Emerging from darkness, the two men in black stood partially concealed in shadows just beyond the light from the streetlamp.

Harry expected her to react, but Officer Guy nonchalantly returned to her car, quickly surveyed the area, then slipped behind the wheel.

She can't see them.

The cruiser made a U-turn and pulled away, driving right by them.

From behind the initial two, came others. Clad in black, they moved like shadows, barely discernable in the darkness.

My God...how many are you?

Whispers emanated from them like blasphemous prayers as together they walked in an uneven line, moving closer, their wide stares piercing Harry's logical mind and laying waste to whatever semblance of reality remained. He wanted to run, to scream, but stood cemented in place, mouth agape as their bright wet eyes cut the darkness, embers burning white-hot against the backdrop of night and traces of moonlight.

"No," he said, as if this might somehow stop what was happening. "*No.*"

A strange buzzing sound cut the night just before the streetlight burst, showering the road with a fine misty spray of glass that caught the moonlight and fell to the ground like diamond dust. And then darkness crashed down like a sudden and violent explosion, rolling over everything and anything in its path, pulling it all down into the blackest, impenetrable depths of night.

Even as Harry slammed the door and locked it behind him, he could hear footfalls rushing toward the house in a single frenzied wave.

But as he backed away from the door, certain his mind had irrevocably shattered, the only sound that remained was the dragging of a small lame stump of a leg as it slowly scraped pavement...again...and again.

9

Harry stood by the recliner, poised to strike, baseball bat clutched in his hands. He'd switched the lights off again, submerging the house into darkness and immediately giving him a clearer view through the bay window. But now there was nothing to see but night, the road, trees and Rose's house sitting dark and empty across the street. Though he was lightheaded and his heart was beating at a frightening rate, he did his best not to breathe too deeply for fear he might cough. He needed to be quiet and still. The sounds of footfalls had ceased, as had the horrible dragging sound, and just when he was certain the strangers would converge on the house, bursting through the windows and kicking in the front door, the night fell silent. He waited awhile longer but the assault never came.

He moved farther back into the room, to the deeper darkness in the corner, the bat still held high and his eyes wide as he imagined them all huddled around the house, surrounding it like an army of shadows.

And that bandaged *thing*, where the hell had that gone?

If you just go to sleep, this will stop.

Was it listening just outside the door?

If you've had enough, sleep.

A series of savage pains suddenly tore through his temple, causing him to lower the bat and bring a hand to the side of his head. As the pain worsened he felt sick to his stomach, and everything went blurry, drifting past his field of vision at rolling angles.

Just sleep. That's all you have to do.

Somewhere far off he heard the baseball bat hit the floor, and his skull felt like it had shattered from a sudden and violent impact. He staggered and nearly fell, hands gripping either side of his head as if to prevent it from bursting apart.

Dark and unfamiliar corridors from his nightmares blinked before him.

The pain stopped. Quickly, like it appeared. A mild tingling behind his eyes was all that remained.

Breathless, Harry collapsed onto the couch.

Eventually the room stopped moving and his vision cleared. The fear remained. "If I go to sleep," he said quietly, voice slurred, "they—*this*—won't really be gone. Not while I sleep, not when I wake up, I—I just won't be able to see any of it."

None of us can control whatever microscopic organisms exist in nature all around and within us...

"You'll still be here," more forcefully now, certain they could hear him. "Like those disgusting bugs and whatever else the human eye can't see. None of this ever goes away. It's always here. *You're* always here, moving around, watching, crawling all over us. We just can't see you. Sleep changes nothing."

Harry made his way to the bay window and peeked out.

The strangers were gone.

"Of course they are," he said, laughing like the lunatic he was certain he'd become. "They—of course—you're just fucking with me now, right? It's all a game isn't it? You're trying to drive me crazy, to scare me to death to—"

The cordless began to ring. He stared at it, knowing he had to answer. *I'm even afraid of the phone now. They're trying to frighten me into complete emotional and physical paralysis. And they're succeeding.*

He crossed to the command center, scooped up the handset and hit the button. Rather than say hello he waited, listening to the static on the other end of the line.

"Mr. Fremont?" asked a male voice he didn't recognize.

Sounds like an older man.

"Mr. Fremont?" the voice asked again.

Under normal circumstances the voice probably would've been comforting, but on this night the tranquil tone and reserved delivery struck him as decidedly creepy instead.

"Mr. Fremont, can you hear me?"

"Yes," Harry replied, voice gruff and strained. "Who are you?"

"I'm Doctor Bonnet."

"I don't..." He swallowed, nearly coughed. "I don't know any Dr. Bonnet."

"I'm your doctor."

"My doctor's name is Poole. Tim Poole."

"I'm caring for you now."

"Where's Doctor Poole?"

"He has other patients to tend to. How do you feel?"

"I...I don't..." He ran his free hand across his forehead and through his perspiration-soaked hair. "Not very well, I...I'm so tired and..."

"Try to sleep. It's all right to sleep."

Harry felt his body tremble again, but differently this time, as if in response to hundreds of tiny insects scurrying across his skin, along his arms and legs, up his neck, across his face, everywhere. "Are you one of them?"

"One of them?"

He cradled the phone with his chin and scratched at his flesh with both hands, but the sensation kept moving, spreading across his body and running from his touch like a mass of cockroaches escaping to darkness. "You know exactly what I'm talking about!"

"You need to stay calm and rest."

Harry backed into the corner of the room, his scalp itching now, the insides of his ears—were they crawling around in there too?—even his mouth felt like there were hordes of tiny creatures swimming in it, which of course there were, their legs tickling the insides of his cheeks and scuttling over his tongue, along the gums between his teeth…nesting there… burrowing deep into the tissue... climbing slowly up behind his eyes, tentacle-like antenna scraping the sensitive underside of his eyelids. "Who are you?"

"My name is Doctor Bonnet."

It's all in my mind. I don't really feel them—they— they are *there but I don't feel them, it's—that's not possible.* "I already talked to Doctor Poole earlier and I—I didn't call you." Harry scratched manically at his head. "I know every doctor in Tim Poole's practice, there's no Doctor Bonnet."

"It's all right, we can talk later. You need to sleep."

"Tell me who you are!"

"It's important that you remain calm, Mr. Fremont."

"Then answer me."

"My name is Bonnet. I'm a doctor. I'm here to help you."

"No you're not."

Static suddenly filled the line. Loud at first, it gradually lessened until the line went quiet. Harry defiantly remained on the phone, but several seconds came and went and the man said nothing more. "What do you want with me?" he asked. "Why are you doing this? Can you…can you make this stop?"

No answer came, but the person on the other end had not hung up.

Harry hit disconnect and threw the phone at the recliner. It bounced off the back cushion and came to rest on the seat as he frantically ran his hands from his head down the length of his body, clawing and swatting the unseen bugs from his flesh.

They're everywhere, they—Jesus Christ—they're all over me!

Spinning about in a crazed pirouette he lost his balance, toppled over and slammed the floor. The den shook as he flopped onto his back. He lay there a moment staring at the white ceiling. Strange swirls seemed to appear from deep within the paint and primer beneath, moving in odd patterns and directions, gliding and slithering before his eyes like tadpoles crazily skimming the surface of a pond.

Wait...

He squinted, straining to see more clearly.

They're not on the ceiling...

He scrambled to his feet, pitched forward and nearly fell again.

They're in my eyes!

Harry clenched his fists and ground them into his eye sockets, teetering and stumbling about the den like a crazed marionette. Despite the horror and adrenaline rush, the exhaustion was overwhelming. The room tilted and spun, his temples pounded and he was suddenly short of breath and seconds from unconsciousness.

He dropped to his knees. The carpet moved before him and it took every ounce of energy and control he had left not to completely shatter and break apart. "I just—I—I have to sleep," he blubbered, "I can't do this anymore. I'm so exhausted, I can't, I—I can't think, I—I have to sleep, I need to sleep, I..."

His eyelids dropped like black curtains.

Fight—don't lie down, don't—you—you have to fight this you—get on your feet you sonofabitch—get up.

"No," he mumbled, eyes mere slits now, the world around him hazy and dim. The skin-crawling sensation weakened...receded...left him. He remained there a moment, soaked in perspiration and thoroughly drained. "I need to sleep. I need..."

In the distance he heard a strange sound. The cordless was ringing again. He crawled to the recliner, wiped his mouth with the back of his hand, then struggled up into the chair and collapsed onto his back, out of breath and still horribly lightheaded. "Tell me who you are you sonofabitch."

"Harry?" Kelly's voice, tight and worried. "Is that you?"

Pain and disgust overpowered the initial relief he'd felt upon hearing the sound of her voice. He needed so desperately for Kelly to comfort and save him, to do what she had done so many times over the years, to let him know she was there and she loved him and everything would be all right. But it all felt so empty now, a useless fabrication they'd told themselves and each other for years finally revealed for the lie it was. Was Kelly truly the person he'd believed her to be, or just a myth, a creation of his own need designed to deflect the truth and convince him she was exactly who he wanted and needed her to be?

"Harry?"

"Of course it's me," he said.

"Why did you answer the phone like that?"

"I'm sick, remember?" He planted his feet deeper into the carpet and pushed until his body slid up into a seated position. "I'm a sick, sick man."

Kelly sighed. "What's going on? Why aren't you in bed? It's late, you should be asleep. And what's with that message you left? You scared the hell out of me. Is everything else all right?"

"No," he said, gripping the arm of the chair to steady himself, eyes fixed on the bay window and ocean of night beyond. "As a matter of fact everything else is not all right. Everything is decidedly fucked up."

"What's wrong?"

"You tell me."

"Look, I'm working. Tell me what's going on. I don't have time for drama."

"Sorry to bother you with trivial matters like our marriage and my sanity."

"What does that mean?"

"You're clever, figure it out."

"This is a very important trip," she said, sighing again. He could picture her pinching the bridge of her nose and closing her eyes like she so often did when frustrated. "If I can nail this account it'll mean a lot of money for the company and one hell of a bonus for me. I can't have these distractions, OK? I'm sorry you're not feeling well and I'm not there to help, but you're acting like a child. Take your medicine, go to bed and get some sleep, what's the problem?"

He'd never felt quite so alone. There, inside a cocoon surrounded by night and those that moved within its darkness.

But I'm not alone...I know you're there...

"I'll be home on Monday," Kelly said when he gave no answer. "If you're still not feeling well I'll make you chicken soup and fluff your pillows and all that good stuff. I'll make it all better when I get home, I promise. Until then, handle it. You're a grown man. It'd be nice if you'd start behaving like one."

"Are you really in San Diego, Kel?"

"Of course, I—why—where do you think I am?"

Maybe she's just lost her way...

Visions of his wife came to him again, wrapped in memories good and bad, all of them smashed together into a hellish mosaic clouding the boundaries of pleasure and pain. He could hear sounds behind her but they became muffled by a series of exaggerated exhales. Rather than answer her question he asked another of his own. "Guess who came to see me today?"

He heard a quiet scratching noise, slow and steady along the outside of the front door, like a long jagged fingernail scraping the fiberglass.

"I don't know, sweetheart, who?"

They're listening...

"Searcy's wife stopped by."

"What?"

"You heard me." The bat was still on the floor where he'd dropped it.

"Gloria came to the house? Why?"

He reached down for the bat, picked it up and leaned it against his leg. "She wanted to talk to me about you and her husband."

"Here we go." Kelly laughed but it was laced with irritation. "Let me guess, she thinks we're having an affair, right?"

"Yes, she does." His fingers curled tighter around the bat.

"And you're actually entertaining what that loon said? Are you kidding me? Harry, Gloria's certifiable."

"Maybe so, but that doesn't make her a liar does it."

"She has a severe drinking problem. She was smashed when she came to see you, am I right? The point is the woman's a walking disaster. She has serious mental health and emotional issues. She thinks Aaron cheats with every woman he knows. She accuses him of this kind of thing all the time, and lately she's been on this kick about Aaron and me. She's beyond paranoid. Frankly I don't know how Aaron puts up with it. Like they say, love is blind."

Yes, that is what they say.

He pictured her walking down a city street in San Diego. He couldn't help but wonder if Searcy was there too, walking right beside her. "Are you having an affair, Kelly?"

"You better be kidding."

"You didn't answer the question."

"I shouldn't have to."

"Answer me."

"Go to bed, Harry. Hopefully when you wake up you won't be such an asshole." The only response she received was silence. "What is the matter with you? Why would you ask me that?"

The old black tape along the baseball bat grip stuck to his fingers. He tightened his fist around it. "Answer the question."

"No, I don't think I will. It's a ridiculous question and an insulting question and a mean and nasty and hurtful question that should never be asked by someone who allegedly loves me."

"Amazing," Harry said, struggling to his feet, leaving the bat behind but keeping an eye on the door. "You're the one screwing me over and you've somehow managed to make me the bad guy."

"Nah, you're doing a fine job of it all by your lonesome. This is the second time you've come at me with this accusatory bullshit, and I'm tired of it. I know you don't like my job and the travel and all that—fine, OK, fair enough—but to accuse me of this bullshit, and with Aaron of all people. Jesus. And you base this on what exactly, the drunken ramblings of Gloria Searcy? That's all it takes, huh? When did our marriage become so fragile? One quick visit from that paranoid, alcoholic bitch and suddenly I'm a liar and a cheat? You sell me down the river and side with her just like that? Nice. Really nice."

"She called your hotel. They have no record of you two staying there."

"I don't believe this." Kelly gave another lengthy sigh. "Lately whenever Aaron travels he tells Gloria to call his cell and instructs the front desk not to put her through if she calls the hotel."

"Why would he do that?"

"Because the woman calls every five minutes if he doesn't. He'll get back to his room and there are literally twenty or thirty messages in a two or three hour span. He'll call her back and it's nothing. He keeps his cell on vibrate as it is because she calls that constantly too. She's just checking up on him, or she has some ridiculous excuse, but it's never anything important. She's nuts, Harry. She's a fucking train wreck."

"Does he instruct the front desk to tell her you're not registered too?"

"With the accusations she's been throwing around lately it wouldn't surprise me in the least if he did. Otherwise she'd probably start badgering me when she couldn't reach him."

He stood near the door, listened. The noise had stopped.

But I know you're there. I can feel you.

"You said yourself I should call you on your cell rather than at the hotel."

"Because I thought it would be easier for you to reach me. I'm rarely in my hotel room. I can't believe we're having this conversation."

She's lying. Don't let her off the hook.

"Every time I've spoken to you on this trip it's been on your cell," he reminded her. "No one's ever answered the suite number you gave me."

"OK, I'm on foot but only a couple blocks fro the hotel. Would you like to call me back at the suite in five minutes? Then I can prove to you I'm really in San Diego. You know, since there's such compelling evidence that I'm not."

"Why was this trip so last-minute?"

"You need to call the doctor back, that fever's boiling your brain."

"Answer me goddamn it!"

"Where the hell do you get off speaking to me this way? Who do you think you're talking to?"

"I'm not sure anymore."

"Neither am I."

She's stalling...trying to think of an answer...

"Our top competitor is coming to pitch these guys next week. I wanted to get the drop on them and get here first. I was confident if we did I could close the deal before they even had a chance, but there wasn't time to play around and go through the usual rigmarole. We threw it together and made the move. I want this account."

Her explanation seemed reasonable—they all had so far—but Harry couldn't shake the feeling that hiding somewhere within all that truth were more lies. "And you get what you want, don't you," he said, "one way or another."

"These innuendos are getting really tired."

"When Gloria couldn't reach Searcy she called Brody Fay to get info on where you two were staying," he told her.

"Oh for Christ's sake, she's calling Brody at home now? Wonderful. Aaron's going to be mortified."

The postnasal drip had kicked in again. As Harry swallowed, a scratch tore across his throat and he began to hack.

"I don't like the sound of that cough. Seriously, maybe you should call the doctor back."

"Don't worry about it," he gasped, forcing his way through the cough. "Brody Fay had no idea what Gloria was talking about. He knew nothing about any San Diego business trip."

"I'm not surprised."

"You expect me to believe the senior V.P. of the company doesn't know you two are on such an important trip?"

"Given the present circumstances at the company, yes, I do."

"He backpedaled and tried to cover for you."

"Cover for what?"

"Why do you suppose he'd do that Kel, any idea?"

"My guess is he was embarrassed."

"I bet."

"Harry, listen to me very carefully. Aaron just turned sixty-five. He's retiring at the end of next year and hasn't yet made a decision as to who his successor will be. Brody's expecting to get the position but it's not going to work out that way. He's not the most competent guy, so Aaron's been leaving him out of the loop lately, particularly in terms of the day-to-day activities of the other executives. He's been reduced to more of a figurehead than anything at this point. So no, he wouldn't necessarily be aware of this trip, it doesn't surprise me in the least."

"Did you fuck Searcy?"

"You've got to be kidding me."

"Do I sound like I'm joking?"

"No, unfortunately you don't."

"It's an easy question to answer. Or at least it should be."

"There's nothing between Aaron and me. Nothing. OK?"

"You're sure about that?"

"We're friends and coworkers. That's all."

"Have you been fucking him all these years? Do you still crawl under his desk whenever he asks?"

"My God, what a *charming* slew of questions."

"Oh cut the shit, Kelly. Pull that pretentious routine with the people you work with, not me. I've known you too long. I know you too well."

"And yet you believe this nonsense."

"Gloria said in your company this is common knowledge."

"What is? What exactly is common knowledge? Please, enlighten me."

"That you've been doing her husband for years."

"*Doing?* Wow, classy."

"Sorry, it's not easy to find class in your boss bending you over his desk."

"Do you honestly expect me to defend myself against this bullshit?"

"I expect the truth."

"You know what? Fuck you. You're my husband. You're supposed to protect and stand up for me. You're supposed to defend my honor."

"You never needed me to do any of those things. You were always more than capable of doing them yourself."

"Well somebody had to."

"I never failed you in those areas and you know it."

"No, but you're failing me now."

"Asking for the truth? Don't you think I'm entitled to it?"

"After all these years I assumed you already knew it."

"Did you fuck Aaron Searcy? It's a simple question. Answer it."

"No. Why the hell should I?"

"Do I have to keep going?"

"You don't have to do anything."

"But should I?" The sounds of traffic filled the void that followed.

"I wish you wouldn't."

"And why is that?"

He heard her swallow, draw a deep breath and exhale. "I don't see the point. We love each other, we're happy, we have a good life. Why do you want to destroy that?"

"I don't want to destroy anything. It's being taken from me, ripped right out of me, and I'm trying to salvage whatever scraps are left." His eyes moved to the bay window. "Whatever bits are still real."

"Harry, you're exhausted and so sick with the flu you can barely string a coherent thought together. I'm a million miles away and right in the middle of— it doesn't matter—just try to get some sleep, all right? I love you. You know that, I know you do. *I love you.*"

He couldn't decide whether to close his eyes or keep them open. No matter what he did, all he could see was her.

"Did you hear me?"

"Yes. I heard you."

"I said I love you." Her voice broke. She tried to cover it by clearing her throat. "More than anything in the world, and I'd never do anything to hurt you."

"Then why have you done this?"

"Done what, Harry? I haven't done anything."

It suddenly turned quiet, as if something had purposely engineered the silence. He moved closer to the bay window and stared into the night, heart pounding. "I think maybe you're not who I thought you were. I think maybe you're someone else. Someone I don't know at all."

"I'm the same person I've always been," she said, a level of desperation in her voice he'd never before heard. "I'm your wife and the mother of your child."

"That's when you're here, with me, with Garret. Who are you when you're not here? Who are you then Kelly?"

"The same person you fell in love with."

"No you're not. I see glimpses of her now and then, but that's about it."

"None of us stay exactly the same. We all age, we all grow."

"So who are you now? What have you grown into?"

"A whore apparently."

It's all dying it's—I'm dying—it's all coming down—so quietly. The world is crumbling to pieces without a sound...

"This isn't my fault, I—"

"Fine," she interrupted, "is that what you want to hear? Nothing's your fault. You're incurably innocent. It's all me. I'm a tramp and a liar. I steal too. Sometimes I even jaywalk, litter and give arbitrary strangers handjobs all at the same time. I'm an outlaw slut of epic proportions."

"You think this is funny?"

"I think it's sad."

Pain ground along his jaw and up into his temples. "Yes, it is."

"But clearly it's what you want."

"I want the truth."

"You decided what the truth was before you even gave me a chance."

"I'm giving you a chance right now."

"No, you're trying to hurt and humiliate me."

"You've done that to yourself. You did it the first time you pulled your panties down in that fucking asshole's office. You did it the first time you let Searcy and that job rule your life, the first time you allowed him to turn you into someone else, an entirely different personality, one apart from me you thought I'd never know about."

"Stop," she said softly, "just stop, will you?"

"You did it the first time you let the old you die, the real you."

"Harry please," she said, voice shaking as her tough exterior deteriorated.

The rain...I wish the rain would come back...

"I know I haven't been perfect, Kelly, but I was always faithful. Always."

...come back and wash this all away...

"I haven't been perfect either," Kelly said. "But I'm not the slut you and your new best friend Gloria are trying to make me out to be."

...wash it all away...and wash us clean...

"Do you have any idea what you've done? *Any* idea?"

"You're breaking my heart."

Tears filled his eyes. "Then I guess we're even."

"Is this really what you think of me? Is this really who you think I am?"

"Right now I have no idea who you are, no idea who anyone is."

"You can't possibly believe this."

"You're not working a client, Kel. It's me. I know you're lying."

"Lying about what?"

"You and Searcy."

"I am not going to argue this with you," she said sluggishly, as if she'd suddenly grown extremely tired. "I'm not doing it. I can't. I just can't."

"I have to go."

"Fine, we—we'll talk when I get home."

"I may not be here when you get home."

"Don't say that. You don't mean that."

Suddenly Harry was freezing again. The night was coming closer, filling in the gaps, taking his air, wrapping around him like a cage of razor wire as memories of dark blood trickling from beneath Gloria's scarf haunted him. "I can't stop it," he mumbled.

"Harry," she said, "this isn't me, this—this isn't us."

"Our life is a lie."

Maybe all of life is a lie. Not just ours—everyone's—all of it, lies we convince ourselves are true because we want and need them to be more than the states of nirvana we aspire to. We need a reality we can believe in, something we can see and touch and experience, something we can hold on to when we feel alone and hopeless...

"You can't really believe that."

"You killed me, Kelly. You killed me. I'm already dead."

"I'm coming home," she said. "I'll cancel the rest of our meetings and see if I can catch a redeye tonight.

This is ridiculous, you're delusional."

"I have to go," he said again.

"Wait—"

"I love you, Kelly. Despite everything, I really do. Sometimes I wish I didn't. I wish I could stop. But I can't." Tears streamed his face, but like the words falling from his mouth, he made no move to stop them. "I remember when we fell in love. You were so young. God, we both were. Just kids really. You were so beautiful, and you had this amazing innocence. I loved you the minute I saw you. And I knew you loved me. We had something special, something most people never know. And you took it all away, Kel. You tossed it aside like garbage, you just gave it away. You let that fucker have it, you let him turn you into someone you're not, you allowed yourself to become his little whore and you killed me, you killed us. I think the saddest part is that you still don't seem to have any idea what this has done to you, how it's changed you. You're not the same person you were when you started working there, Kel. That place changed you, *he* changed you, and you just sat back and let it happen. But what you'll never understand is that you didn't just break my heart, you destroyed how I saw you, how I saw me, how I saw the world. Everything. You threw it all away for nothing. *Nothing*."

"Harry, you can't punish me for not being who or what you wanted me to be. Things change, people evolve."

"Evolve? *Evolve?* Are you fucking serious?"

"Neither of us are exactly the same people we were when we met. But I'm not some demon from Hell. I'm still me."

"No," he said, "somewhere along the line you became someone else. And I still can't stop. I still love you. What I never knew until now is that for all these years you've used that to your advantage."

"Harry—"

"But has it ever occurred to you how much suffering that's caused me?"

Something moved across the windows, slipping from one to the next like a ghost.

"This is ridiculous. You know I love you. You have to know that."

"Yes," he said, watching as the phantom crept by the bay window, up along the ceiling, then down the walls in a wide shaft of light. "In your own way I know you love me. So why did you let someone like Searcy and some job—and I'm sorry Kel, but at the end of the day that's all it fucking is—ruin you, ruin your life, ruin your family? Why would you grant him—it—so much power? It's so deep, it's so twisted and sick and dark you can't even see how unhappy it's made you, how miserable you really are, how riddled with guilt and regret."

Lights—headlights, it—someone's turned onto the street.

"If you love me then why are you doing this?" she asked. "It isn't fair, I—"

"I want it all back."

"Harry, listen to me. Nothing is lost."

The light faded as darkness returned to the corners and ceiling.

"The whole world's lost."

"No it isn't. It doesn't have to be."

"Goodbye, Kel."

Outside, no sign of the others. They had retreated, returned to shadow.

"Don't you mean goodnight?"

But across the street was a car that hadn't been there before.

"Something's happening. I don't know what it is yet but...there's something here, something evil. It's showing me things, frightening things. And you're just one more part of what's happening tonight, one more piece of the puzzle. I know that now."

A familiar car.

"I've tried to hate you," he said. "I can't."

"This is crazy, what—why are you doing this?"

For the briefest moment Harry saw Kelly as he'd always imagined her, as he'd always believed she truly was. And then it—she—was gone. "Goodnight, my love. Sleep tight."

"Harry wait—"

He disconnected and dropped the phone. It rolled along the carpet and came to rest a few feet away. The chill running through his body worsened.

So cold, he thought. *Like the dead.*

Harry rubbed the tears from his eyes and the car across the street came into clearer focus.

Rose was home. She'd just pulled into her driveway.

10

A circle of light pierced the darkness.

The lantern fixture over Rose's front door had come to life the moment the motion sensor detected her movement in the driveway. Dressed casually in jeans and a raincoat, she left her car and walked around to the rear of the vehicle, looking remarkably refreshed and alert despite the late hour. After popping the trunk she leaned inside and appeared to either rummage around or attend to something inside.

She's stumbling right into the middle of a hornet's nest and has no idea. I've got to get her off the street.

Harry grabbed the bat, then hurried back to the window. Rose was still leaned over into the trunk. He looked to the house, no one on the roof. Normally he'd have been able to see the adjacent section of road but the exploded streetlight left the surrounding area submerged in darkness. He had to risk it.

But they could be anywhere...

As he returned his attention to Rose he saw something above her shift, a subtle movement along the roofline. Heart racing, he went to the door and yanked it open. Night spilled in, bringing a soft but chilly breeze along with it. Harry's lungs burned as his eyes darted back and forth, anxiously searching the darkness for any signs of the shadow people.

The cul-de-sac was quiet and now Rose's roof appeared clear, empty.

He stepped outside tentatively, a stranger on foreign ground, and looked around. Satisfied the others had retreated to shadow, he moved rapidly as his weary legs would carry him down the driveway, breathing in a steady rhythm and trying not to cough. "Rose!" he said in what came out like a loud stage whisper.

She looked back over her shoulder. "Harry?"

He'd made it to the street. "I need to talk to you."

"What are you doing up so late?" she asked, pulling her head from the trunk. "Is everything all right?"

"There's something happening." He crossed onto her property and made his way up the short section of driveway, looking behind him, then up and down the cul-de-sac and finally beyond her to the roof. "We can't stay out here. You have to come with me, OK? Don't question me, just do it and I'll explain—"

"What's the matter?" As she got a better look at him, Rose stepped back, closer to her car. Hands held down in front of her, fingers nervously interlocked, she glanced at the baseball bat and swallowed so hard it was audible.

Realizing he'd frightened her, Harry stopped a few feet from her car. Rose's house stood before them, the eave of the roof cutting the black sky. Overhead, the moon watched. Silent…still…lifeless…"We need to get inside," he told her. "Right now, we have to do it right now."

Hazel eyes blinked nervously behind eyeglasses. "What's with the bat?"

"Please, Rose, don't ask any questions, just do as I say. We have to go."

"Go?" A rush of breath left her laced with confused laughter. "Go where?"

"It's not safe out here." Harry looked around, frantically attempting to cover as much ground as he could in every direction. They might attack from anywhere, at any moment. "The police were here twice today."

"Why? What's going on?"

"We can't stay out in the open," he said, reaching for her. "You need to come back to the house with me and I'll explain everything."

Rose leaned back, farther away from him and his outstretched hand. "What are you doing? Where's Kelly?"

His throat tightened and he began to cough. "She's away on business," he gagged. "You have to hurry. Please Rose, for Christ's sake, they're all around us."

"Who is?" She looked around restlessly. "What are you talking about? You're freaking me out."

He swiped sweat from his forehead as chills fired through him. "I—I know, I'm sorry but—there was someone on your roof earlier, OK? We need to get off the street it's not safe."

She stared at him, baffled.

"Goddamn it, I'm not playing fucking games! We have to get out of here!"

Rose hugged herself. "I think you better go home now, Harry."

"All right, look, it…" He paced about madly, knowing it was only a matter of time before the night came alive and took them. "A man, a—there are these men all over the neighborhood and—they wrote these strange symbols in the closet and—I know it seems crazy but—Rose—I don't think they're *human* and they—I know how it sounds but please listen to me."

She looked as if she were waiting for a punch line.

"They're watching us right now," he told her. "We have to get inside."

"You look like you've been up for days. Go home and get some sleep."

He watched the slope of her roof. Had something just moved across the periphery of his vision? "Don't turn around," he whispered. "They're on the roof."

"You're hallucinating."

"You don't understand."

Run. Just run. Get back to the house where it's safe. Leave her.

Rose combed a strand of blonde hair behind her ear and tried on a smile equal parts apprehension and compassion. "Harry, did you know it's believed hallucinations and unexplained visions originate in the same part of the brain that produces dreams?"

"What?" He shook his head as if to dislodge something. "You want to *chat*? Have you heard a word I've said? We can't stay out here!"

Rose's uneasiness turned to something more composed and elusive. "Truth is doctors and scientists have no idea what dreams or hallucinations really are. They're reality, but also a mystery. Maybe it's all in who does the dreaming, huh?"

"I'm not dreaming."

"Are you sure?" A quiet shuffling sound drifted from the far side of the roof. "Strange things are happening, or at least it appears that way, right? That's what you said, isn't it?"

Harry nodded, tightening his sweaty palms around the bat.

"How do you know for sure it's real or not?" she pressed. "Normally aren't you asleep by now? How do you know what really goes on after dark? How do you know what happens just outside your windows or just beyond your doors? You don't. Could be someone standing in your yard, in your driveway, looking in or at your house every night. You'd never know. They could be all around you—in the trees, on the roof, in the yard, in the street—and you'd have no idea."

Behind her, something rustled about in the trunk.

Harry craned his neck in an attempt to look beyond her. "What've you got in there?"

"You just haven't been able to see them until now." Rose made a subtle lateral move, effectively blocking the still open car trunk. Any compassion or sense of humanity she'd projected previously had left her, and there was something different about her face. Something wrong. It had changed. Slightly... barely perceptibly...but it *had* changed. Had she been quite that pale before? And weren't her eyes noticeably wider and suddenly animated with a look of cruelty? "There are patterns of sleep, of thought, sense, sound and sight; patterns in the universe only clear to you when you haven't slept in a very long time and begin to experience the agony of wakefulness. But like all pain, it eventually reveals truth."

This time it was Harry who took a step back. "What's in the trunk, Rose?"

"You should've slept while you still could."

"These...*things*...do you know what they are?"

She cocked an eyebrow. "Don't you?"

Harry's head spun and his legs nearly gave way, but he stood his ground. "The symbols everywhere—the glyphs—what are they? What do they mean? Are they a warning?"

"They're not for you."

"Who then?"

"It's their mark. It's how they find their way."

"To what?"

She smiled in a way he had never seen Rose smile before, her lips curling back into a vicious grin. "To you."

Whatever was in the trunk bucked again, and Harry caught a glimpse of something wrapped in a bloodstained sheet writhing about violently, as if trying to escape. An inhuman groan escaped it, and it struggled again to free itself. Unable to look away, Harry watched as the thing jerked up into a sitting position and the sheet fell away to reveal the bandaged face beneath, it's oddly familiar eyes desperate and filled with terror.

"Did you think it would last forever, this life of yours?" Rose asked. Above and behind her, dozens of figures in black crawled over the roof, scurrying across the shingles like an endless wave of swarming insects barely visible against the backdrop of night. "Didn't you know it would end? Didn't you know one day there'd be a price to pay? Did you think you were special, entitled, *blessed?*'

Grimacing, he looked behind him. The street between the houses was clear. In the trunk the bandaged freak twisted and turned its way farther out of the sheet, moaning like a wounded animal as it tried to squirm over the edge and onto the driveway, hideously savaged stumps for legs trailing behind it.

From somewhere farther down the cul-de-sac the sound of a large pipe scraping pavement cut the darkness. The bandaged thing screeched and struggled along the ground for purchase, flopping about like a giant worm.

Rose released a hideous laugh as the skin on her face and neck blistered like it was being burned— branded—by some unseen device. The scarred flesh began to form intricate patterns, becoming rows of glyphs seared into every inch of visible flesh.

Harry stumbled back, managing to hold the bat aloft despite the violent convulsive trembling throttling him from head to toe. "You're not Rose."

With the same demonic grin, she bowed her head forward, glasses falling away as her eyes slowly slid up and locked on him. Unearthly growls and the excruciating cries of imprisoned souls shrieking in agony emanated from some black pit deep inside her, and when she spoke, her voice was raw and gurgling, dripping with evil. "And you're not Harry."

* * *

He slammed the door behind him, threw the lock and pressed his back flat against it, chest heaving and rattling as sweat poured across his face. Visions of dark corridors blinked in his head, the ceilings lined with panels of mostly extinguished fluorescent lights, the floors an industrial tile, worn but shiny, the walls a dull white. A hospital, he was certain now, it was definitely a hospital. And at the far end of the dimly lit hallway stood a man in a white coat, a doctor whose features remained concealed in shadow.

The hideous sound of Rose's voice echoed in his head.

"And you're not Harry."

I know who I am, I—I'm Harry Fremont, I—she's one of them, they're trying to drive me crazy, I—

An unnerving clatter drew his attention to the darkness at the top of the stairs. Someone was trying to force open a locked door.

They're trying to get in through the closet again.

Stifling a cough, he pushed away from the door, sank into a crouch to avoid being seen through the bay window and hurried to the kitchen.

The mudroom was empty. The coyote had bolted.

They're in the house.

Bat in hand, Harry spun back toward the den, trying to figure out what to do next, his mind a jumble of thoughts and memories and nightmare images he still couldn't quite make sense of.

The only light on in the kitchen was on the stove. Had he left that on? He staggered over to it, flicked it off...waited...listened...tried to breathe through his mouth. The night and the house again fell silent.

An itch tickled his eyebrow, crawled in a jagged line down toward his cheek. His eyelid twitched. With a sweaty palm he pawed at his face but the feeling remained, sweeping over him, down over the top and sides of his head, along his forehead and onto his nose, mouth, chin, throat and neck.

No. Wait. Not an itch. A sensation of touch.

But not human touch, something far more subtle barely making contact with his flesh in a strange rhythm, like a bevy of invisible silk scarves had been thrown into the air all around him and were delicately, gradually descending, brushing against him one after the next as they fell.

Harry whirled, holding the bat with one hand and waving the other around in horror as if to clear the area of spider webs. "Get away from me, get—get away, get off, get off!"

As he stumbled into the den the feeling left him, the phantom scarves vanishing like smoke. Breathlessly, he ran his hands over his body to make certain whatever touched him had left nothing more in its wake than perspiration and fear.

A now familiar scraping sound crept up through the floorboards.

He looked down, listened.

Something was in the cellar, dragging that same strange piping he'd seen before along the concrete floor.

They're in the basement.

Harry slid over to the front door, stepping lightly so as not to alert those below of his movement. The frantic urge to flee was overwhelming, but he knew running was no longer an option. Perhaps it never had been. They'd found their way into the house but were outside too, countless numbers of them lying in wait just outside that door. Even if he made it to his car and his head and vision miraculously became clear enough for him to drive, where would he go? There was nowhere to escape to. There was no help. Not the police, his friends or family, a neighbor or even a stranger on the street could help him. He was alone. He knew that now, understood it as fact. His only choice was to follow the noises down into the cellar and investigate them. Clearly whatever was making them wanted him to do just that, and there was little point in continuing to avoid the inevitable.

The wind rustled the trees and gently shook the house, but there was something more. There, just beneath the surface, another sound, a second sound bleeding through from somewhere very far away. Scratchy and hollow, it was barely audible above the erotic whispers of the wind, faint but unmistakably human, a male voice emerging as if from the needle of an old phonograph. Was it in his head or just outside the windows? Harry couldn't be sure.

"We found some very strange things in the house..."

He stood perfectly still and breathed through his mouth, trying desperately to figure out where the otherworldly voice was coming from.

"Things that indicate he was deeply disturbed..."

The television blinked, the light from the screen puncturing the otherwise dark room. The satellite signal was back but there was still no audio. Hadn't he switched it off earlier? How had it come on by itself? A rerun of an old sitcom bent rays of light across his face and along the walls but offered no clues.

"Audio recordings, bizarre writings on the walls and in the closets..."

The voice wasn't coming from the television, he was sure of it.

"Odd photographs..."

His eyes searched the framed photographs scattered about the room. He squinted but was barely able to make out the various faces on display, as if they were slowly fading into oblivion, memories once real advancing toward myth. *They're all dead*, he thought. *Everyone in those photographs is dead.*

The voice faded, swallowed again by a scratching sound reminiscent of a phonograph needle stuck in a groove.

Just as it too faded away, the phone began to ring. He traced it to the floor where he'd dropped it earlier. He crouched, picked it up, hit the TALK button and brought the phone to his ear. Through the crackle of distortion, a woman's voice came to him, spoken in a soft and dreamy whisper, as if from a great distance.

"I have a secret."

Gloria? Or just something mimicking her?

"Gloria?" he said, his voice weak. "Is that you?"

"There's been a murder."

He remembered the blood running from behind her scarf, a sudden trickle from her temple down across her cheek. "Gloria, have you done something?"

Static...

"What have you done? Answer me, what have you done!"

"I'm afraid," she said, voice breaking. "I don't know where I am anymore."

The line went dead, then just as quickly began to ring again.

"Who's there?"

"Harry!" Another female voice. "Harry what's going on?"

"Jasmine?"

"Don't play stupid with me! I'm done with bullshit niceties. Where is she you bastard?"

"What do you mean? I—"

"Answer me! *Where* is Kelly?"

"I don't know."

"I know something's happened! I know it! I tried to call her like you said but her cell keeps going to voicemail. I left her two messages and she didn't return either of them, even one I sent as urgent. I called a few coworkers and they have no knowledge of her going on any business trip to San Diego. Since then I've called every friend and family member of hers I know and not one of them has seen or heard from her in three days. *Three days*, Harry!"

"I…I've spoken to her. I spoke to her earlier today."

"Liar! I swear to God, if you've hurt one hair on her head you'll—"

"No, I…" He could barely breathe. "You know I would never…"

"No one's seen or heard from Aaron Searcy in days either."

He swallowed, hard. "So?"

"Cut the crap, Harry. I know you knew what was going on. Kelly told me she knew you were becoming suspicious and she was worried about how you'd react if you found out. She was planning to cut it off after this weekend—you—tell me you didn't do anything stupid!"

"I don't know what the fuck you're talking about."

"14 Beach Street. How about now? Know what I'm talking about now?"

"Excuse me?"

"You heard me. 14 Beach Street, Sippican Shores, on the Cape."

"I've never been to Sippican Shores."

"You're lying. 14 Beach Street."

A sharp pain slashed across his temple. "Is that supposed to mean something to me?"

"I tried Aaron's cell and I even tried the house phone there. No answer. It's like they just fell off the face of the Earth three days ago."

I haven't slept in three days.

"Something's wrong, you sonofabitch, I can feel it. You're lying."

"*I'm* lying?" he said. "You knew about this all along and let it go on, let the two of them make a fucking fool of me and pretended all was right with the world. You came into my home, *my* fucking home, knowing what was happening and acted like everything was fine and you've got the balls to call *me* a liar?"

"I'll drive out there and check on them if I have to, don't think I won't."

"Fuck you, Jasmine. You're the liar and a phony and a piece of shit."

"I'm calling the cops, asshole."

"Do whatever you have to do."

"Fucking bastard, you'll burn for this."

The television died and the room returned to darkness. Harry stood trembling, the phone pressed to his ear. But there was no longer anyone there.

He disconnected. Something told him he needed to retrieve the card Officer Guy had given him, and though he wasn't entirely sure why, he very calmly found the card, got a dial tone, then punched in the number.

"Donna Guy."

"This is Harry Fremont."

"Hello Mr. Fremont," she said through a sigh. "Is something wrong?"

"Yes," he answered. "I think there's been a murder."

Something shuffled about in the cellar below.

"A murder?"

"Yes, possibly more than one."

"Where?"

"Fourteen Beach Street, Sippican Shores."

"How do you know this?"

"I don't."

He dropped the phone, and as if in a trance, walked back into the kitchen. He reached for the door next to the pantry, a nondescript, rarely used, easily overlooked door on which Kelly had hung a calendar featuring baby animals. An adorable puppy stared back at him, the dog posed in a field of daises and brilliantly green grass.

He reached out, touched it. The little dog looked so real.

Happiness often did.

Warm snot dribbled down the back of Harry's otherwise dry throat. Stifling a cough, he pulled open the door. A dank and musty smell wafted up along the open wooden stairs, lingered a moment and then dissipated. Harry watched the deeper darkness awhile then flicked the switch just inside the door. The fixture above the stairs remained off; a dark smudge along the top of the bulb suggesting it had burned out at some previous point. There was another light on a pull-string mounted to one of the beams in the center of the basement, but there was no way to activate it remotely. In order to illuminate the area he'd have to descend the stairs in total darkness, negotiate his way to the center of the cellar in pitchblack, then locate the hanging string.

Gripping the bat, he took a step down. The staircase shook a bit beneath his weight. Another step and then another. Harry looked back as if to be certain the open doorway to the kitchen was still there. Satisfied, he took another step closer to the bottom of the stairs but in his mind he saw that door slamming shut behind him, locking and trapping him in the blackness, sealing him in a horrific tomb of cement and dirt and cobwebs from which he could never escape.

Something moved in the darkness below. Quietly… subtly…a shifting of weight perhaps, the slow slide of a foot, an exhale of breath…

Harry froze, straining to see. "Who's there?"

It's all the thoughts in your head, the horrible thoughts and possibilities and scenarios that won't leave you alone, that won't die no matter how hard you try to kill them… fear…joy… torment…ecstasy…misery…

Something pale moved in the far corner of the basement, a blur of off-white shifting through the darkness.

He took the last three stairs into the bowels of the house and stepped down onto the cement floor. A deep inhale drew in the usual array of stale basement odors, but amidst the familiar, something foreign.

Slowly, he reached out for the string, hoping to find it dangling there.

But before he could grasp it the bulb came on, swinging and swaying back and forth from the end of the cord it was mounted to, painting the walls and corners with swaths of light before moving away, panning to and fro like a prank in a funhouse, revealing quick glimpses of all that was down there with him.

The pale faced man in overalls huddled a few feet away and struggling with a long length of pipe he was attempting to fit together with other pieces... The patio furniture stacked and pushed into another corner...the lawnmower and lawn chairs...the oil furnace...

And in the far corner, a woman in a full slip, once white but stained and faded with perspiration and speckles of blood. Her hair and makeup was mussed, eyes wild, hands pressed against the cement walls as if for purchase, or perhaps searching for a way out. As the bulb swung past, Harry saw the bloody bandaged freak lying still near her bare feet.

"Kelly," he heard himself say.

She turned, looked back over her shoulder at him, sorrow in her once-beautiful blue eyes.

The bulb came to a stop, illuminating most of the basement now, leaving only the corners in shadow. Something overhead in the rafters crawled away, Harry heard its legs clicking as it went. His eyes moved to the pale man, who had finished his work and now stood staring at him, those unnaturally wide eyes boring into him, seeing places he wanted no one to see.

Kelly fell back against the wall, arms dangling at her sides as if broken. "That's how they take you down there," she said in a slurred voice.

Harry considered the strange network of pipes that ran to the wall and down into the floor, all of them fitted together, turned and fastened one to the next, a maze of thick moist pipes just large enough to fit an animal or perhaps a child but...

"First they make you fit." She motioned faintly with her chin to the swaddled thing at her feet, her face contorting into a grimace of terror. "Then they take you down."

The man stepped back and away, retreating into one of the corners where the darkness still lived and could conceal him. Only his large, wet, slowly blinking eyes remained visible.

At the same time Kelly stepped out of her corner, allowing more of the light to touch her. She squinted as if she hadn't seen light in a very long time. Her flesh was covered in a thin sheen of perspiration, and like her slip, sprayed lightly with blood. The exposed tops of her breasts shook as she stumbled forward, looking like an unsuspecting performer suddenly thrust into the spotlight.

Maybe she's just lost her way.

Behind her, deep in the corner, sat a man in a chair Harry recognized as Aaron Searcy. His pants and underwear were around his ankles, but his shirttails, though tented by an erection, covered his genitals. He stared straight ahead with a demented smile, like some sort of deranged mental patient, his large horse-like teeth shining through the darkness. Kelly glanced back at him, bowed her head and returned to the corner. Sitting on the basement floor next to him, she slid her hand up over his calf, along his thigh and beneath the shirttails.

The familiarity and comfort between them was more appalling than any act they could commit. That she could touch him with such nonchalance, so casually and effortlessly savaged him like a hatchet to the chest.

As Kelly's hand moved up and down, slowly at first and then faster and faster still, the shirttails fell away but Searcy remained still, grinning maniacally as she masturbated him.

Nearby the bandaged freak began to moan and writhe about. Neither Kelly nor Searcy paid any attention.

Through rage, tears, and then, as he angrily wiped them away, something horribly cold came awake in him, slithered about and nested.

It was in that moment that Harry tried to remember the quiet. He'd known it once, hadn't he? Hadn't *they*? Comfortable silences where no words were necessary, where a subtle sigh or change of position, a sideways glance or a whisper of skin brushing skin said everything, made everything all right and life worth living. It had never been the noise, not even the laughter or tears of joy they shared, but the silence, the quiet, the unspoken that had been the true measure of their love. That utter and complete silence when Harry knew he was loved and everything—*everything*—would be all right.

"I want it all back."

"You can't have it back," Kelly said. "It's gone away now."

"There are consequences to what we do. There has to be."

"Yes, we answer for our actions. Not just to others, but to ourselves." She glanced down with disinterest at the cock in her hand. It began to come. She jerked it harder.

"Mmm," Searcy moaned, "that's my good girl."

Harry's legs buckled and he sank to his knees.

"There's been a murder."

"Yes," Kelly said, as if just then awakened from a dream. "I know."

11

It was raining. He remembered it was raining.

It *was* rain, wasn't it? Pouring over them, so warm and wet and slippery and oddly comforting, at once washing and staining them anew as they sat together in the dark with their secrets. He'd dreamed of this, hadn't he?

Harry took her hand in his, felt the rain squish between their palms. It felt so delicate and small, her hand, her precious and beautiful hand, the ring finger still sporting the diamond he'd given her all those years ago. "Do you remember?" he asked softly.

"*Can* you still remember what it was like before?"

"No."

"But you want to don't you."

"Yes."

"Betrayal is a vicious animal."

"So is guilt. So is rage."

"Yes."

"I didn't know, I—"

"You didn't want to know. But you always have."

"No."

"And you will again," he told her, the sole of his thumb gently caressing the top of hers. "It won't be much longer now."

"And then?"

"And then you'll know the truth."

"Will it free us?"

He wished he could see her face, but it remained obscured by the rain. "Only me."

Her hand slipped away. But she was not gone.

She'd been broken into pieces—they both had—and had since patched themselves together like living scarecrows, a conglomerate of ideas and myths and possibilities, of mind storms and things never spoken, precariously held together with glue and rusty staples, their insides hay and grass and dried leaves, once beautiful and alive, now dead, pointless. The concept of torment, of having been tortured by this realization for years and opting to bury it, to conceal it within himself rather than face it for the reality it was had crippled him not only emotionally, but intellectually. Methodically, it chipped away at his sanity and strength, eventually becoming a perfect breeding ground for agony and madness alike.

On hands and knees, Harry made his way into the pool of light on the cellar floor. He fell back onto his ass and sat there, out of breath and sniffling, no longer tired but instead in a state somewhere between damnation and grace. One was not so very far from the other. They were, after all, brethren. Kelly sat across from him, head bowed, her hair matted down and body bathed not in rain but a thick layer of fresh blood, the whites of her eyes pronounced and frightening against a backdrop of crimson. Harry looked to his hands. Curiously, they had finally stopped shaking.

The shadow creatures crawled about like predatory insects, circling the pool of light, coming close but never quite crossing into it, their growls and shuffling bodies echoing along the cement foundation, Harry's torment alive and embodied and stalking him even now, relentless and unforgiving.

"Get away!" he screamed. Those closest retreated to darkness but continued circling like the ravenous wolves they were. "Get away!"

"You can't suffer for someone else's sins," Kelly said, her voice gurgling, mouth and throat full of blood.

"That's what most people suffer from, other people's sin."

"Sin," she repeated back, "seems such an archaic word."

"What should we call it then?"

"Maybe we shouldn't call it anything."

"I've dreamed of this," Harry said. "I've dreamed of this blood."

"So have I." She reached for him with a look in her eyes he had not seen in a very long while, her hand falling just short, the fingertips dripping crimson. "I'm so sorry, sweetheart."

"So am I."

"It's very late."

Something flopped into the circle of light. The bandaged thing, stained still with blood and dirt—filth—emerged from the shadows, moaning frantically as it worked its way across the floor until it reached Kelly. Up close and in the light Harry could see the legs had been hideously severed or perhaps torn or gnawed away, the bloody jagged stumps dressed hastily in soiled bandages.

That's how they take you down there. First they make you fit.

Then they take you down.

Kelly reached for it tenderly—reminding Harry of how she'd once reached for Garrett when he was still a baby—and dragged the thing onto her bloody lap. It reached for her as well, its arms clinging to her neck as if fearful she might let it go otherwise. Behind the bandages, the same strangely familiar eyes shifted and locked on him.

And then he knew.

With bloody fingers Kelly carefully peeled the bandages from its head. The others came closer, breeching the circle, watching…

Like listening to one's recorded voice and finding it surprisingly foreign, sometimes gazing into one's own eyes produced a similar confusion.

As the last strip fell away and the true horror, pain and devastation on Harry Fremont's face was revealed, they snatched him away, tearing what remained of his body from her arms and taking it with them back into darkness. He screamed and cried out, but his attempts at words failed, sounding as if his tongue had been removed, or perhaps as if his jaw had sustained crushing injury.

Despite the darkness, Harry could make out glimpses of the others dragging what was clearly him toward the labyrinth of pipes.

"Jesus Christ," he said, looking away. "Am I in Hell?"

Kelly closed her eyes, becoming one with the blood. "Not quite."

In the nightmares they came in a single wave of violence and savagery, pale faces and wide eyes no longer focused on rooftops, intricate networks of pipes, the mutilated version of his soul writhing in agony and terror or this most curious of nights, but him. He scrambled up the cellar stairs toward the sparse light in the kitchen, crawling like a tired old cat up the wooden steps, the bat no longer wet with perspiration from his hands, but blood. His mind urged him to go faster, to push harder, but his body had virtually nothing left.

Right on his heels, he could hear their jaws snapping; feel their fingertips brushing his ankles, but he somehow made it to the landing, rolling across the tiled floor and frantically kicking the cellar door closed just in time.

Gripping the edge of the island, he pulled himself to his feet. The door burst open in an explosion of flailing arms, open mouths sporting razor teeth and a chorus of primal screeches…and those horribly wide, moist, nearly childlike eyes, ablaze with purposeful fury.

But those were the nightmare memories. In the moment he'd found himself on the roof of his house with no knowledge of how he'd gotten there. Bathed in moonlight, he stood near the edge and looked down at the driveway below. Behind him, crawling up over the gutters and out the attic window, the shadow people followed...slowly...knowingly.

In the clear night and fresh air there was almost something peaceful about it. A surrender of sorts, the prey recognizing in its final moments that the chase had ended and all that remained was that which had been inevitable from the very beginning.

Harry gazed up at the moon. Smiling through his tears, and without looking back at the others, he opened his arms as if to embrace the night sky, and stepped into oblivion.

* * *

Through the darkness, a lonely private street...at the end of a long and winding driveway, a beautiful summerhouse waits atop a small hill overlooking the ocean.

14 Beach Street.

Inside, where furniture and voices and living things once resided, there is now empty space and silence. Only the ocean crashing nearby shore can be heard above the echoing footfalls of Harry's shoes as he strides through a large vacant room consisting of bare walls, dull hardwood floors, high ceilings and windows without curtains. And there, on the floor, is Gloria Searcy, the same scarf wrapped about her head, the same trickle of blood staining her cheek and neck. Only now Harry can see the wound clear through the material and into her shattered temple, a wound caused by some blunt object, a bat, perhaps. She speaks without looking at him.

"I have a secret."

"Kelly's bleeding," he tells her. "She's badly hurt, she's bleeding."

Gloria nods, dead eyes fixated on the floor. "There's been a murder."

"What have you done?"

"I'm afraid. I don't know where I am anymore."

"Is this your house?"

"There was a time when it was our special getaway down by the beach, a romantic summer place just for the two of us. That was a long time ago, though."

"And now?"

"The passage of time is a strange thing, don't you think? It bends and flows, kind of like water. And just like water, what you see doesn't even begin to scratch the surface of its mystery." She smiles but it seems to pain her to do so. "He brought her here. Here, where he used to bring me. That's why I told you. I wanted you to come, to see, to know."

Harry notices a door at the far end of the room, slightly ajar. Like the rest of this place, it seems oddly familiar. He moves toward it.

"Don't go in there," she warns. "You don't...trust me...you—you don't want to go in there."

He paces like a caged animal, hands pressed to his temples. "What have you done? God help us, what—what the hell have you done?"

"What have you *done, Harry?"*

There comes a point where you have to see the truth, Harry...

Gloria begins to laugh. It is a horrible, hideous cackle that pulls back the curtains fogging Harry's mind to reveal him entering this place days before. Bat in hand, testing the front door, finding it open, stepping through the threshold and into this very room. Somewhere nearby, a stereo is playing. Bruce Springsteen is belting out "Tunnel of Love" but in the next room Harry hears people arguing, shouting at one another.

You have to see it even though you don't want to...

Gloria has beaten him here.

Even though it's disgusting and awful and hurtful...

And in the other room, Searcy, a towel wrapped around his otherwise nude body, tries frantically to explain what is happening to his irate wife as Kelly stands to the side, near the corner of a mussed bed, dressed only in a slip and partially concealed in shadow. She looks as if she's already gone elsewhere, her physical presence little more than a memory, a whisper still drifting through empty rooms, forgotten hallways.

You don't understand yet, but you will…

Kelly looks up and sees him, and as their eyes meet, something inside her withers and dies. "Harry," she says.

Gloria and Aaron turn and look at him in unison, unaware that his face will be the last thing either ever sees.

"Now hold on one minute, Harry, there's no reason we can't be civil here. We're not children." Searcy starts toward him. "Just put that bat down and we'll get this all straightened out."

Through the rage, the blood, the screams, the gut-wrenching sound of wood smashing flesh and bone, Gloria brings him back. "I didn't want you to kill him," she says. "I wanted you to hurt him, to make him feel and understand what his lies did, the violence they caused. I wanted him to know what I—and you—had been enduring for years, and I wanted him to live with it for the rest of his miserable life, just like you and I had to live with our pain and shame and embarrassment. I wanted the prick to drown in it, and I wanted Kelly to do the same. But I never meant for you to do this…not this…"

"You're lying, I—I wouldn't hurt anyone."

He sees Gloria then, running to him, trying to stop him from bringing the bat down again. Though it's too late, she runs to him anyway, screaming "Stop!" But he doesn't stop, he has crossed a line where reason and restraint— even consequence—no longer apply or occur to him. At his feet Searcy lies dying in a bloody heap, his face and head smashed in, his arms and chest and legs already bruising where the bat struck again and again. Overcome with violence and rage, Harry spins toward Gloria as she runs for him, and swings the bat at her. It isn't until it connects with her skull with a sickening clang that he realizes what he's done. She staggers, looks at him with a combination of fear, confusion and shock and then topples, falling like some boneless, weightless thing blown over by a gust of wind. She hits the floor, her hand reaching for her temple. It comes back slick with blood so dark it borders on black. Harry wants to drop the bat but can't.

It's fused to his hand. Gloria smiles as if she can't quite believe what's happening and then collapses facedown into a pool of blood. Harry looks to the bed. He still cannot remember, but Kelly too is collapsed in a bloody mess. He sees a flash in his mind, a brief moment when his eyes met Kelly's and she looked at him with acceptance if not outright submission. Almost as if she knew what was coming and that for her there would be no escape. And with that knowledge, came a level of peace.

"I would never hurt her," Harry mumbles. "I couldn't, I—I'm not capable of hurting her. I love her more than life itself."

He remembers her raising a hand, holding it up like a crossing guard signaling incoming traffic to stop, or perhaps it's instinctual, a reflexive attempt to deflect what she knows is coming. Her diamond and wedding band catch the sparse light through the nearby window. It is the last thing Harry remembers before he swings the bat and connects with her head, the last thing he remembers before she falls to the floor where he hits her again.

From a faraway corner of his crippled mind, he sees Garret as a little boy watching him, a crumpled juice box and a baseball mitt at his feet.

Sometimes love runs so deep it hurts, but when it turns to anger or even violence it becomes something else entirely.

Doesn't it?

"We're all dead," Gloria tells him.

The memories fade. "Is Kelly alive?" he asks through a blur of tears.

Gloria slowly traces the floor with bloody fingers.

"Is she alive?" he says, screaming it this time, his voice booming in open space.

Finally, she looks at him. "Are you?"

* * *

Night…it was still night. The first thing he saw was a blurry vision of his car and Kelly's SUV beyond it. Pain surged through his body, coming from somewhere very deep inside him, and he tasted blood. Lots of blood. He'd hit the driveway with tremendous force, and even before he attempted to move he knew he'd been severely injured. His head hurt horribly, like it had shattered and was now held together by loose flaps of bloody wet skin that had once been his face.

Something moved into his limited frame of vision.

My God, the coyote…

It stood next to him, nervously sniffing the air, eyes panning the area for potential threats.

He's protecting me, watching over me.

As if it sensed something, it turned its head and looked closer at Harry, so close its nose nearly touched him.

Suddenly Harry sensed it too. He was sure of it. He knew those eyes, the soul behind them and the look of recognition. His old friend.

"Marlon?" he asked weakly. Was that even his voice?

I'm sorry. I've done all I can.

Slowly, the coyote backed away.

Harry tried to move his arms. One shifted, the other refused to budge but throbbed with pain. With a grunt he struggled as best he could to pull himself up, to raise his head and attempt to at least get to his hands and knees.

The coyote was gone, returned to the dark forest from which it came.

Get up, I—they're coming, I have to get up.

His entire body began to shudder as he tried to push himself up, the pain agonizing, his vision still blurred but getting better, enough to make out a reflection in the moonlight. Along the side of his car, a face. His face but…

I can't. I can't make it. I want to sleep. I need to sleep.

A shattered face, broken and torn, slowly morphing.

There is no rest from torment, Kelly…

Now a once beautiful face.

…from pain…pain inflicted by actions that must be answered for…

Blonde hair caked with blood.

…from feeling what he felt, to live what he lived…

Blue eyes barely alive yet strangely aware…

...on that last night...to know...to understand...to truly understand...

Finally aware...

Dropping from the roof, the shadow people fell about her broken body like spiders descending on webs, closing on her until there was nothing left but night and the horrific wails of the damned.

12

But still, the dreams persist.

"Mr. Fremont?"

When I think of you now—really think of you—I see you for what you are. A disease, an infection that slowly killed us both, a plague that changed the woman I loved more than anything in this world into someone I no longer knew, an illness that took hold in me and turned me into someone capable of unimaginable violence. For what? Tell me, for what? Why her? Why me?

"Mr. Fremont, can you hear me?"

There is a version of our lives before you, and a version after. One includes someone I knew and fell in love with. The other leaves mere scraps, a near-stranger in her place. For so many years I slept, waited and listened, and eventually came to understand these things. I came to drown in them.

But I never planned to drown alone.

"My name is Doctor Bonnet."

I learned to put my pain, anger and suspicion aside, to pretend they weren't there, to trick myself into believing all was well. It was easier that way, I suppose, to simply pretend I didn't see what was right in front of my eyes. It was safer to play along, to look the other way, to think happy thoughts and focus on something else. But there's always something below the surface. Always.

You should've thought about what was beneath mine.

"Can you hear me? Mr. Fremont?"

Be it a wall, a floor, earth, flesh, darkness...peel any of them back and beneath their exteriors and outer layers a network beyond what can readily be seen and touched is revealed, there all along but existing unseen, hidden. And what resides beneath rarely resembles that which conceals it. Maybe the key to happiness is to never look deeper than those surfaces.

To never know the difference between what is real and what are lies.

"Mr. Fremont? Can you hear me?"

Like all else, it comes down to destiny. I know that now. There is what we want, what we do not, and what must be. And no one—nothing—can stop what must be. Once cornered I knew you'd understand the torment you'd caused, and how little it takes for an unassuming person to turn rogue and ravenous with violence. You'd see it alive and thriving in me, an unclean spirit possessing the soul of a wounded man for whom the bleeding never stops.

And never is a very long time.

"My name is Doctor Bonnet. I'm caring for you now."

Once, a long time ago, things were special, sacred. The love we shared, our union, and then the birth of our child—such an amazing gift—so pure and perfect, he made us whole, or at least it seemed that way. All of it held intrinsic meaning. And still, it was lost. Taken. Given away.

We had to answer for that.

So did you.

"Mr. Fremont, do you understand?"

I'm awake.

"You've been badly injured, Mr. Fremont."

God help you.

"Very badly injured."

God help us all.

* * *

Dreams no more, and yet he could not yet see, not quite. Swirling blurs of light and shadowy shapes drifted about as if submerged and floating in murky liquid. A steady beeping sound called to him from very far away as all else began fading into view, focus finally arriving to reveal a windowless hospital room, two of the four walls consisting of large windows beyond which he could just barely make out a large desk or counter area of some kind. His eyes blinked, cleared a bit more, looked to the drab walls, what little of the glossy floor he could see, the low lights everywhere providing just enough illumination to see the outlines of various machines all around the bed on which he'd been placed. And quiet, it—why was it so quiet? Only the incessant beeping continued, a bit louder than before but steady. In the next few seconds he came to realize it was beeping in time with his heart. He should've found this comforting, why then did it frighten him so?

He attempted to lift his head for a better look at himself, but he couldn't seem to budge. He drew a slow breath, let it out, then tried again. He could not lift his head from the pillow, and something was irritating his nose, a tube or some sort of plastic contraption had been stuffed up there and attached to one of the bedside machines. He wanted it out, it—he tried desperately to bring his hand up from his side and tear the tube away but he couldn't get his arm to respond. He looked down. His arms were right there at his sides, but both were concealed in casts.

They're broken. I've broken both my arms.

The beeping increased...louder...faster.

The fall from the roof—or had he jumped—he remembered now how he'd watched the paved driveway race toward him as he plummeted through the moonlit night.

He tried again.

I can't...I can't move, I—Jesus Christ—I can't move.

Struggling to control his panic, he squeezed shut his eyes a moment, took another deep breath, then reopened them.

He decided to start with something simple, like wiggling his toes. He tried and though it felt as if he were doing it, when he strained to see his feet, he could make out only a thin brown blanket pulled taut across his torso.

I'm hurt. I'm hurt bad.

He looked beyond the curve of blanket where he knew his thighs to be. Where the blanket should've been tented it remained flat all the way to the foot of the bed.

The beeping grew rapid as a prickly pain rever berated through his legs and down into his feet...

God no, no, I—

...lower legs and feet that were no longer there.

He was screaming. He could feel himself screaming. But all that came from him was a hideous squealing grunt, as his face was wrapped in bandages, the bones beneath shattered; his jaw broken and immobile.

The fall had shattered his entire body, but—had he broken his legs so severely they'd had to be amputated? Could that be?

How long had he lain there in the driveway, bloody and broken, before someone found him?

Garret, my—my boy—where are you? I'm so sorry, son, I—

Something moved in the far corner of the room. In the dim light he could not make out any specifics, but when he frantically looked to the door he was able to see a long, empty and relatively dark hallway that led to his room. The nurse's station through the window was also unmanned and quiet.

But he was no longer alone. Perhaps he never had been.

The shadows peeled back as if from unseen hands, and the strange dark contours of something unnatural emerged. Odd symmetrical angles, dripping with moisture, an entire network pieced together, there in the darkest corner of the room.

That's how they take you down there.

Eyes bulging with horror, he looked to the ceiling.

First they make you fit.

Something black scurried overhead like an enormous crab.

Then they take you down.

Harry felt tepid breath against his face, as if someone were panting right next to him, their face pressed to the side of his. He couldn't turn his head but he frantically slid his eyes to the side. Someone…some*thing* was there…

"That's the power of love, Harry."

Kelly, I—help me, I—

"It makes you believe things even when they're not true."

Something dropped from the ceiling.

"And you don't care."

Hands, I—I don't want them touching me, get— please, I—get their hands off me, get them off!

"Because it's such a powerful feeling you can't let go."

The room shifted, the ceiling slid past and suddenly he was falling, dropping to the hard tiled floor in a tangle of tubes and wires and bandages. He could hear the labored breath of those moving in the shadows, those pulling him, dragging him toward the pipes.

"You don't ever want to be without it again."

One large opening, dripping wet like the mouth of a giant eel, coming closer, so close he could smell the foulness within.

Don't, just—let me go, I—don't—please don't, I—

His screams went unheard as inhuman hands lifted him, offering his mangled body to the gods below, pushing him into the opening, forcing him as he writhed and groaned in protest, sliding deeper into slime and darkness as glimpses of the room blinked in the distance, his wife watching next to the bed in a slip sprayed with blood, her head a mask of gore but for the loving smile pursing her split lips.

13

Like life, place and time, it had all been reduced to a blur, a memory. It came from that place deep down inside where pretense cannot survive, where there are no rules or judgments, restraint or second-guessing, where one is only alive and aware without shackles, a place at once defined, realized, mysterious and intricate, horrifying and beautiful, a labyrinth of dreams and shadow wrapped in veils of emotion so raw and true none of it could be deciphered or experienced beyond the visceral.

Perhaps, in the end, that's all anyone needed.

Stay with me...

Had he heard the hypnotic grumblings of thunder just then?

Kelly, as he liked to remember her. So young, an All-American girl-next-door with a bright smile and gorgeous blue eyes, the most innocent and trusting eyes he'd ever seen. Eyes filled with such happiness and love it seemed she'd never be able to contain it, and yet...

My God, how I loved her.

Her hair had been pulled back into a ponytail that day, like she so often wore it then. Not yet married, he'd stopped by her house to see her. It was a Saturday and she was in the yard playing with some neighborhood kids, all of them younger than she was. Just as he remembered, they were throwing a Frisbee back and forth, and Kelly was laughing, having more fun than anyone. She ran over to him and kissed him quickly on the lips, saying something about the kids tiring her out, but she didn't seem tired at all. She seemed at peace. And now that he had joined her there, even from the sidelines, she seemed whole. He watched her leap for the Frisbee, running and laughing and throwing it back with such abandon, a girl on the verge of womanhood so sure of herself and so happy and yet.there was something else too, something more just beyond that naïve and childlike surface.

Stay with me...Kelly, stay with me...

If only Garret could've been there too, the dream would've been perfect. But he was years from being born.

So were they.

It wasn't until the scene faded away, swallowed by the darkness, that Harry realized Kelly was still next to him and that she'd been watching it too.

Kelly, come on now...stay with me...I need you to stay with me.

A red light whirled, slashing the darkness and illuminating their faces with each pass. She looked ghoulish now. They both did. But when she reached for his hand Harry let her take it, her flesh soft, wet, sticky.

"You know how they say your life flashes before your eyes when you die?" she asked, her voice strained and struggling for breath. "Maybe it's not your life at all, but a tiny bit of someone else's. Someone you loved; someone who loved you. That way you know. You understand—truly understand—because the last thing you feel is what they felt, what that love did to them, good and bad, the joy and the pain. And maybe in the end it cleanses you both."

"Stay with me," Harry said, and though he meant it, he realized it was not his voice but someone else's, someone neither of them knew and yet someone with whom Kelly would share the most intimate moment of all. “Please, I need you to stay with me.”

I’m losing her—we—we’re losing her!

Her hand slipped free of his, dropped away, and as the darkness took her the red light began to fade, its circular sweeps coming slower and slower until it blinked off and all was quiet.

And finally, long after dark, in desolate silence, Harry Fremont slept.

THE RAIN DANCERS

For Terry Wright

"The evil that men do lives after them;
the good is oft interred with their bones."
—William Shakespeare

1

The dreams began not long after the decision was made to return to town to settle things. I hadn't dreamed of that town or that house in a very long time, but in the weeks leading up to my return, I was confronted with a recurring nightmare so unsettling I didn't mention it to anyone. Instead, I sat with it, alone and in the dark. I could feel it as if it were a living thing. Slithering about, summoning forces none of us fully understood, making it real, making it so. And there was no stopping it.

Not now. Not ever.

* * *

Sometimes I wonder if things would've been different had it not been raining so heavily that night. Would he have still appeared at the door as if born of the rain, an orphan even the night didn't want? What would've happened if I'd never answered the door or refused to let him in? I wonder.

But I did. I did let him in.

He arrived in darkness, in the middle of a violent downpour.

I was in the kitchen when I noticed headlights gliding along the otherwise dark wall. The house was located in a rural area, on an unmarked and heavily wooded road few people ever came to, especially at night. The road was a dead end, and this was the only house there, a modest Cape my wife had grown up in and my father-in-law had occupied until his death a year before. At Betty's insistence, we continued to pay the utility bills, and although it sat empty the entire time, everything was still in place, just as it had been the night Earl died. I'd arrived in town early that morning to clean the place out and get it organized and ready to go on the market. Located near the end of the road, it was roughly one hundred yards in, off a two-lane state highway that ran through town. Unless one was looking for the house or already knew where it was, most drove right by the unmarked road without even realizing it.

Looking back, there seemed some thing strange about that particular night. Nothing I could put my finger on per se, just a vague sensation that the world around me was askew, that something wasn't quite right. Somewhere within all that darkness and rain it seemed as if nearly anything was possible. A night made for magic, everything felt dreamlike and mysterious. Or perhaps that's simply the way I chose to remember it, and that in hindsight I allowed such things into the mix to justify my own feelings. What I did know was that although our reasons were different, neither one of us wanted to be there. We hadn't been back since Earl's funeral—Betty couldn't bring herself to return—but we'd put it off long as possible. It was time to put it all to bed, to get the house in order, sell the property and move on with life.

Standing in the kitchen that night, watching those headlights slink down the otherwise dark road, there was no mistaking I felt something odd. Even before I knew who it was or what he wanted, I knew what I was feeling, how powerful it was, and how I'd never felt it quite the same way before.

Fear. I was beset with pure, unadulterated fear.

And I hadn't the slightest idea why.

As I moved to the window next to the front door, flipped the outside light switch and leaned in close to the rain-blurred pane, my eyes adjusted. A large, relatively new pickup truck had pulled into the driveway behind my car. As the headlights went out, I pictured Betty going through things in the cellar, and for some reason felt the need to call her name.

She didn't respond.

The driver's side door to the pickup swung open, triggering the interior light. Though it was only on for a second or two, it revealed a quick flash of an older man dropping down out of the cab before slamming the door shut.

I checked my wristwatch. It was only a little after seven-thirty, but due to the storm and the fact that it was early November, it had already been dark for a few hours and felt later. I watched as the man moved across the driveway to the stone walk leading to the front door. He was tall, just over six feet, with a thin, rangy build. Despite the downfall, he seemed unaffected and moved at a slow but steady pace until he'd reached the house. Before he could knock or ring the bell, I opened the door. All that separated us was a storm door.

The man smiled and waved at me as if we were old friends. He wore a battered baseball cap, an old pair of cowboy boots and a yellow rain slicker over an unassuming plaid flannel shirt and Dickies workpants. "Evenin'," he said, loud enough for me to hear him through the door.

At closer range he was a lot older than I'd originally thought. He appeared to be in his early seventies and had a disarming, gentle manner that led me to believe he was probably harmless. But still, I had no idea who he was. "Hello," I said. "Can I help you?"

"I hope so, son," he called above the rain. "Looking for Betty."

I nodded, but he must've realized from my expression that I was going to need a little more from him than that.

"Sure am sorry to bother you." His voice was deep and smooth but laced with a faint trace of southern accent, like a radio announcer from an old country-western show. "I'm an old friend of Betty's family. Haven't been in town for years. I'm back for a visit and heard from a mutual friend that her father

Earl had passed on awhile back and that you were in town to settle his business."

After a slight hesitation, I opened the door. "Come in."

"Much obliged." He stepped inside, bringing a gust of wind and a spray of rain with him. "Great Gosh Almighty, nasty night out there, isn't it?"

"Quite a rain," I said.

He made sure the storm door closed and latched behind him. "Apologize for showing up unannounced like this," he said, "but when I heard Earl had passed I felt it only right to stop in and pay you and your lovely bride my respects." He offered his hand. "I'm Bob Laurent."

We shook hands. His palm had the coarse feel of someone who had worked as a laborer for a very long time. "Will Colby."

"Pleasure to meet you, Will." He gave my hand a firm pump then let go. Laurent's eyes were an arresting blue, particularly set against his leathery skin, which was perpetually tanned and wrinkled, probably from years of working outdoors. Otherwise his features were hawk-like, his face long and angular, nose crooked and beaked, lips thin and pale. "Heard Earl's death was sudden."

"Yes, it was very unexpected. A heart attack." I switched the overhead light on and stepped deeper into the kitchen. Laurent followed. "He managed to call an ambulance but died later at the hospital."

He frowned. "Had no idea. What a shame."

"It happened a little over a year ago," I explained. "Getting the house in order so we can put it on the market."

"No interest in living here, huh?"

"Afraid not. I have a place in New York."

"New York," he said, as if he'd never spoken the words before and thought he'd try them out. "Betty turned into a city girl, did she?"

I smiled but offered nothing more.

He shrugged as if it didn't matter and said, "Earl and I go way back. Gosh, I've known your wife from the day she was born. I knew she'd lost her mother years ago. Matter of fact, that's the last time I was in town, for the services. Long time now. Fine woman, her momma."

"Unfortunately I never had the pleasure of knowing her." Betty's mother had died of cancer when Betty was sixteen. When Betty and I met, in our early twenties, her mother had already been gone for years. Laurent apparently wasn't exaggerating when he said he hadn't been back to town in a long while. Twenty-six years was a long stretch between visits.

"Earl and Jan were good people." He looked away, as if remembering something else, then sighed heavily. "As I say, hadn't heard the news about her father until just today. How's little Betty holding up?"

Had we been discussing something else, his moniker for my wife would've made me laugh. *Little Betty is forty-three years old*, I felt like saying, but I let it go. After all, the last time he'd seen her she was only thirteen. "She did well as could be expected," I said. "I know from personal experience you never completely get over the death of a loved one, but they say time makes it somewhat easier."

"Sometimes," Laurent said softly. He removed his baseball cap to reveal badly thinning gray hair styled in a comb-over. "Sometimes not."

"True enough. Let me get your coat for you."

He wiggled out of his raincoat and held it out for me cumbersomely; clearly embarrassed that it was dripping all over the floor. "Geez Louise, I've gone and made a mess."

"Not at all. It's just a little rainwater." I took his hat and slicker, hung them on hooks just inside the front door then motioned to the kitchen set. "Please, Mr. Laurent, have a seat."

"Only if you promise to call me Bob." He smiled, showing faded dentures.

"Bob," I agreed. The inexplicable fear I'd initially felt had subsided, but in its wake was an equally baffling sense of unease. "Make yourself comfortable."

"Thank you kindly." He pulled a chair away from the table, sat down and crossed his spindly legs. "Sure do appreciate the hospitality, Will."

I jerked a thumb toward a closed door on the kitchen wall to my right. "Betty's down in the basement. I'll go get her."

"You've got yourself a real good girl there." He winked at me. "Always used to say little Betty was the sweetest berry in the patch."

I had no idea how to respond to that, so I smiled politely then excused myself. I slipped through the door and escaped down the cellar stairs to find Betty halfway up the staircase herself.

She cocked an eyebrow, narrowed her eyes and gave me her best *is-someone-here?* look.

I nodded, took another step down so she could hear me, and whispered, "There's a man upstairs. Bob Laurent. Says he's an old friend of your father's."

Betty thought a second. "What was the name?"

"Laurent. Bob Laurent. Old guy, seventies, tall and thin."

"Huh. Sounds vaguely familiar, I think, but…"

"Said he's known you since you were born. Hasn't been back to town since your mom died and apparently he was visiting and heard about your father. He's here to pay his respects."

"Great." Betty pushed her bottom lip out and blew a renegade strand of hair up and away from her eyes. "I look awful. Let me straighten myself up a little." She was dressed in a pair of sweatpants, a T-shirt and a pair of ratty sneakers. Her hair was pulled back in a ponytail, but for a few renegade strands hanging in her eyes. "Tell him I'll be right there."

I returned to the kitchen, closing the cellar door behind me. "She'll be right up," I said. "Can I get you anything? We don't have much, just a few things we brought with us and some leftover pizza we had delivered this afternoon."

"Thank you, Will, but I don't want to be a bother."

"No bother," I assured him. "Something cold to drink maybe?"

Laurent pursed his thin lips. "Golly, are you two going to have anything?"

I couldn't quite figure out if his over-the-top downhome politeness was genuine or not. "I've got some beer in the fridge."

He pointed at me and grinned. "You're on."

I plucked a couple bottles from the refrigerator, twisted off the caps and handed him one. "There you are."

"Sure is nice to sit and have a cold beer with friends now and then." He looked around, taking in the small room. "Spent an awful lot of time in this house. Surely did. I've got so many good memories here."

I was glad someone did.

"Yes, sir, I spent many an hour sitting right in this kitchen with Earl just shooting the breeze."

Before I could think of a comeback, the cellar door opened and Betty sauntered in, looking as if she'd just that moment realized someone was there.

Laurent sprung from his chair with impressive speed for a man his age, crossed the kitchen in two long strides and wrapped her up in a huge bear hug. "So good to see you, sweetheart," he said, still holding her tight.

Over his shoulder, Betty looked at me with a befuddled expression I read as: *I have no idea who this is.* I suppressed a chuckle, had another swallow of beer and flashed her my own look. *Well I sure as hell don't know him.*

When Laurent finally ended the hug, he took her by her shoulders and held her back and away from him a bit. "Let me get a good look at you, girl." His eyes roamed over her from head to toe. "Little Betty. Still the beauty." Betty blushed, but before she could say anything he pointed at her and said, "Remember I used to call you my little strawberry? Who's the sweetest berry in the patch?"

She grinned helplessly. "Me?"

Laurent laughed, slapped his knee and turned to me. "Didn't I tell you? I was just telling Will here how I always used to say that."

I raised my bottle in salute, as I hadn't the foggiest idea what else to do.

"So," Betty said, doing her best to appear familiar, "how have you been?"

"Never mind me." Laurent turned serious. "I'm truly sorry to hear about your father."

"Thanks."

Laurent gave a sullen nod. "He's with your momma now."

"I know."

With his arm around her, he led Betty to the kitchen table. He pulled out a chair and she sat in it, then he slid into the one next to her. What was odd was that he chose the closest side of the table, which meant once they were sitting down they both had their backs to me.

Rather than join them, I remained where I was.

Behind me, wind tossed rain against the window over the sink, spraying the pane with a quick drumming sound. Suddenly, I was confronted with a strange vision of the woods behind the house in the darkness and rain, and a sense that someone or something was watching the house, watching us.

Baffled, I sipped my beer and banished the peculiar visual from my head.

Laurent was relaying a story about how years before he and Betty's father had gone on a hunting and fishing trip up in Maine. As he told Betty the story, he nonchalantly slid his arm around her. I didn't think much of it at first, but he did seem awfully comfortable physically with my wife. *Maybe he's just one of those touchy-feely types*, I thought. I wasn't sure I liked this latest development, but Laurent hardly seemed the stuff of predator or dirty old man, so I let it go and listened to him babble on about what fun he and Earl had on their fishing trip. Betty was enthralled, and if Laurent's arm bothered her, she gave no indication.

As the story continued, with Betty injecting an occasional question, very slowly, Laurent's hand began to move from Betty's shoulder down to the center of her back. His palm went flat and he began to rub from side to side, so slowly at first that the motion was barely perceptible. But within seconds, the strokes had become longer and more pronounced, his fingers tenting then walking along the middle of her back.

Was he really doing what I thought he was doing? I hoped not, because he appeared to be checking to see if she was wearing a bra.

I waited to see if Betty reacted. She didn't.

Unsure of what to do—if anything—I strode over to the table, keeping my motion deliberately casual so as not to project a sense of upset or urgency. Neither Betty nor Laurent noticed me, so I rounded the table and slid into a chair directly across from them. I hadn't noticed previously one way or the other, so I glanced at Betty's chest, and through the thin T-shirt saw that she had a bra on.

The moment I sat down, Laurent removed his arm and shifted positions in his chair so he could comfortably see both of us. It was a smooth move, and one designed to appear as if he were accommodating me. As he continued his story his eyes bounced between us, back and forth, but I was no longer listening to him. I was focused on Betty. She seemed unaware of what Laurent had done, which led me to question my interpretation of what I'd seen. I leaned back in my chair, pretended to be riveted with his story and ran through it all again.

I reached the same conclusion. I wasn't wrong, and knew it. Laurent had absolutely been feeling for a bra. Stranger still was the fact that he knew I was standing behind them and would see what he was doing. Yet he'd made no move to hide it, not really. Why would he think this was acceptable behavior? Why wasn't he concerned that one or both of us might react badly to such a move? But what truly stumped me was why Betty hadn't reacted to it at all. Certainly this couldn't be the first time in her forty-two years that a man had felt around her back for the presence of a bra, so she had to know what he'd been up to. I could understand not making a scene or overreacting, but why not nonchalantly get up and move away? She easily could've stopped what he was doing without being confrontational, aggressive or even rude, but chose instead to do nothing.

Then again, so had I.

"Listen to me going on and on," Laurent said, staring down fondly into the mouth of his beer bottle. "Didn't mean to ramble, I promise you I didn't. Just like the Mrs. says, I get going and never know when to stop."

"Don't be silly," Betty said, gently touching his wrist. "I'm glad you told me the story, I'd never heard it before. Sounds like you both had a great time."

"We surely did." He patted her hand. "Your Dad was happiest when he was hunting or fishing, you know that."

She nodded, and though her eyes had turned slightly moist, she was smiling with a genuineness I'd rarely seen since her father's death. "He always loved the outdoors," she said. "He adored being out in nature."

My feelings shifted the more I studied my wife. Her level of comfort, facial expressions and physical mannerisms while interacting with Laurent led me to believe she now remembered him, but I couldn't be sure. One thing was certain, however, his story—some silly routine about romping through the woods with her father in wet socks or some nonsense—had touched her. From what little I'd heard, it wasn't anything profound, but then, maybe that was the point. I tried to think about my own father, who I'd lost five years before. My fondest memories of him were largely puerile, and at least on the surface, quite trivial. It was always nice to remember the dead fondly, of course, particularly those we loved, but when it came to Betty's father it was a struggle for me because we'd never been close. We were simply too different. I never detested him to the degree he hated me, but I didn't like the man either. I was indifferent when it came to my father-in-law. While he wasn't completely void of good qualities, more often than not I'd found him disagreeable. But he was Betty's father, and she loved him, warts and all. And good for her, I'd never taken that from her or tried to convince her otherwise. I simply couldn't play along when it came time to fondly reminisce. I'd support her the best I could while remaining neutral, if not a bit removed, and in some ways she probably resented me for it, though I knew she understood how complicated the dynamic was for me when it came to her father.

"How about you, Will?" Laurent asked, breaking my concentration. "Are you a hunter and fisherman too?"

There was a twinkle in his eye that led me to believe he already knew the answer. "Afraid not," I said. "I find hunting barbaric and unnecessary in today's day and age, particularly as sport. Survival is one thing, but I can't understand how anyone derives joy from killing something."

"Well it's really not about the killing."

I held his gaze, which was quickly becoming annoying. "Oh no?"

"Maybe for some, but not for me. And I know it wasn't about that for Earl, neither. Wasn't about that at all."

I could sense Betty's discomfort. She knew where this was headed, as she was well aware of my views on hunting. Interestingly enough, she shared my feelings on the topic, but had always given her father and his hunting buddies a pass, as if what they did was different somehow. "Really?" I asked. "What's it about then?"

Betty flashed me a look. *Will you drop it, please?*

"Well, it's more about the way you get to be a part of that, the—what's the word when you're with your friends and enjoying the same things together?"

"Camaraderie?" Betty offered.

"Right. *Camaraderie*, that's what it's about. Being out there with all that beauty and enjoying yourself. Know what I mean?"

"Then why not bring cameras instead of guns?" I asked. "If it's really about enjoying beauty then why destroy that beauty with violence? If it's not about enjoying the kill then why incorporate killing into the equation at all?"

"Then why what now?" Laurent frowned then just as quickly chuckled. "Sorry, Will, I'm a simple fella, you lost me there."

He knew damned well what I meant, but I let it go. "It's not important."

"A man's opinion is always important."

"What about a woman's?"

"Even more, if you know what's good for you!" Laurent barked out a laugh and clutched Betty's shoulder. "Am I right?"

"Absolutely!" Betty laughed along, but I could see in her eyes how irritated she was with me. "Can I get you another beer, Mr. Laurent?"

"You go right ahead and call me Uncle Bobby just like always or I'm liable to think I'm a broken down old man you youngsters have to call *mister*." Laurent winked at her then grinned in a manner I suspect he thought looked doting.

"It's been a long time since someone called me a youngster, so first of all, thank you for that." Although Betty seemed confused, graciously as ever, she hid it well with polite, accommodating laughter. "Secondly, how about that beer, *Uncle Bobby*?"

Laurent rose to his feet, moved to the end of the table and playfully poked my shoulder. "Isn't she just the sweetest thing ever?"

"Absolutely adorable," I said through a tight grin.

"I remember when you were just a little one," Laurent said, shaking his head as if he still couldn't believe it. "You were the prettiest gosh darn thing I'd ever seen. The Mrs. and I moved away not long after. Let me see now, I guess you must've been thirteen or so by then. Didn't see you again until a couple years later when I came back to town after your mom passed. You were sixteen and prettier than ever. And you know what? You've hardly aged a day."

"Oh stop," Betty gushed.

"So," I said, "what brought you back to town this time?"

Laurent hesitated a moment, almost as if he were trying to think of an answer. "Came to visit some old friends. Ed and Cathy Hamilton. Betty, you know Ed and Cathy, they were friends of your father's too."

"I've known them since I was little."

"Yep, Ed mentioned he saw Will at the store buying cleaning supplies."

"We've only met once, at Earl's wake," I said. "Surprised he remembered me."

Rather than answer me, Laurent snapped his fingers and pointed at Betty. "That reminds me! I almost forgot to tell you about Davey. You two were hot and heavy there for awhile."

Betty swatted at the air as if to knock the words away. "That was ages ago, I haven't seen Davey in years. After we broke up, he ran off and joined the Marines. Last I heard he was married with kids and living out west somewhere."

"Turns out he just moved back to town."

"Did he?"

"Sure did. Got to see him while I was visiting with his folks. He's been out of the service quite awhile, got himself one of those fancy computer jobs, fixing them or some such thing, afraid that's all way over this ole country boy's head."

"Strange. Ed never mentioned Davey was back home."

Laurent shrugged. "He's divorced now, but his ex and kids still live in New Mexico where they were all living before the breakup. When Ed told me you were in town I happened to mention to Davey I was coming to see you and he made me promise to tell you hello from him. You ought to give him a call before you head back home. I bet he'd love to hear from you after all these years."

I was always at a distinct disadvantage when it came to these types of discussions because Betty had been born and raised in town and I had not. No matter how much time passed, where we lived or where we didn't, far as the locals were concerned, she was a townie and I was an outsider. As for the Hamilton family, I'd met them at Earl's wake but probably wouldn't know them again if I fell over them. And while Betty had briefly mentioned Davey over the years, I'd never met him or even so much as seen a picture of him. All I really knew about him was that he was an old boyfriend she'd had, sort of a teenage puppy love type thing, as she described it.

"Maybe I'll run into him before we leave," Betty said.

"He'd love it, I can tell you that. Now, about that beer, I will take another, thank you. But first, if you'd be so kind as to let me use the restroom, my tired old bladder and I would be forever grateful."

Betty nodded in my direction and I took the cue. Leaving my beer bottle behind on the table, I escorted Laurent into a short hallway off the kitchen. "Right in there," I said, pointing to the first door on the left.

"I remember, but appreciate it, Will."

As he slipped into the bathroom and closed the door behind him, I headed back out into the kitchen fast as I could and found Betty pacing over by the sink.

"Did you get *Uncle Bobby* his beer?" I said, trying not to laugh too loud.

"Quiet, he'll hear you." She slapped my forearm. "I can't believe you went on one of your anti-hunting tangents."

"It was hardly a tangent. I was just trying to make conversation, *my little strawberry.*"

"I'm serious," she said, but she was trying not to laugh herself. "Look at him, he's a sweet old guy and obviously means well. No need to be rude."

"Good news, though, Davey's back in town. Be sure to give him a call now, he's available. Maybe you guys can have dinner and catch a movie before we leave."

"A girl can dream." Betty smirked at me. "Wiseass."

I stole a quick glance back over my shoulder to make sure he wasn't coming. "And what's with all the touchy stuff?"

"What do you mean?"

"He had his arm around you, and at one point when he had his hand on your back, I'd have sworn he was—"

"Oh Will, please. He's a hundred and eight, a harmless old man."

"I'm just saying it was inappropriate for him to—"

"Keep your voice down," she said in a loud whisper. "What's gotten into you tonight? This is awkward enough, I don't need you behaving like a jealous high school kid because some old friend of my father's put his arm around me for two seconds and mentioned an old boyfriend I haven't seen or spoken to in decades."

I let it go and tried to convince myself to at least be open to the possibility that I'd misread the old man. "Fine. Sorry, I didn't mean to—"

"I'm sure he'll have one more beer and be on his way." Betty reached into the fridge for a fresh bottle.

"Sounds like he and your dad were pretty close at one time," I said.

"Yeah, that's why this is all so strange."

Thunder rolled.

"Why, because you didn't remember him at first?"

The rain kept falling, slamming the house.

"No," Betty said gravely. "Because I still don't."

2

The dreams were so vivid I started to wonder if I still knew what was real and what wasn't. Was I truly asleep when these things happened, or was I awake?

Worse, did it matter?

In a dark and dreary room, I found myself lying on an old dusty bed. But I wasn't alone. There were others there too. Standing around me as if holding some sort of silent vigil. I couldn't see them, but I could smell them. I could feel their souls touching mine, all of us becoming one, a strange and hideous hybrid of good and evil, sanity and madness, innocence and guilt, a foul entity chewing through my skin like a thousand tiny insects. And somewhere deep within the decadent lunacy, like a pinpoint of light surrounded by endless darkness, a chance for deliverance still burned.

* * *

The light out back came on, illuminating the backyard with a powerful spot Earl had installed over the deck. It was motion-activated, the type animals routinely trip after sun-down. Assuming this was no exception, I looked out through the rain-blurred window over the kitchen sink and scanned the yard as best I could through the heavy downpour. "Probably a raccoon or something," I muttered, but I saw nothing moving, save for the rain and some bouncing tree branches waving in the wind.

I turned back to my wife. She was still over by the table, holding Laurent's beer like an abandoned waitress. "How could you not remember this guy?"

"I don't know, major brain fart? Early Alzheimer's maybe?"

"If he lived in town and was as close to your dad as he claims—for that matter so close to you that you referred to him as *Uncle Bobby*—it hardly seems possible for you to have absolutely no recollection of who he is."

"I think you're taking this way too seriously. I was just a kid, OK? My parents had lots of friends. I don't remember all of them. Do you remember all of your parents' friends from when you were a child?"

"I don't remember all their names, and might not necessarily recognize them on sight, but I have memories of who they were, particularly if they were close friends. And I'd remember someone outside the family I called *Uncle*, I can tell you that. It's not like you were a toddler when you knew him, he said you were thirteen when he and his wife moved away and sixteen the last time you saw him. How could you not remember him at all now?"

"He's an old man." Betty shrugged. "He must have his dates and times wrong. Who knows? Maybe he has me mixed up with someone else."

"You mean you *weren't* the sweetest little berry in the patch?"

She laughed reflexively and suggested I go fuck myself.

I wanted to laugh it off too, but couldn't. There was something wrong about this, something wrong about Laurent. And none of it was funny. "I'm not kidding," I said. "If half the things he said weren't creepy enough—and trust me, they were—if you truly have no clue who he is then I'm concerned. Maybe it's time I asked him to leave."

"Please don't do that."

"But what if he's not telling the truth?"

"Will. Stop. I mean, honestly, for God's sake. He obviously knew us. I was just a teenager when my mom died. It was very traumatic. I don't remember much about that entire period. I blocked a lot of it out. You know that. And besides, his time-frame could be off. Regardless, I'm sure he won't stay long anyway. He said himself he was just paying his respects. Let's just get through this, be nice to the poor old coot for a few more minutes and that'll be that. OK?"

I looked deep into her eyes. "You really don't remember this man at all?"

She paced about awkwardly near the table. "I don't know, maybe a little. Like I said, his name sounds vaguely familiar, I think."

"You think."

"Yes, I think."

A troubling notion drifted through my mind. What if Laurent was telling the truth and Betty was lying? But why would she claim to have no idea who Laurent was? It made no sense. Then again, what possible reason would there be for Laurent to lie? I dismissed the concept and assured myself no one was lying. It was a simple misunderstanding, a confusion of dates and times, or, as Betty suggested, perhaps he'd been forgotten along with most everything else from a horribly painful period in her childhood. That was far more likely. Wasn't it?

Then why wasn't I buying it?

I felt a rush of nervous energy surge through me. What was wrong with me? The situation was odd, surely, but hardly warranted the levels of stress and paranoia I was experiencing. "Fine," I said. "One more beer and we wrap it up."

Betty motioned to the window behind me with a tilt of her head.

The light out back was still on.

"It went out a second ago then just came back on," she said. "There's something wandering around out there."

I nodded, eyes straining to see through the rain. "Strange. Don't animals generally hunker down during storms like this?"

"Something wrong?"

Laurent was standing a few feet away, just inside the room. He'd startled me because I hadn't heard him coming. I hadn't even heard the toilet flush. I told myself the wind and rain had muffled his movements. "No," I finally answered. "The spotlight out back keeps coming on is all."

"Motion-activated?" he asked. When I nodded he said, "They're a real pain in the neck. Night like this, any number of things could set that thing off."

Betty came closer. "Your beer."

"Why thank you, pretty lady." Laurent took the bottle, had himself a healthy swig then joined me at the window. "That a mulberry tree out there?"

"Yes," Betty said. "My father planted it years ago."

"Thought so. I was always a working man, spent years in the landscaping business. Hard work, but I always enjoyed working outside. Nothing like being outside, working with your hands, sweating under a bright sun, putting your back into it and earning an honest dollar. Know what I mean, Will?"

Although I'd spent the majority of my adult life residing in cities, I too had grown up in a small and predominantly working-class town, and had heard this sort of drivel about *working men* for years. As if laborers were the only ones that worked for a living and were therefore of purer stock than those of us who earned our livings in other ways. What they did was *real* work. Everyone else coasted through cushy, faux jobs while enjoying undeserved salaries they hadn't truly earned. Ironically, I'd always had respect for laborers and what they did, but that respect was rarely returned. More often than not I encountered prejudice against me due to my profession, and for not being one of them. This was no different.

I knew that. So did he.

"I'm a college professor," I answered pleasantly. "But yes, I'm familiar with working hard and earning a dollar. Whether that dollar qualifies as *honest* is, of course, entirely subjective. Know what I mean, Bob?"

"Speaking of mulberry trees," he said, smiling coyly. "Have you two ever heard the story about how their berries came to be red?"

"Can't say as I have."

"Something tells me it's an interesting story," Betty chimed in.

"Matter of fact it is, and it's a love story to boot."

"Oh, love stories are my favorite." He winked at her. "I know."

"Then by all means, do tell."

"It's a love story, but so you know, it's sad too, like a lot of love stories. What's the word they use? Tragic. That's it, *tragic*." Laurent made it a point to look directly at me. "Sure you want to hear it?"

I met his gaze, unwilling to be the one to look away first. "Absolutely."

"Well, once upon a time," Laurent began, slipping his free arm around Betty and guiding her back to the table, "there was a boy and a girl that grew up and lived in the same neighborhood. They fell in love and wanted to get married, but their parents didn't approve and tried to keep them apart. Now, as fate would have it, the houses the boy and girl lived in were real close to each other, so close that their houses shared a common wall. On one side of the wall was the boy's bedroom, and the girl's was on the other."

When they reached the table, Betty dropped into a chair. Laurent remained standing over her. I drifted a step away from the sink but purposely kept a bit of distance.

"Turns out, there was a little crack in this wall," Laurent continued. "And these two found it. At night they'd whisper back and forth to each other about how they were in love and how one day they'd run away together and be happy."

"How romantic," Betty said, smiling at me.

I nodded but said nothing.

Laurent sipped some beer then belched silently. "Thing is, nice as that wall was, they couldn't touch or even see each other, so they knew if they were going to be together, they'd have to do something. Just so happens that on a lonely old country road on the outskirts of town there was this big mulberry tree. One night, they decided they couldn't be apart anymore, and agreed to meet out there by the mulberry tree not long after midnight. The boy told her to be careful because out there in the middle of nowhere there was no telling what they might run into, especially so late at night. He told her he'd be sure to get there before she did and bring a knife with him just in case."

From the corner of my eye I saw the light out back go out.

"Well the girl snuck out of the house and walked a few miles to the tree and waited. It was a chilly night so she brought a coat along, slung over her arm. She waited a while for the boy to show, but before he did, in the moonlight she saw a wolf step out of the woods and start down the road towards her. The wolf had just killed and eaten something, you see, because his jaws and face were covered in blood." Laurent took another pull of beer, relishing Betty's rapt attention. "Now this poor girl was scared out of her wits, and much as she wanted to wait for her true love, she couldn't just stand there and let a wolf attack her, so she turned and ran. Afraid the coat might slow her down; she dropped it there on the road and ran off into the night. Well the wolf grabbed hold of that coat, tore it to pieces and left it bloody and shredded at the foot of the mulberry tree. And—you guessed it—right about the time that wolf wandered off the boy showed up. He sees the wolf running back into the woods and when he gets to the mulberry tree all he finds is the girl's torn and bloody coat. He figures because he got there too late and wasn't there to protect her, she got attacked and eaten by the wolf. Of course he's just beside himself, doesn't want to live without her. So he picks up her coat and starts kissing it, telling her how sorry he is and how he killed her sure as that wolf did. The boy takes his knife and cuts his throat. The blood sprays all over the tree, turning the berries dark red."

Betty was hanging on his every word, watching him intently.

"Just about this time, the girl decides, scared as she is of that wolf, it's worth the risk to be with the one she loves, so she turns around and goes back. She gets there just in time. The boy is dying but still alive. With his last breath, he looks into her eyes, the most beautiful eyes he's ever seen, and with a smile, dies in her arms. *Your love for me killed you*, she says. *Everyone's tried to keep us apart, and not even Death's going to get away with it.* And with that, she falls on the same knife and dies under the mulberry tree beside him. See, the berries are like a memorial for all time to remember those two. In the end, the two *were* together forever, but in death. Some say their families felt so bad over keeping the two apart that their bodies were cremated and put in the same urn, so they could be together in that way too. And *that*," he said, raising his beer bottle up, "is why mulberry fruit is a deep, dark red."

"Pyramus and Thisbe," I said.

He and Betty looked at me, stone-faced.

I'd lied. I actually *was* familiar with the story. I should've let it go, and normally would have, but for some reason I wanted to embarrass him. "The story you just told. It actually has its origins in classic Greco-Roman Mythology. The boy and girl were Pyramus and Thisbe. And it wasn't a wolf, but a lion. The original story came from Ovid. *Publius Ovidius Naso*, to be precise. He was a Roman author, known primarily, though not exclusively, for his erotic poetry. He also wrote *Metamorphosis*, a classic poem in Greek and Roman mythology. He was quite prolific, and his work has influenced such literary heavyweights as Shakespeare, Chaucer, even Dante and Milton." I gave him the best condescending smile I could muster. "But that's a nifty down-home and westernized version you've got there, Bob. Lots of fun, and nicely told."

Betty looked like she couldn't decide whether to crawl under the table or beat me to death with one of the kitchen chairs.

An awkward silence filled the air.

After a moment, Laurent began to laugh. "I admit I've got no idea what any of that means—all I was doing was telling one of my grand-mamma's old stories—but I tell you what, Will, I believe you!"

Betty laughed along, lightly slapping the table for effect as she shot me a dagger-laced glare apparently designed to burn directly through my skull. "Yes," she added, "you'll be pleased to know we're both *thoroughly* impressed."

"Just trying to be helpful," I mumbled. I already regretted what I'd done. I'd embarrassed no one but myself and knew the moment Betty and I were alone she'd call me out for it. I just couldn't help myself. There was something about this man that caused me to instinctually dislike and distrust him, and that brought out the worst in me. But what concerned me most was that Laurent seemed well aware of this and was purposely trying to provoke me. I could see it so clearly, how could Betty be oblivious?

"So where did you and your wife move to?" I heard Betty ask him.

"South Carolina. Beautiful down there, let me tell you. Ever been?"

"No, never have."

"How about you, Will?"

"I've driven through a couple times." I finished my beer, set the bottle in the sink then went to the fridge and against my better judgment, got myself another. "But that was years ago."

Laurent nodded, as if he deemed my answer acceptable. "So you've only been in town since this morning?"

"Yes," I explained. "Been putting this off for months but now it's time to get this place cleaned out and on the market."

"Maybe you've been putting it off because you got more to do here than settle Earl's affairs."

"What do you mean?"

Laurent grinned and shrugged.

"I could've kept the place as a rental, I suppose," I said, ignoring his cryptic comments. "But it needs a lot of work, so it made more sense to just sell it off. Besides, keeping this house would've been...difficult."

"Wouldn't be the same without ole Earl wandering around in it, that's for sure." Laurent stretched dramatically, like his body had grown painfully stiff. "Probably best you stay down there in New York anyway."

"Got at least another day of work cleaning this place out and doing some dump runs," I said, hoping he'd get the hint. "Between that and donating the rest of the furniture and whatnot to the local Salvation Army, the place should be ready to put up for sale. Still quite a bit to do though."

"Well, nice as this is," he sighed, "I've bothered you long enough this evening. Time to get a move on."

"Don't be silly." Betty touched his wrist. "No bother at all."

"Thank you, darlin', but I really should get these old bones moving."

"Be careful in this rain," Betty said. "Especially making such a long drive like that, sounds exhausting."

"It is, but I'll be fine. Hoping once I get through this mess it'll be smooth sailing." He powered down the remainder of his beer and set the empty bottle on the table. "Hope you two don't have to drive in this mess tonight."

"No," Betty told him, "we're spending the night here."

I wished she hadn't shared that information, but it was too late to stop her.

"Good. Stay safe." Darkness crossed his face. "You have my deepest sympathies on the loss of your dad. Earl was a good friend and a fine man."

"Thank you so much." Betty rose to her feet. "It's been great to see you…again."

"You too, darlin'. And Will," he said, thrusting a hand at me, "a pleasure."

We shook hands. His grip was a little stronger this time, subtly more forceful. In response, I squeezed a bit harder myself. "Pleasure's mine, Bob."

"Thank you for inviting me into your home." He continued to pump my hand. Neither of us loosened our grips. "A man should only go where he's invited. Always found that to be the best policy, least for me anyhow."

Seemed an odd thing to say, but then nearly everything that came out of his mouth sounded odd to me. I responded with a quick and decisive nod then released his hand. "Drive safely now."

"You bet." He gave Betty another big hug then kissed the top of her head, the way a parent might, and made her promise she'd take good care of herself.

Arm-in-arm, they sauntered to the door. Laurent took his raincoat from the hook, slipped it on then pulled his baseball cap on tight and waved back at me with a smile I could only describe as smug.

And then he was gone, released back into the rain from which he'd come. The door was closed and it was just the two of us.

Betty immediately went on the offensive, as I knew she would. She wasn't being nasty, she was only trying to understand why I'd behaved the way I had. What she didn't realize was that I was struggling to understand it too. I didn't want a fight, so I made an effort to prevent things from escalating.

"What was all *that* about?" she asked, arms folded over her chest.

"I don't know."

"You made a total ass of yourself. Why were so rude to the poor man?"

"I'm sorry, I just..."

"You just what? Why would you behave that way? He could *not* have been sweeter to us. You don't even know the man, and here you are—"

"Do *you* know the man, Betty?"

She calmed a bit and considered my question. "The name Laurent does sound familiar, but honestly, I can't seem to place him at all."

"You remember the name but not him."

She made a funny face. "Weird, huh?"

"Maybe he's not who he says he is."

Her expression left no doubt as to her thoughts on that theory. "And why would he lie about who he is? Why take the time to stop here and pretend to be someone he isn't? What point would there be in that? Seriously, do you hear yourself? Sweetie, come on. Obviously he's old and confused, has his dates and times mixed up. Even if he did move away around the time my mother died, like I said, I've blocked a lot of that out. Wouldn't that make more sense?"

"Do you remember calling one of your father's friends *Uncle Bobby*?"

She looked as if she were thinking about it, which struck me as odd. "No," she finally said. "Maybe I've just forgotten."

I watched the headlights of Laurent's truck disappear along the dirt road before vanishing completely in the storm. "Well, doesn't make much difference now, I guess. He's gone."

She reached out and gently rubbed my back. "You OK?"

"I don't know what got into me tonight." I sighed and gulped some beer. "I thought the guy was creepy right from the start, and I didn't like the way he was running his fingers along your back like he was checking to see if you had a bra on and—"

"You really think that's what he was doing?" Betty bit her lip in an effort not to laugh. "Honestly?"

"Don't you?"

"No, sweetie, I don't."

"Fine," I said, waving at the air between us, "then I must've been mistaken. I'm sorry, I'm tired and—"

She gave me a quick kiss. Vintage Betty, she never stayed angry long. "That cellar was grotesque. Think I'll call it for today and take a shower. Want to go to bed early? That way we can get an early start tomorrow. The sooner we get this finished the sooner we can get home. Plus, there's snuggling to be had. Serious going-to-bed-early snuggling."

I felt myself smile. "Sounds good."

"Just one condition. You take a shower too. You worked up as big a sweat as I did today, and you know me, I'm partial to funk-free snuggles."

"We could always take one together."

"Then neither of us will get clean."

"I'm thinking of the environment here. Conserving water and what not."

"Uh-huh." She grabbed a suitcase she'd packed for us from the other room and headed upstairs. "Be down soon."

Once she'd gone I found myself at the window watching the night, the rain and the darkness. Laurent was gone, but I could still feel him there, lingering.

Like a bad odor.

A man should only go where he's invited.

A chill crept through me. There, then gone.

Pretending the cold beer was to blame, I sipped some more and watched the night a while longer.

I have no idea how I knew, but right then, I did. I knew. I *knew* I'd not seen the last of Bob Laurent. He'd come to this house for reasons far deeper than paying his respects. And he was far from done with us. He'd be back.

Soon.

3

In the dreams, teardrops fell like rain from a black sky, every path led to nowhere, and in the dark, the vague silhouette of a man danced at the edge of a shadowy forest with the jerky movements of a marionette, its inhuman face white as chalk, its eyes ringed in black. A demonic clown eerily skipping through the pain and horror of a night gone mad, it greedily lapped the falling tears with its bloody tongue, like the agony the rain represented might somehow sustain it.

Then it looked right at me, right through me. And it saw the truth.

* * *

Betty and I not only hailed from different areas of the country, we came from divergent backgrounds as well. My father was an engineer, my mother an executive with a clothing company. Ours was a middleclass family, back when the middleclass still existed. Betty's was working-class. Her father was a mechanic, her mother a school bus driver. I have two older sisters and an extended family. Betty is an only child with few relatives. My family was never wealthy, but we were relatively comfortable. Betty's family lived paycheck-to-paycheck and struggled financially. Education was a given in my family. Didn't matter where you went to college or even what you studied, just that you went and made something of yourself. In Betty's family, she was the first to earn a college degree, as few had even graduated high school, much less attended college. No one was any better or worse than anyone else, our families and lifestyles growing up were simply different. Each had its own sets of advantages and disadvantages, positives and negatives, and while some members of both families struggled with those differences, Betty and I never had. It was largely irrelevant to us. We were together, happy and in love. That's what mattered.

The decision to live primarily in cities was a joint one, and while I rarely missed living in a small town, from time to time Betty did. We'd spent close to the first two decades of our marriage living all over the eastern seaboard, mostly following my career path from university to university, and Betty's career as an accounting executive at a series of huge corporations that paid well but left her little time for anything else. For Betty, returning to her hometown even for the two or three days it would take to settle her father's home, represented a chance to truly put that part of her life behind her once and for all. Earl had been the last tie to town she had, and now that he was gone there was no reason to hang on. It was more complicated for me of course, not only because my relationship with Earl had always been strained, but because this town was a small, insular community of people who had lived there for generations and viewed those who hadn't as oddities, nuisances or threats. During the wake and funeral I'd been disrespected, ignored, ridiculed and treated like some sort of lowlife by waves of townsfolk I didn't even know. Betty didn't notice much of it, she was burying her father after all, why would she? But even when she did she dismissed it as the ignorance of the locals and suggested I do the same and not take it so seriously or personally. Easier said than done. Particularly when so many of them had gone out of their way to be rude to me for no apparent reason.

Although Betty had always been relatively close to her father, there was a bit of distance between them as well. They were very different in some ways (and frighteningly similar in others), and their relationship struck me as decidedly lopsided, with Betty as submissive caretaker to her father's ironfisted patriarch of one. And as sweet and accommodating as Betty was, Earl was difficult even with her, and I witnessed firsthand how debilitating that could be for her. It was hard enough being his son-in-law; I couldn't imagine what it must've been like to be his only child. Luckily, we'd always lived fairly far away from him, so our time together was largely relegated to holidays and the occasional visit.

Despite their difficulties, Betty and Earl loved each other, and his death devastated her. I'd lost my father years before, also unexpectedly, so I knew what she was going through and how long the process of recovery was. If it could even be called recovery, since one never truly recovered from the death of a parent. Instead, one learned to live with the wound it left behind, a wound that never completely healed. Time had helped, however, and although the topics of pleasant memories and fond reminiscences were sometimes awkward (as I had virtually none when it came to Earl), I did my best to allow Betty those things. While I couldn't participate without being disingenuous, and therefore appearing insensitive or disrespectful, what I could do was support her and be there for her to the best of my ability. And I thought I'd done a fairly good job of it, at least until Bob Laurent pulled into the driveway.

I remained in the kitchen, finished my beer and paced, trying to figure out why he'd had such a strange effect on me. All the while I watched for headlights out front and for the spotlight out back. Neither appeared.

Pipes rattled. The shower upstairs was on. I pictured Betty under the hot water enveloped in steam, her body wet and slick with body-wash. Even after years of marriage I was still wildly attracted to her. To others she most likely appeared to be a tidy thirty-something woman (though she was actually early forties), a classic girl-next-door type who wore little makeup and didn't have to, and looked as good in an old pair of jeans and a T-shirt as she did in a business suit. But to me she was a heart-stopping beauty that got sexier and better with age, and one of the most intelligent and decent human beings I'd ever known.

In many ways I envied her. While she'd always maintained her natural good looks and fit body, I struggled to stay in shape. I looked my age, and was secure with that, enjoyed it even, but despised how my body had betrayed me. I'd once been slim and strong with little to no effort, but now, as I drifted further and further into middle age, my body was turning on me, fighting me at every turn. In the end I suppose it was my own damn fault, as I'd once played tennis and basketball regularly, and had always been an avid walker and bicyclist. Now I rarely exercised, didn't eat right as often as I should have and spent far too much time planted firmly on my ever-expanding ass. Betty, on the other hand, generally took care of herself, had always been a runner and still logged three miles five days a week, rain or shine, summer or winter. Although we both drank socially, she'd never smoked a cigarette, and other than some pot in high school, she'd never been a drug user. I gave up drugs in my late twenties, but tried nearly all of them. Again, we were very different, and from different backgrounds. But we were good together. And we were happy.

We'd always been happy.

I had a slight buzz but decided I'd switch from beer to wine. Just minutes into town I'd made a liquor store pit stop, and a nice red had been chilling in the fridge for hours. I poured myself a glass, downed it, then poured another and decided to relax and get lost in a novel I'd brought along until Betty was done with her shower.

But then a rumbling sound shook the entire house.

I looked to the window.

Headlights appeared at the end of the road, bouncing in the darkness.

By the time I'd reached the window by the front door it was apparent that the headlights belonged to an enormous flatbed tow truck. Chained to the back was Bob Laurent's pickup truck.

Heart racing, I watched as the tow truck maneuvered precariously about the narrow dirt road, eventually executing something of a three-point turn that left it facing back in the direction of the highway. After a moment the light in the cab came on, revealing the driver—a young skinny kid in a hoody—and Bob Laurent. They shook hands then Laurent hopped down out of the truck. With a wave back to the driver, he casually strolled through the rain toward the house, lugging an old suitcase along with him.

As the truck charged off into the night, I opened the door to find Laurent chuckling and shaking his head. This time he didn't wait for an invite, he simply reached out with his free hand, pulled open the storm door and stepped inside.

"Darnedest thing," he said breath lessly. "Truck gave out on me."

"Gave out?"

"Died," he said, setting his suitcase down and slipping out of his coat. "Was running fine earlier. I got a couple miles from here and she took to sputtering. I pulled over, switched her off but couldn't get her started again. Don't have one of those cell thingies, even though the Mrs. keeps telling me I need one, but as luck would have it I wasn't far from the fire station, so I got myself over there and one of the boys on the nightshift called me a tow. Not sure what's wrong with her, just bought the darn thing, but the kid driving the hook said none of the mechanics over to Sully's are on until morning. You know Sully's?"

I stared at him dumbly.

"Only repair shop in town," he said. "Sully was a good man. Heard he passed on few years back. His son runs the garage now. Anyway, I won't know what the damage is 'til morning. Looks like I'm stuck in town another night."

"I don't mean to be rude," I said as sincerely as I could, "but is there some reason you had him drop you here?"

"It was either here or Ed and Cathy's, and their place is clear over on the other side of town. Besides, the kid didn't have to give me a ride at all, but since he was kind enough to I didn't want to push it, know what I mean? Figured your place was closest." He shut the door behind him, hung his coat and hat on the hook and gave me a maddening grin. "Sure hope you don't mind."

"No," I said, clearing my throat and stepping aside, "come in."

Leaving his suitcase behind, he accompanied me to the kitchen. "Awfully sorry to be such a pest tonight."

"Can't be helped. We all have car trouble now and then."

He pointed to the glass in my hand. "Having some wine, are you?"

"Would you like some?"

"Not much of a wine drinker, but I thank you." He glanced around. "Where'd Little Betty scamper off to?"

I could still hear the shower going. "Upstairs."

He listened, pointed to the ceiling. "Having herself a shower?"

"Yeah. Another beer?"

"That'd be just fine, Will. Thank you kindly."

I went to the fridge, got him a beer and handed it over. "So is there someone you want to call or…"

"Well," he said, pausing to take a long pull, "thing of it is, Will, there's not really anybody *to* call."

I felt my gut tighten. "What about the friends you came to visit?"

"Ed and Cathy's is even smaller than this place, and…well…with Davey back in town and staying with them until he can find his own place, afraid there's no room for me."

"Surely you must know plenty of other people in town," I said evenly. "There must be someone who can help."

"I know you." He winked. "But I sure do hate to impose. I'm sure we can figure something out."

I thought about it a moment. "There's a little motel just over the town line. We passed it on the way in. It doesn't look too bad, and I bet they have very reasonable rates. I could give you a lift and you could spend the night there."

"This is real embarrassing, but I'll be honest with you, Will."

I cleared my throat. "All right."

"I've never been one for credit cards and such, don't even have one. And I only brought a small bit of cash with me. I'm already worried if the truck costs too much I might have to get ahold of Edith and have her wire me money. So, much as I hate to admit it to you, I just don't think I can afford a motel room."

Pipes rattled overhead as the shower shut off. Without really thinking about it, I pictured Betty stepping from the shower and toweling herself off in a fog of steam. By the expression on Laurent's face it wouldn't have surprised me if he'd done the same. He looked up at the ceiling like he expected to see some sort of religious vision, staring with wide eyes and his mouth hung open. After a moment, his eyes slid shut and he had another sip of beer, savoring it as if he'd never tasted anything quite like it before.

"Would you excuse me a moment?"

The sound of my voice snapped him out of his trance. "Sure." He slowly licked his lips. "If you don't let Betty know I'm back she might wander in here all powdered up and bare-assed. Wouldn't want that, now would we?"

"No," I said firmly, though I could feel my voice shaking. "We wouldn't."

I left the room without another word, but by the time I reached the end of the hallway Betty was already rounding the newel post at the base of the stairs.

Dressed in a heavy terrycloth robe that reached nearly to her ankles, her hair was up and wrapped in a towel. She looked perplexed. Wide dark bruises ran around her throat and neck. We both pretended not to notice them. "Thought I heard you talking," she said softly.

"It's Laurent again," I whispered. "He's in the kitchen."

"What happened?"

Gently taking her by the elbow, I led her back toward the stairs, explained the situation and relayed the conversation we'd had.

"So what are you saying, he wants to stay here?"

"That's what he's implying."

Betty made a face but I knew her well enough to know she was actually considering it. "Well, I mean, if he has nowhere else to go, I guess—"

"Look, I don't want this guy here, and certainly not overnight."

"Sweetie, he's harmless."

"We don't know that."

"He's older than dirt, what do you think he's going to do?" She frowned. "We can't just put him out, babe."

"He seems pretty resourceful to me, I'm sure he'll figure something out."

"With no transportation?"

I drew a deep breath, held it a moment then let it out. "I offered to drive him to that little motel just outside town—whatever it's called—you know the one, but he isn't sure he has enough cash to cover the room and fix his truck. So why don't we pay for the room? I'll drive him over there right now."

"How much have you had to drink?"

I thought about it. "Few beers and a couple glasses of wine."

"You shouldn't be driving then, particularly in this storm."

"Betty, I'm fine."

"You may be fine but if you get pulled over and—"

"I'm not going to get pulled over."

"But if you do and you fail a Breathalyzer then you're legally drunk and you'll be arrested. You can't afford to have a DUI in your position. It's not worth the risk."

"Then I'll phone the motel, pay for his room with a credit card and call him a cab to run him over there. We'll pay for that too. How's that?"

"Sounds like a plan." Betty cinched the belt on her robe up tight. "I'm just not going to put an old man and family friend out in the rain, OK?"

"Suddenly he's a family friend?"

"You know what I mean."

"No, actually, I don't. I'm not even sure you know what you mean. He may have known your father but I don't have a clue as to who he is and I'm still not convinced you do either. For Christ's sake, we know nothing about this man other than what he's told us. And as I said, I'm getting a bad vibe from him."

"I'm not going to turn away someone who was a good friend to my dad just because you've decided to get in touch with your inner paranoid schizophrenic."

"Hopefully you won't have to, OK? Let's get him a cab."

When we returned to the kitchen Laurent apologized profusely to Betty for having returned, then rose from his chair and gave her another huge hug. "Well don't you smell nice?" he added. "Pretty as a flower."

While trying not to projectile vomit, I let Betty present him with my plan.

"Y'all want to pay for a cab *and* the motel?"

"It's not a problem," Betty assured him. "We're happy to help."

"Well, I…I surely don't know what to say. That's awfully nice of you folks. But you've got to let me send you the money it costs once I get back home. Please."

"Sure," I said. "Sweetie, what's the name of that cab company?"

She told me. I snatched my cellphone from the clip on my belt, dialed 411 and got the number. It began to ring. And ring. And ring. Finally an answering machine picked up and a scratchy recording informed me they were closed. "Great." I disconnected. "They're closed. So much for that plan."

"I'm assuming they're still the only one in town," Betty said.

"In this bustling metropolis I'd say that's a safe assumption."

"Far as I remember the next closest was a few towns over and even if they're still in business and open, I doubt they'd come this far." Laurent let out a loud and dramatic sigh. "But just the same, I surely do appreciate such a kind gesture."

I killed my glass of wine in the hopes it might help even me out and keep me from getting upset. "You're sure there's no one else in town who could help?"

Betty threw me a disapproving look.

"I'd be happy to hunker down in the car out in the driveway," Laurent said with a straight face. "That way I wouldn't be in the house and—"

"That's ridiculous," Betty snapped. "For God's sake, we're not going to have you sleeping in the car."

"No, now Betty, I understand Will not being comfortable with a stranger staying the night. You and I know each other, but Will and I just met."

After more death-glares from my wife I said, "It's not that, Bob, I just—"

"Tell you what," he said, cutting me off. "I've been enough of a bother to you both this evening. I'm sure I can make other arrangements. I'll just grab my suitcase and get right on out of your hair. I can walk back to town and figure something out from there."

"No." Betty turned to me. "Will, he cannot walk all that way in this storm."

"No," I begrudgingly agreed, "of course not."

"I think we've exhausted our options here." This time Betty spoke directly to Laurent, as if I was no longer part of the conversation, which I suppose I wasn't. "I can make up the couch in the den for you and in the morning we can get you down to the garage to see about your truck."

"Much as I appreciate that," Laurent said, suddenly looking like an abused and abandoned puppy, "I don't want to stay if y'all aren't comfortable with me being here."

"It's fine," Betty said, putting a hand on his shoulder. "Truly."

"You sure you're all right with it, Will?"

I wasn't but nodded anyway.

"You're *sure*?" he pressed.

"Yes." I clenched my jaw. "It's fine."

"Then it's settled," Betty announced. "You'll stay the night."

Laurent put his hand out. "Thank you, Will."

I shook his hand. Quickly.

"And you too Betty." Laurent drew her into another hug.

Our eyes met. Very slowly, one of his hands lingered near her lower back then slid down just enough so that his fingertips were touching her ass. I could tell he was purposely making very light contact so Betty wouldn't feel him through the robe, and as she hugged him back he smiled at me over her shoulder. It was a triumphant smile, void of humor or kindness and laced instead with an air of superiority and gleeful depravity. Perversion.

Do something his eyes dared me. *Say something. Go ahead. Do it.*

It was then that I realized there was more to his brilliant blue eyes than I'd noticed previously. The color served as a distraction, but for the first time I saw beyond that. There was something wrong with his eyes, something horribly wrong. It was as if they were disconnected somehow, distant and present all at once, like the eyes of something that was alive but shouldn't have been.

In that moment, Bob Laurent barely seemed human.

Despite my discomfort, I held his stare with one of my own. One designed to let him know I had his number and understood exactly what he was up to.

Problem was, beyond the obvious, I really didn't.

And he knew it.

4

In the dream, the children were always there too. They looked human until they turned to me and I saw that they had no faces. No eyes, nose or mouth—not even ears—just a flat stretch of smooth skin where those things should have been. Like they weren't quite finished. Or perhaps those things had been brutally scraped smooth intentionally. As if, in some way I couldn't yet understand, they'd been erased as whole and unique human beings, and these abominations were all that remained; deaf, dumb and blind mutations.

They had no ears. Yet they could hear.

They had no mouths. Yet they could scream.

They had no eyes. Yet they could cry.

My God, I thought. Could any of this really be happening?

Frightening as it was, the possibility that it was all in my mind was even worse. It meant this was about me and no one else. It meant I'd slipped off that wall I'd been balancing on since this nightmare began. It meant I'd finally fallen over the side. And there was no way back.

* * *

Nothing seemed quite real. I'd never felt so vulnerable and unsafe, even in this house, where I'd never felt particularly welcome or comfortable to begin with. Now it was as if I'd been caged in a zoo and only just then become aware of it. It was like I was trapped inside a mirror looking out, a helpless reflection watching the night play out before me. Laurent was clearly goading me, but why? What could he possibly have against me? We didn't know each other, had never even met. What did he want, and why was he purposely trying to provoke me with his behavior around Betty? Much as I wanted to tell him to keep his goddamn hands off my wife and his inappropriate comments to himself, I knew that's exactly what he was hoping for, so he could feign innocence and I'd look like even more of an ass. But *why*, what was the point? I wasn't about to give him the satisfaction of playing into his hands, but at the same time, I wasn't sure how long I'd be able to stop myself from reacting, particularly if he continued ratcheting up his behavior, gradually tightening a vise I couldn't ignore forever.

I put the wine away. No more drinking. My mind was already fuzzy and I was feeling no pain. I needed to be alert and aware from here on out.

I lingered in the kitchen doorway, trying to sort my thoughts while keeping an eye on him. He'd joined Betty in the den as she made up the couch for him with a sheet, blanket and pillow she'd found in the linen closet. I was only half-listening, but he was in the midst of another heart-warming saga, this one about a party he'd attended here when Betty was just a little girl, and what fun they'd all had. He even recited the country music tunes he and Earl had loved and how they'd played records and gotten so drunk they both started singing along with George Jones, making fools of themselves and not caring in the least.

I focused on Betty. She loved every minute of it, listening to these stories she'd never heard before from a man who portrayed himself as someone that truly loved her father. That didn't concern me. What did was the way she so effortlessly slipped into the role Laurent wanted her to play, that of innocent *Little Betty*, a blushing beauty so taken with him and his self-serving compliments that she didn't know any better than to smile and bow her head and giggle and fawn over every word like an attention-starved teenager. Where was my wife, the educated, savvy and sophisticated woman I knew and loved, the one who'd see this for the bullshit it was in a New York minute? Who was this woman-child so easily swept away by a strange old man and his pandering tall tales? It was as if an internal switch deep inside her had been thrown, as if Laurent knew exactly where it was and how to manipulate it, how to arm it when she was interacting with him and how to switch it back off when she was dealing with me.

But that was ridiculous. No one had those sorts of abilities. The entire thing was absurd, yet that's exactly what was happening.

As Betty bent forward to straighten the blanket on the couch, her robe opened just enough to reveal a hint of cleavage. Laurent casually adjusted his position so he'd have a better view then glanced back over his shoulder at me and winked.

"Will and I are going to sleep in my old room," she told him. "And we could've put you up in Dad's bedroom, but we donated the bed this afternoon, there's nothing to sleep on."

"This is just fine, darlin'."

"It's a comfortable couch. Shouldn't be too bad for one night."

"I appreciate you going to all this trouble." He hugged her yet again, purposely crushing her against him harder and longer than was necessary.

If it bothered Betty she didn't show it. In fact, she reacted by returning the hug and going on and on about how it was the least she could do.

There was no question. This was a different Betty, a Betty I didn't know because she'd existed prior to my meeting her. That's why in Laurent's presence she seemed like a stranger to me as well. This was a dated version of my wife, a version Laurent was able to resurrect whenever he wanted to. All he needed was some silly stories about her father, a few inane compliments and as many inappropriate hugs as he could get away with and there she was, back from whatever grave Betty had left her in.

That made me odd man out. With my own wife. In an unforgiving old house I had no connection to or feelings for, and no memories of but for those unpleasant times I'd had no choice but to be here. In some ways it wasn't that far off from when we'd come to visit over the years. Only it was bearable when I felt that way in Earl's presence. After all, he was her father. Who the hell was Bob Laurent?

"Besides," Laurent said, snapping me back, "I'm having so much fun I don't know if I'll sleep tonight anyway. It's just so good to see you again, Betty, and it's been a pleasure meeting and getting to know you, Will, who'd want to sleep on a night like this? Heck, I feel like a kid at a slumber party!"

"Well if it's going to be a sleepover," Betty laughed, "we need to get in our jammies and have popcorn!"

"You already got your jammies on, girl!" Laurent slapped his knee. "Least I hope that's what's under that robe!"

Betty playfully feigned shock. "I'll never tell!"

"What are you trying to do, kill this ole boy?" As they continued laughing he turned to me. "Will, I guess we need to get our nightclothes on!"

I forced a smile. "You go right ahead." My head was reeling. I couldn't believe we were having this conversation, jokingly or otherwise. "I'm all set."

Betty gave me a look. *Don't be such a grouch, he's only kidding.*

"Maybe we ought to just settle for the popcorn and some more beer!" Laurent managed through another burst of laughter.

My wife followed suit.

Rain pummeled the house. It had slowed for a bit but had regained its strength in the last few minutes. I couldn't recall the last time I'd experienced such a prolonged and violent rain.

"Look," Betty said, her tone suddenly serious as she pointed at the window behind me. "It's doing it again."

The back light had come on.

Rain sprayed the window, drumming the pane in a steady rhythm as I moved closer and peered out. I don't know what I expected to find, but all I could make out was rain and shadows, glimpses of the backyard and a blurry tree line leading to dark forest beyond. Nothing seemed out of place, and everything looked just as it had in daylight. But in the storm, and bathed in the eerie liquid glow of the spotlight, the world beyond the window took on a surreal and alien edge, like I'd caught sight of a version from some alternate reality.

"Why does it keep doing that?" Betty asked softly. "Something must be setting it off."

I turned from the window. "There's nothing out there, don't worry about it." That's what I said, but what was going through my mind was the fact that the light had only done this while Laurent was in the house. The entire time he was gone it hadn't come on. Not once. Everything else had been the same—the storm, the night—he was the difference. Ridiculous as I knew it was to even consider that Laurent could somehow be causing the light to come on and off, I couldn't shake the idea that at a very minimum, it had something to do with him.

Betty slid in next to me and gazed out the window as if in a trance, her eyes slightly squinting at the night. "Something," she muttered. "There's..."

"What's wrong?" I asked, gently touching her arm. "What is it?"

"I don't know, I...I'm not sure, I...thought I remembered something."

"Storm's spooking everybody," Laurent said. "World's not the same when it rains. Everything changes."

The sound of his voice snapped Betty back from wherever she'd gone to. She blinked her eyes rapidly and stepped away from the window. The confusion on her face drifted away as she looked to Laurent. Their eyes met and locked. "Yes," she said, "you're right, I—I think that's it. The storm, it..."

I stepped between them. "Sweetie, are you all right?"

"Of course," she snapped. "Shouldn't I be?"

Stunned by her venomous response, I froze. "I just—"

"I'm going upstairs to dry my hair then put something on for the night," she said, staring at me dully. "I really shouldn't be running around the house with nothing on under my robe. We have company."

I nodded, unsure of why she'd felt the need to say that aloud. It seemed wholly unnecessary to make such an announcement when she simply could've excused herself, gone upstairs and taken care of what she needed to do. Which is exactly what she normally would've done.

But nothing was normal about this night. Not anymore.

"You go and do what you need to do, little one," Laurent said. "Will and I can sit and have another beer and chat awhile. Isn't that right, Will?"

"Yeah," I answered. "Sure."

Laurent winked at Betty.

She winked back. "You boys play nice." As she crossed the kitchen, left the room and headed up to our bedroom, the outside light went out.

It took everything I had not to follow her, but I forced myself over to the table and motioned to a chair. "Have a seat."

He did, a silly grin plastered on his face. His presence threw everything off. Nothing felt the same, or as it should, and the longer Laurent's invasion into my life continued, the stronger the sensations became.

I took a seat across from him and placed my hands on the table.

"Not going to leave me drinking all by my lonesome are you?" he asked.

"I think I've had enough for tonight."

He placed his beer bottle on the table. "Then maybe I have too."

"Don't feel you need to stop on my account."

"You two always drink like this?"

"Like what?"

"Well, we've all had quite a few tonight already. And the night's young."

"Just being sociable, Bob."

He leaned back. "It happens."

"What does?"

"People that been together a long time, like you and Betty for instance, fall into certain patterns of...well, let's call it *comfort*. But they're not always healthy patterns. Like drinking. See what I mean? You both throw back the beer and wine pretty easy. Bet you do the same with the heavy stuff too, am I right? I'm thinking you're a scotch man, being a teacher type and all, going to all those faculty parties and whatnot."

He was right but I wasn't about to admit it.

"And I'll bet Betty's a vodka drinker," he said.

Lucky guess, I told myself. Sure, Betty and I drank socially but neither of us had a problem. We had a couple drinks most nights but that didn't mean anything; lots of people did that. "What's this all about?" I asked. "Why are you here? What do you want? Why are you trying to goad me?"

"Why am I trying to what now?"

"Look, do us both a favor and drop the hillbilly bumpkin act, all right? It's just you and me now so there's no reason for your good-ole-boy routine. You know what I'm asking you and you know damn well what *goad* means."

Laurent smiled like I'd amused him. He grabbed his beer bottle and drank the rest of it down. "Well lookie here, the dog's got some fight in him after all."

I felt a warm tingling sensation spread through my body. "Why would you want me to fight with you?"

"If a man came into my house and did to my wife what I've already done to yours, I'd knock his dick in the dirt."

"I'm not some kid on a schoolyard. I don't get into fistfights."

"Too good for that, huh? Above it, are you?"

"Yes, I am."

"Civilized, right?" he chuckled, bowed his head and thought a moment. "Or just maybe that's code for being a prissy little faggot, a scared pussy-boy."

"What do you want?"

"Never understood why people use the word pussy when they mean to say weak. Pussies are strong. It's amazing the beating they can take."

I grit my teeth. "You think I'm afraid of you?"

"I think you're afraid of everything."

"Why are you here?"

"Just an old family friend lost in the storm is all."

"Bullshit. Betty's not even sure who you are."

"She knows exactly who I am," he said evenly. "She's remembering."

"What do you want, Laurent?"

"Just here for a little fun." He smiled with his eyes. "Betty always was fun. You should've heard ole Davey Hamilton going on about her today. They were quite the item when they were younger, you know."

"We all have old flames," I said. "So what?"

"Davey sure does have some great stories about her. Come to think of it, plenty of boys in town do. Guess nobody's got to tell you, but damn, that girl sure can suck dick, can't she? She always loved it in her mouth, natural born cocksucker, that one."

I sprung to my feet, fists clenched before I'd even thought about it. I was so angry my entire body was trembling. I hadn't come so close to hitting another human being since high school. "Get out."

"Aw, you don't want to do that, Will. Betty wouldn't like it."

"When she hears what you've just said she'll—"

"What'd I say? That Davey sure did have some nice things to say about her? Well, *gosh*, Will, I'm awfully sorry, I didn't realize you had a temper like that and would react the way you did to some old stories from a few boys that dated your wife before she even knew you. But if I've offended you somehow, I truly didn't mean to and I hope you'll accept my apology." He winked, crossed his arms over his chest. "You going to throw me out for that?"

"I'm going to tell her what you really said."

"You think she'll believe you?"

"Yes I do. She's my wife."

"Maybe she won't want to believe it. Ever think of that?"

I stood there shaking, wanting nothing more than to put my hands around his scrawny old neck. "Why are you doing this? There must be some point."

"Sit down, boy. We both know you aren't going to do anything."

I remained on my feet.

"I know your type, Will, know it well. Always had a good life, good family and a good home. Or at least that's how it looked on the outside, right? Behind closed doors it wasn't quite the *Leave It To Beaver* world y'all made it out to be publicly, was it? Dad drank a little too much, popped a few too many pills to keep the darkness away, yeah? Pumped a little strange on the side while everybody looked the other way and pretended he didn't. Mom saw doctors about her depression and took pills of her own, pills that made her a zombie stumbling through her own life. Two older sisters that couldn't get out fast enough. One married young and moved across country. You still barely see her and only talk on holidays on the phone. The other's got a thing for the ladies, was always something of an outcast growing up and hit the big city by the time she'd graduated high school. Lives with another woman out in the desert now, with some dogs and an adopted son. You tell yourself you're closer to that one but it's all a lie, isn't it? You haven't seen her in years. And when's the last time you saw your mother, Will? Long time, huh? You like to pretend you miss your old man—and maybe in your own way you do—but the two of you never got along. You were a disappointment to him and he was a disappointment to you. You had all the advantages, made the most of them, went to school, studied and worked hard and got ahead. Fucked around in college with plenty of babes but none of them meant anything to you. Married your first true love, made a life together. Couple cats and dogs over the years but no kids, so you two settle in and you do the whole married thing. You live the life. And now, you blinked and a couple decades are gone. You're both into your early forties and it's all slowing down. The payoff you thought would be there isn't, it's just more of the same, day in, day out, the same, one day blurring into another. This is it, and you know that now. It doesn't get any better than where you are right now. That's why you drink the way you do, so when you tell yourself your lies, you might just believe them. You tell yourself this is the part of life where you're supposed to be able to slow down a bit and smell the roses—and it is—but that's all been taken away, hasn't it. *Given* away. You've never been as alone as you are at this moment, and it tears you to pieces because you still think you should've been able to stop it, to make it all right, to save the both of you. Sound about right?"

I swallowed so loud it was audible. "How do you know about my family?"

"I know everything, Will. It's part of who I am."

"And who are you?"

"It's not the *who* you should be worried about." Laurent began to laugh.

My stomach clenched as fear clawed at me, ripping me apart from the inside out. "*What* are you?"

His laughter stopped as quickly as it began. He leaned forward on the table, glaring at me, and when he spoke it was quietly and through clenched teeth. "Everything you're afraid I am."

I suddenly felt lightheaded and nauseous. The room tilted and I grabbed the edge of the kitchen table for fear I might otherwise topple over. "Tell me what you want."

He pointed a long and crooked index finger right at me.

"Why?" I gasped, my voice a tight croak. "What am I to you?"

"I'm the death of you both."

Behind me, I heard the stairs creaking. Betty was coming.

Laurent's lips slowly curled into a devilish grin as he motioned to the other room. "Did you know when they were just young'uns Davey used to fuck her right in that den, on that couch she just made up for me? Oh they used to put on a real good show, let me tell you. And all the while poor ole Earl was passed out drunk right upstairs."

I rounded the table, stood over him. "Get up. Get up and get out. Now."

He licked his lips with a pale tongue. "Yes sir, Davey used to give it to her doggie-style real good, nice and deep, right up that cute little ass of hers. Betty still like a nice hard cock in her ass, Will?"

I don't remember attacking him, only that he was suddenly in my grasp. I had hold of his shirt with both hands, had evidently yanked him up and out of his chair and was in the process of shaking him back and forth like a madman.

"Will, I—what's wrong?" he shouted fearfully. "What have I done?"

I threw him down and he crashed to the kitchen floor. The back of his head slapped the wall on the way down and he let out a muffled groan as he collapsed and rolled onto his stomach, crawling toward the door and begging for mercy. I straddled him, my rage rising, and cocked my fist back with the intention of slamming it into his skull.

"Will! What are you doing? Stop it, for—for God's sake—stop it!"

Betty's voice, shrill and laced with anger and fear.

I staggered back, or maybe she pushed me, I can't remember. I only know that I found myself a few feet away as she crouched down next to Laurent, who looked dumbfounded and horrified, his face flushed and twisted into a grimace of pain.

"My God, are you all right?" she asked him.

"I-I think so," he stammered.

"He's fine," I growled, my heart racing. "Get up and get out, Laurent."

Ignoring me, Betty asked him if he could stand. He said he believed he could if she helped him. While I paced over by the sink she managed to get him to his feet and help him back to his chair at the kitchen table. He made a dramatic effort to swallow and said, "Thank you, Betty. Thank you kindly."

She spun toward me. "What the hell is the matter with you?"

"Will," Laurent said before I could speak, "I apologize if I offended you, I—I never meant to, my friend." He looked to Betty with imploring eyes. "I'm sorry, Betty, I had no idea Davey Hamilton was such a sore subject."

"Davey? Again with this?" She moved toward me with a level of anger I'd never before seen in her. "Are you serious?"

"You have no idea the things he was saying about you."

"I told a couple stories Davey told me and I guess it upset him, I—I never meant any harm, Will, please accept my apology, I—gosh, I feel just awful about this. I don't know you well enough and I should've—"

"Shut your mouth." I tried to step around Betty but she blocked me. "I'm not going to tell you again, you lying sack of shit. Get out."

"You stay right where you are," Betty ordered, pointing at him with one hand and grabbing hold of me with the other. "Excuse us a moment."

I allowed her to drag me into the living room.

"Are you out of your mind?" she asked, trying to keep her voice down.

"Listen to me, he wanted me to do that. He's been trying to get me to attack him all night, he—"

"He *wanted* you to attack him."

"That's right."

"A frail old man wanted you to physically assault him."

"He's been egging me on all night then acting differently with you. He said horrible things about you, do you understand? Nasty things about back when—"

"I don't care what he said. Argue with him then. Tell him to leave."

"I have several times now. You keep letting the sonofabitch stay."

She pinched her nose up by her eyes with her fingers and sighed. "My point is that you do not physically assault a man that's old enough to be your father. Technically you're grandfather. You don't physically assault anyone, but especially not a defenseless old man."

"He's not as defenseless as you think he is."

"You could've killed him. You're lucky he isn't seriously hurt. And you better hope he doesn't press charges. That's assault, what you just did."

"He wants to call the police, I'll give him something to call them about."

"If I'd wanted to be with the type of man who goes around hitting people I easily could've found one. They're a dime a dozen. You were never like that."

"I'm still not. I—goddamn it—I—that's the first physical confrontation I've had in thirty years! He had it coming. He's not who you think he is, Betty."

"What is happening to you?"

"I'm telling you, this man is…"

"What? He's *what*?"

"This is what he wants. What's happening right here, right now."

She shook her head as if this was all too much for her to process. "What could he have possibly said that could've caused the intellectual, peaceful man I know and love to behave this way?"

"I was defending you." My frustration was to the point where I wanted to put my fist through the wall, but I controlled myself. If I flipped out again Betty wouldn't even hear me. "He said some awful things about you."

"Maybe that's just how you took it. I'm sure he didn't intentionally—"

"He said Davey Hamilton used to—"

"Oh for crying out loud. Look at me. I dated Davey Hamilton when I was a fucking teenager. It was a million years ago. You're getting upset about some story about an old boyfriend. Really? We're back to this foolishness?"

"He said when you were younger Davey used to have anal sex with you in this room on that couch while your father was passed out drunk in bed upstairs. I've been putting up with his inane innuendos and touchy-feely bullshit all night. When he said those things about you I'd had enough. I snapped, I just—fuck him—I let him have it."

Betty watched me for several seconds, her eyes blinking slowly. She looked like something inside her had died, something vitally important, and the strange trance-like state she'd been in earlier returned.

"I don't know who this man is, what he wants or how he knows the things he does," I said. "But I think he's dangerous. He's been trying to get a reaction out of me since he got here. I finally gave him what he wanted. The bastard had it coming. He needs to leave. I want him out of this house."

"It's my house," she said softly, her eyes moist. "My father left it to me."

I had no idea how to answer that. I wasn't sure if I should be angry, insulted or both. "Fine," I managed. "I want him out of your house then."

She opened her mouth but said nothing.

"Why would you want him to stay when he said those things about you?"

"Because it's necessary," she finally said, her voice quiet and distant.

"I don't understand."

"I don't…I don't either." She wandered away, toward the stairs. It was then that I first realized she'd changed into pajama bottoms and a sweatshirt.

"Where are you going?"

"Upstairs," she said, again as if she'd suddenly become mesmerized. "I have to change my clothes."

"You already did."

"The things he told you," she said. "They're all true."

I closed my eyes and held them shut a moment. "It doesn't matter," I told her. "Not to me."

"And Davey didn't tell him those things." She slowly climbed the stairs. "He'd never do that. Not ever."

"He must've. How else could Laurent have known?"

She answered without looking back. "He was there."

5

The dreams did more than frighten me. They began to linger beyond sleep and confuse me even when I was awake, and the lines between paranoia and justified concern became so blurred I was no longer certain which was which. To distrust others is one thing, but to distrust oneself is horribly unsettling because it forces you to walk to the very edge of sanity and question whether you're truly still teetering on the precipice, or if you've already tumbled off into genuine madness.

I knew the truth. Deep down, I knew it. I knew who was alive and who was dead. And just like the lies, just like the rain, I couldn't outrun any of it.

* * *

I didn't notice the woman until she spoke to me. The funeral home was mobbed with a steady line of people coming to pay their respects, and I'd been in there with Betty for more than an hour. The townies had all been respectful and pleasant as could be to my wife, but had consistently either ignored me or gone out of their way to be rude. I needed a break, needed some air, so I'd grabbed a bottle of water and headed outside for a few minutes to catch my breath and collect myself. Alone in the stillness of the parking lot, I'd let my mind wander away from this place and time, these people, and I hadn't seen the woman approaching. She stood to my right, at the base of the steps leading inside, and although I knew she'd said something to me I hadn't heard enough to make any sense of it. "I'm sorry?"

"You're him?" she asked. "The one that married Betty?"

"Yes, I'm Betty's husband." I offered my hand. "Will Colby."

She briefly considered my hand before accepting it. Her palm was fleshy and cool, but what held my attention was the palpable sense of sorrow the woman exuded, a sadness not only emotional, but physical. "Sharon Lodge."

"Friend of the family?" I asked.

Short and stocky, the woman was roughly my age but had a posture that left her hunched slightly forward, like perhaps she'd sustained some sort of back or neck injury at some point. Her clothes were inexpensive and dated, and she wore no makeup. Her face was drawn and pale, the skin loose, her eyes heavy-lidded and sleepy, and her dull brown hair, littered with flecks of gray, was combed straight back and away from her round face in a severe style that seemed in direct contrast to her otherwise sedate appearance. In her hands she held a bulky tan pocketbook that looked heavy and awkward, especially when she took one hand and gave my wrist a gentle pat. "Hasn't been easy in there for you, has it," she said. It wasn't a question.

"I've had more pleasant afternoons." I managed a weak smile. "But this isn't about me. I'm doing my best to keep that in perspective. Did you know Earl well?"

"Well enough. Town this size, everybody knows everybody. No way around it. He was a good man. Not the easiest to get along with, but a good man. Was never right after Betty's mama died. Took to drinking too much. In a way, when her momma died Earl did too. He never knew it was happening."

I wasn't sure I'd heard her correctly. "Never knew *what* was happening?"

"There's a rain coming." The woman looked to the sky and the dark band of clouds rolling in over the horizon. "You leaving right after the funeral?"

"Yes, but we'll be back at some point to clean out the house and settle Earl's affairs. We've already decided to sell the property."

The woman gave a firm nod to indicate she agreed with the plan. "Take Betty back on out of here. Stay gone this time. Now that Earl's gone there's nothing here for her but bad."

I didn't necessarily disagree, but the woman's demeanor seemed a bit melodramatic. "Were you a friend of Betty's?" I asked.

"Grew up with her. Lived here in town with her." The woman slowly climbed the steps to the funeral home. Once she'd reached the landing she looked back down at me. "Died here with her too."

Her words didn't immediately register, and once they had I was more confused than ever. "I don't—I'm sorry—did you say you *died* with her?"

"What you ought to do is get her out of here before that rain comes." Baffled but intrigued by the strange woman, I asked, "Why's that?"

"That's when he comes. If she's here he'll know. He'll come for her first."

Nervous amusement turned to concern. "Who?"

"Betty was always his favorite."

"To whom are you referring, Ms. Lodge?" I climbed a couple steps but kept a comfortable distance between us so as not to appear aggressive. She stared at me as if she hadn't understood the question. "What are you talking about? I don't understand."

"I know." She nodded, eyes wet with grief. "People come and go. Live. Die. But the evil people do…it just is. Sometimes it hides, waits awhile, but it's always there. Watching. It never leaves a place, never leaves *us*. Something that's not alive don't die, it can't. Not ever."

I followed the woman inside but before I could ask her another question Betty waved me back over into the receiving line, as another wave of people filed in to pay their respects. Sharon Lodge came through the line, shook hands with Betty then hugged her for what seemed an inordinate amount of time. I noticed she whispered something in her ear but I wasn't able to make out any of it.

Later, I relayed to Betty the bizarre conversation I'd had with her.

"Poor Sharon," she said. "You noticed how heavily medicated she was, didn't you, that awful look in her eyes, like there's nobody in there anymore? God, it gave me the creeps. What a tragedy."

"She was out of it, no question."

"I heard from a few people at the wake that she's had a tough time. Apparently she's had several nervous breakdowns, a couple suicide attempts and is under the care of a psychiatrist who keeps her on some pretty powerful psych meds."

"But what was she talking about?"

"Who knows? She probably isn't even sure."

"You don't know who she was talking about?"

"I haven't a clue. She's sick."

The woman had spooked me a bit at the time, but after talking with Betty I forgot about the encounter, chalking it up to exactly what she'd said it was, an old childhood friend that had become a sad and mentally ill woman babbling about things that only made sense in her own demented mind.

I hadn't thought of that conversation in over a year.

Now, standing in my father-in-law's kitchen, amidst boxes and clutter, Bob Laurent sprawled in a chair at the table and still playing up his reaction to my assault, I still had no idea what Sharon Lodge had been talking about that day. But I did know *whom* she was talking about.

Rain pounded the house, coming down like bullets. Somewhere far away, thunder growled as it rolled across the heavens.

Laurent and I watched each other but didn't speak. I could feel tension running through my body like electrical current, and although it wasn't hot in the house, I began to perspire. My mouth was dry, and a level of anger I hadn't known I was capable of continued to bubble just below the surface, threatening to burst free at any moment. I didn't want this. I didn't want any of it.

"Leave," I finally said. "Or I'll make you leave."

Laurent slowly straightened up in the chair, drawing in his long legs as he leaned on the table. "Hope you're a better professor than you are a badass."

"Get out." I kept my hands at my sides but curled them into fists.

"Big fighting man now, huh? You a tough guy all of a sudden, Will?"

"Tough enough to kick your scrawny old ass."

"Thought you were above all that."

"I'm not going to tell you again, Laurent. Get out."

"You don't want me to leave. Not just yet. Curiosity's a bitch, ain't it?"

I bit my tongue but the question came anyway. "Who the hell are you?"

"You already asked me that. And I already answered." He smiled at me with his dentures. "Problem with your type, Will, is that you think you got it all figured out, the world, the universe, the light, the dark. You tell yourself you don't have any questions 'cause you already know everything. You're so goddamn brilliant and educated. Only you're not. You don't know shit. And you don't ask the questions you really want to ask because you're afraid of what the answers might be. That's why you never ask the right questions. The ones you really want and need to ask. It's only one of the reasons I love your type. People like you not only make me possible, you make me strong, make it so I can move through the world with impunity. How's that for a fancy word? Yeah, I know a few. Got any idea how easy it is to hide when no one thinks you exist in the first place? It's beautiful, your arrogance. It's like fucking oxygen to me."

"You think you're something more than a man?"

"I think you're something less than one."

I remained where I was. "I met Sharon Lodge at Earl's wake."

"Did you now?"

The sonofabitch was amused. "She told me about you."

"Stupid drugged out bitch doesn't even know where she is half the time." He chuckled, his face no longer hidden behind the mask of innocence he'd worn previously. Bright blue eyes wide and alive with excitement, he reveled in the mayhem, the rage, the violence, the decadence, and was doing everything in his power to drag me down into that trough of filth and degradation along with him. "She was always the weakest. The ones like her drowned in it. It destroys them. If they live they end up like her, alive but dead inside, goddamn walking corpses. Some do their best to take it on, thinking it'll heal them. It doesn't. Others try to forget, bury it so deep they almost do, and then move on. But none of them ever escape it. None of them ever escape *me*. I'm always there. Never too far." He smiled the most depraved and unsettling smile I'd ever seen. It sent shivers through me, and he knew it. "Betty was always the strong one. She was always my favorite. It's coming back to her. Slow, but it's coming. She's fighting it, the memories, the truth, the things she knows aren't just the bad dreams she's spent her life convincing herself they are. She can't hold it off forever. She knows that. Veil's coming down, Will, and once it falls there's nothing left to protect her. Every ghoul she buried is climbing back up through the dirt, right up out of the graves she put them in, and nothing's going to stop them."

My body trembled with rage and fear. I was in the presence of literal evil. "What did you do to her?"

"What do you think I did to her?"

"Get out."

"You invited me in. You want me to leave you'll have to put me out."

I walked to the doorway, grabbed his suitcase and carried it to the front door. Keeping one eye on him, I opened the storm door and tossed the suitcase out onto the walk. Then, without another word, I grabbed him by the scruff of his neck, yanked him from the chair and bodily removed him from the house.

He offered no resistance, and as I forced him through the door and pushed him out into the storm, he stumbled, lost his footing and fell. He laid there on his back on the stone walk, unmoving, the rain pummeling him, soaking him down. I waited a moment to see if he'd get up. He didn't.

At that moment I didn't care if he was really hurt or if this was just more of his dramatics. I slammed shut the door, locked it, and then hurried upstairs to check on Betty.

I crossed the den and fell up the stairs, crawling on all fours before righting myself and scrambling up through the shadows and darkness at the landing on the second floor. As always, I felt like the intruder here. I'd spent as little time as possible in this house, and nearly all of it downstairs. All these years later I still felt like I was going places I didn't belong, the boyfriend venturing deep into the house to find the daughter's bedroom while the parents slept.

At the far end of the dark hallway was a bathroom, the door open. Earl's old bedroom was to my right, Betty's to my left. Both doors were closed, but a small band of soft light leaked from the crack at the bottom of Betty's door. I remembered the first time I'd come this far, standing in my girlfriend's bedroom, so taken with her and so deeply in love, but more focused on the window overlooking the road, watching nervously for Earl's pickup to come rumbling along in a cloud of dirt and dust.

I moved forward until I'd reached the door. Hesitating a moment, I leaned closer and listened. All I could hear was the storm.

With a turn of the knob I slowly pushed the door open.

"Sweetheart?" My voice was raspy and uncertain.

Betty stood alone in the empty room. Her closet door was open and a light bulb suspended from a cord had been switched on, offering enough light to reveal three floorboards had been removed from the floor of the closet.

The clothes she'd been wearing sat in a heap several feet away. Although barefoot, she'd changed into a little plaid skirt and a white top I'd never seen before, some sort of pseudo schoolgirl's uniform that was far too small for her. Both were badly wrinkled and looked quite old. The blouse was so tight several seams had already split and torn, but Betty seemed unaware of it. She'd put her hair in pigtails, and smeared bright red lipstick in wide frantic swathes far beyond her lips, giving her mouth a clown-like appearance. In her hand she still held a gold tube of lipstick. She looked at me as if she were confused to find me there just then, like I'd come to her from some other place and time, which I suppose I had in a sense. I stood trembling in the doorway, my heart breaking.

"Betty?"

She nodded but her eyes were somewhere else, somewhere dark and foreign, hiding the real her somewhere safe, somewhere far away from this old room in this dark little house, with all its nightmares and secrets.

"Christ," I gasped helplessly. "Baby, what are you doing?"

Betty moved to the window and looked out at the night.

"Laurent's gone," I told her. "I threw him out."

If she heard me she gave no indication. Instead, she reached out with her free hand and gently brushed her fingertips against the pane, as if to touch the night itself. "He used to dance in the rain," she said softly. "I'd see him out there dancing and being so silly, and I'd laugh." She turned, looked back at me, her eyes moist and red. "And then he'd come inside and I wouldn't laugh anymore."

I thought for a moment my knees might buckle, so I steadied myself against the doorframe as my wife and her old bedroom blurred through the tears filling my eyes. Tears not so different from hers, really. Tears born of horror, heartbreak and rage. Hatred welled in me and I wanted to destroy something, anything, to completely annihilate it. *Him.*

I wiped my eyes, crossed the room and looked more closely at the floor of the closet. In the cramped area beneath the floorboards she'd removed there was something more than the old clothes and lipstick she'd found. I crouched down and picked up a small manila envelope. Several old Polaroid photographs were stacked neatly inside. I dropped it without looking at them, rose to my feet and pulled Betty into my arms, holding her tight against me and whispering everything would be all right. She stood there in my embrace, lifeless, cold and silent. Over her shoulder, I looked out the window through the rain at the front walkway below. Laurent was still lying there, motionless.

I don't know how long we stood in Betty's old bedroom on that hellish night, but it was a long time. Neither of us said anything, we just held each other and softly cried awhile. And when it seemed we'd expended every bit of emotion we had, shed every tear within us, she gently broke away from me and wandered back to the window. I joined her there. Laurent still hadn't moved. Maybe he was hurt. Maybe he was dead. I didn't care either way. But Betty wasn't even looking at him. She was watching the night, studying something else, another time and night only she could see. I put a hand on her shoulder, kissed her on the cheek and told her I loved her.

Her hand touched mine. Warm, familiar. "Love you too," she said, her voice barely audible. She was still somewhere else, though, somewhere far away, and I could tell from the dead look in her eyes that we were anything but done with this nightmare.

As rain crashed the house, I left her there at the window, returned to the downstairs, and once in the kitchen, pulled my cell free of my belt and got a phone number for Ed Hamilton.

The line began to ring. I watched Laurent through the glass in the door, my anger slowly dissipating, replaced now with emptiness and the need for resolution.

An older man answered on the third ring.

I asked for Davey, my voice still a bit shaky.

Without reply, I heard the phone being placed down on something hard. A moment later another voice said, "Hello?"

"Davey Hamilton?"

"Yes, this is David Hamilton."

I cleared my throat and tried to focus my thoughts into something coherent. "Hi, you don't know me, but my name is Will Colby. I'm Betty Monroe's husband."

After a few seconds listening to him breathe he said, "Betty Monroe." He spoke her name fondly, but with a trace of disbelief. "I...God, I...I was so sorry to hear about what happened."

"I'm sure she'd appreciate that, thank you, but as you know, I'm in town cleaning out Earl's place and—"

"I didn't know that, actually. Just got back to town recently myself."

"You didn't know I was in town?" I asked.

"Is there some reason I should have?"

"Bob said your father told you both we were in town after he saw me at the store."

"Bob?"

"Bob Laurent."

Silence filled the line for several seconds.

"Who is this?" he asked, his previously pleasant tone replaced with one far more aggressive. "Answer me, who the hell is this?"

"I'm Will Colby, Betty's husband. Bob Laurent came here earlier and—"

"OK, if this is someone's attempt at a sick joke or something, I'm not—"

"It's not a joke, Davey."

"David. No one's called me Davey since I was a kid."

"David then, I'm sorry. This is very difficult for me too, all right? I'm doing my best to explain that Laurent is still here and I think he may be hurt. Now I know he was visiting you and your parents earlier today and that they're friends with him, so I thought I'd give you the chance to come and get him the hell out of here. If not, I'll call the cops and have him removed. Up to you."

He breathed heavily into the phone, and when he spoke his voice had begun to shake as well. "We both know Bob Laurent was not here earlier and he's not there now. Now what the hell do you want and what is this all about?"

"I'm telling you, he's here. I'm looking at him right now. He fell on the walkway and he could be hurt. He hasn't moved in several minutes and—"

"If someone there is injured I suggest you call an ambulance."

"Laurent came here and—"

"What is this? Why are you calling me? If you're really Betty's husband then why would you be calling me with this?"

I was gripping the phone so tight it was beginning to hurt my hand. "I thought...I was hoping you could help me."

"Help you how?"

"Are you going to come get Laurent out of here or do I call the cops?"

"OK, listen to me very carefully. Will, was it? Listen to me very carefully, Will. If someone's been there tonight it wasn't Bob Laurent. If he claims that's who he is, he's lying to you, understand? And if he said he was visiting my parents or me earlier today he's lying about that too. So yes, call the police and have him removed from the property, because while I have no idea what you're talking about or what any of this has to do with me, I do know one thing for sure. Whoever it is that's there with you is not Bob Laurent. Do you hear me? It is *not* Bob Laurent."

"And why are you so sure of that?" I asked.

"Because Bob Laurent has been dead and buried for years."

6

Some things are not supposed to be understood. Some sins are not supposed to be forgiven. Some things that are stolen can never be reclaimed, and some nightmares are never truly over.

And so, we sleep. We sleep and forget and dream of other things, other times, other people and places. We dream of happiness and love and safety, and if we're lucky we find joy in those things and do our best to never wander back to those dark and dangerous woods where truth still lingers, biding its time like a spider patiently waiting at the edge of its web, watching impassively as its prey becomes trapped.

It is then that we realize the spider is not gone. It never truly was. It's been there all along. And now, there is only one resolution.

Either the spider dies…or we do.

Bathed in the tears of the innocent, I gently stroked the scarred and bruised flesh circling Betty's neck, traced it lovingly with my fingers, and remembered what it was like to hold her close once more.

* * *

I began to pace over near the sink. From the corner of my eye I saw the outside light come on in the back yard again but paid little attention. I was more concerned about my racing heart and an odd tingling sensation that was making its way across my chest and into the pit of my stomach. Not so very long ago Betty and I had been going about our business, living our lives and leaving the past behind us. And now that wasn't even an option anymore. I wondered if it ever truly had been. My suspicions that the man claiming to be Bob Laurent was actually someone else had apparently been substantiated, but the question that remained was exactly who this man was and why was he pretending to be this monster from Betty's past.

"You're sure about this?" I asked.

"Laurent disappeared twenty-five years ago," David said, his tone indicating perhaps he'd said more than he'd meant to. "The body was never found."

"Then how do you know he's dead? If he simply vanished then—"

"He's dead."

"How do you know for sure if they never found a body?" I ran a hand through my hair. It came back slick with perspiration. "And how could Betty not know about any of this? Twenty-six years ago she was seventeen years old and still living here, in this house, with her father. That must've been big news in these parts, disappearances can't happen often in this town. And if Earl and Laurent were such good friends then Earl knew about it and surely Betty did. How could she not? For that matter, how could I not know? Wouldn't Earl or Betty have mentioned this to me before? None of this makes any sense."

"She *did* know. We all did."

"Then why didn't she tell me any thing about this?"

"I can't answer that. I'm sorry."

"She didn't remember him. She claimed she didn't anyway, it—it's... complicated."

"I know," he said softly. "Trust me, I know." A match-strike echoed through the line, followed by a quick intake of breath and a slow exhale. "Tell me what he looks like."

"Seventies, tall and lanky. Bright blue eyes."

"It's not possible," he muttered. "It's not—not possible."

Bile leapt from my stomach and gurgled into the bottom of my throat, acidic and nauseating. I reached for the edge of the counter and held on tight. "It's him. Isn't it."

"Bob Laurent is dead."

"Then who is he? How did he know you were back in town? How did he know Betty was? How did he know about Earl and Betty's past? He even knew things about me, my family. At Earl's funeral Sharon Lodge warned me about this, about him. About the rain, how it would bring him back."

I heard David drawing on his cigarette again. "He used to dance in the rain," he said, as if reciting some old poem. "We used to watch him."

"And you'd laugh," I said, trembling. "And then he'd come inside."

"And we wouldn't laugh anymore."

"What's happening, David?"

"God help you."

"Tell me, David. Who is he? *What* is he?"

"A bad dream," he mumbled. "I'm sorry, I have to go. I always loved Betty, please know that, and part of me always will. I know you've been through hell, and I wish you the best, but please, don't call here again. I can't do this. Leave me alone. Just...please...just leave me alone."

A blur of motion caught my eye and I turned to find Betty standing in the doorway to the kitchen, still dressed in that hideous outfit, her mouth still covered in bright red lipstick and her cheeks streaked with remnants of tears. She said nothing, only held a hand out for my phone.

Reluctantly, I gave it to her.

She pressed the cell to her ear but said nothing. She listened a moment then disconnected the call and placed my cell on the counter. "It wasn't just me." Her voice was small and weak, like it required great effort to draw the breath necessary to speak. "The others were a part of it too."

"A part of what?"

"The day he was killed and buried, I buried him too. Here," she said, pointing to her temple. "He was dead and gone and we all moved on with our lives as best we could."

"David said Laurent disappeared."

"He did."

"Then how do you know he's dead? Who killed and buried him, Betty?"

"It was the first time we'd all been together again," she said, like she hadn't heard me. "Us...him...the rain."

People come and go. Live. Die.

"The rain? I don't understand."

"He worked outside. He didn't work when it rained."

But the evil they do...it just is.

"He died in the rain. Now he's back."

"The dead don't come back, Betty."

Sometimes it hides, waits awhile, but it's always there. Watching.

"Not him. It."

"It?"

"The evil inside him."

It never leaves a place, never leaves us.

"But if Laurent's dead then..."

Something that's not alive don't die, it can't. Not ever.

"I thought I was finally free of it," she said, looking to the floor. "But it wouldn't let me go, it—it wouldn't let me go. I couldn't fight it anymore."

The light out back went off then quickly came back on. Betty saw it and her face contorted into a grimace of fear and sorrow as tears again filled her eyes and spilled free. She backed away from the window over the sink, hugging herself and slowly shaking her head back and forth.

"What's out there?" I asked, turning to the window. "What is it, Betty? Who is it? What did you and Davey and the others do?"

I looked out but saw only rain and the powerful floodlight illuminating part of the yard. Turning, I ran back to the door to find Laurent. I wanted answers and he was going to give them to me. If not I'd beat them out of him, but I was going to get them one way or another.

Even before I'd pushed my way through the storm door and out into the rain I saw that he was no longer lying in the walkway. Laurent had finally gotten up, but he was nowhere in sight. All that was left behind was his suitcase, which now lay open and discarded to the right of the walkway.

As the violent rain crashed down on me, cold and hard, I closed on the suitcase then crouched down for a better look. It was empty but for an old rag smeared with swathes of a white paste-like substance and an open jar which lay on its side. I scooped up the jar and spun it in my hand until a label came into view that read: *White Base Greasepaint.*

I looked behind me. Betty stood in the door, watching me like a zombie.

Standing, I grabbed the suitcase and hurled it out into the road then made my way through the heavy rain to the side of the house. The backyard had fallen dark again, and there was no sign of Laurent anywhere.

Soaked, I ran back for the front door, slipped inside then closed and locked both doors behind me. As I stood dripping on the floor, I held up the jar to show Betty. She nodded and took a step back, as if I'd thrust a burning torch at her, then brought her hands to her face and slowly rubbed her fingertips against her cheeks like she was putting the paint on herself. "He wore this?" I asked. "Why?"

"At first to make us laugh," she answered. "Then to make us cry."

"Jesus Christ." I tossed the jar onto the table. "You defended him—all that harmless old man nonsense—you sided with him over me, *protected* him. Why? And how could you go our entire lives together without telling me about any of this? Why didn't you tell me what had happened? I don't—Betty—I don't understand. Help me. Help me to understand."

"It's not about me anymore. It's about you now." She bowed her head and shut her eyes, as if in prayer. "You tell yourself they're only bad dreams," she said, just above a whisper. "I told myself it was in the past and none of it happened—not really—that it was all nightmares and false memories, because none of it could be real. Even though deep down I know the truth—and now, so do you—we bury it, we fight it and push it so far down and tell ourselves every day to forget, that it's all a lie. And eventually, we start to believe it, and that becomes the reality. We survive and we move on and we find a new life, we make a fresh start and a new history with someone who loves us. We make a life where none of those old nightmares and horrors matter, and we forget." She opened her eyes and looked right at me. "We forget because that's what we want, what we need. And while the pain and fear never completely leaves us, while what was taken from us is something we can never get back, what was broken can never be fixed, we hold on tight and we live our lives as if none of it ever happened. Because if we stop to remember, if we stop to look, we *will* see, and then it comes to life again and everything we've built comes toppling down like a house of cards."

"But Laurent is dead," I reminded her. "You and David both insist he's—"

"He was murdered."

"But if a body was never found there's only one way you could know that."

She nodded.

"If he's really dead then how can he be here with us tonight?" A sudden burst of nervous, joyless laughter escaped me. "You expect me to believe he's some sort of—what—ghost?"

"Baby, I know this is hard for you but you have to accept it. You have to let this go. You have to let *me* go."

"What the hell are you talking about?"

"Evil is real, Will. Sometimes you can touch it."

I walked away, came back then walked away again. It felt like I was literally about to come out of my skin. "This is madness. What is going on? I—OK—get your things, we—we're leaving. Right now, tonight."

"I can't. You know that."

I stood there shaking with anger and confusion, trying my best to figure out exactly who was standing there with me. The longer the night went the less recognizable my wife became. "Then I'm calling the police. The bastard is out there somewhere, and I want him off this property."

This time it was Betty who laughed, a pathetic, helpless little laugh. "The *police*? Will, for God's sake, do you really think the police can help? Don't you understand what Davey was telling you, what *I'm* telling you?"

"Whoever was sitting in that chair is a man and nothing more. He—his truck—it broke down and was towed away. Was that all an illusion too?"

"In a way," she whispered. "Like a dream, a bad dream. We need to have them sometimes. They help us see what we need to see, the things we need to know."

Rain sprayed the windows, tapping the panes and summoning us out into the storm. I looked to the window over the sink. The light was on again.

"Fine," I said. "I'll handle this sonofabitch myself."

Betty nodded sadly. "I wish there was some other way. But there isn't."

My wife reached out and took my hand in hers. Slowly, she led me back out the front door and into the rain. Together, we walked around the side of the house to the backyard. The outside light was still on, and at the very edge of its reach the dark forest stood silent and swaying in the storm. The rain pelted us with such force it was painful on contact, but neither of us cared. We'd become transparent. *We* were the ghosts now, transported to another rainy night so very long ago. Yet we were alive. The pain told me so.

I held Betty's hand tight and followed her gaze as she turned and looked back up at the house behind us to the second floor where her bedroom was.

And I saw. God help me. I saw.

The children. Betty. Davey Hamilton. Sharon Lodge. Two others. A boy. A girl. Five in all, they stand in the dimly lit bedroom. A lone candle burns on the nightstand, the flame flickering, bending arcs of light along the shadowy walls and ceiling. The children surround the bed. Bob Laurent lies there before them, his face painted stark white, his eyes ringed in black. On the floor next to the bed are a shattered mug and a puddle of coffee, lying right where he dropped them when the sedative took hold and he lost consciousness.

The children. Knowing what they must do. What they have agreed to do and planned out right down to the very last detail. From the tranquilizers stolen from Sharon's grandmother, to the rope bought at the local hardware store, to the hunting knife Davey's father will not notice is gone and will be back in place before he next uses it. Everything has been planned and agreed to well in advance. And it has all led to this night. This rainy day which slowly became a rainy night. The last day, and the last night any of them will have to endure these things, because on this night Bob Laurent will die. They will see to it. No one would believe such a nice man could possibly be responsible for the horrors he has perpetrated against them. No one needs to know what these children have been put through. They know, and that is enough. They will end it. They have decided. Not one or two, but all five of them, together. Together, they will end this. Together, they will forever carry the scars of what he has done to them, and together they will forever carry the burden of what they are about to do. They will not tell, just as Bob Laurent has always warned them not to do. They have become very good at not telling, at pretending things never really happened. He has taught them well.

Now, they will teach him.

Davey goes first. Holding the enormous knife in both hands, he raises it up close to his chin as his eyes brim with tears, his face pale and ghoulish in the candlelight, and then slams the blade down into Laurent's chest. It sinks in deep then snags on bone, turning the teenage boy's wrists. No one says a word. No one looks away. Even when the body convulses and Laurent's breath catches in his throat and he makes an odd wheezing, gurgling sound. Everyone cries. Quietly. Rain spatters the windows as Davey, choking back the bile, pulls the knife free and hands it to Sharon. She takes it with trembling hands, her face a twisted grimace of rage, then stabs him once, then again, deeper the second time, the blade making a sickening ripping sound. As she pulls it free of him, ribbons of blood fly from Laurent's body. He is still alive, but dying quickly.

The blade is passed to the others and they strike just as they promised they would, plunging the knife deep into the body before finally passing the bloody blade to Betty.

Hands trembling and tears smearing her face, she looks to the others then down at the body. Bob Laurent is dead.

"Do it," Sharon says, a wicked smile curling her bloody lips. "Do it, Betty, do it! Do it!"

Betty shakes her head no, the madness rising, becoming one with the terror and shame.

"You promised," the other girl says. "We all promised."

Davey touches her wrist, strokes it with tenderness. "It's OK," he tells her. "Do it. It's almost over but it can't end until we all do it."

Betty hugs herself and backs away. "He's already dead, there's no point," she says, her voice trembling.

"Finish it," Davey says.

Finally, tears streaming her face, she does.

The rope comes next. They bind his hands and feet with it and then fasten the second length around his neck. When the knots are secure, they roll and wrap the body in a sheet. Dark blood quickly stains it, seeping through. Together, they carry the body out of the bedroom, down the stairs, through the house and out into the night.

They cross the backyard, through the heavy rain, and move into the forest behind the house. Nearly a mile in, they come to an old stone well that has been abandoned and unused for nearly a century, forgotten and overgrown deep in the woods. As planned, they have already loosened the stones and prepared the well for their purposes.

Drenched in rain and blood, the children remove the stones one by one until the opening is large enough to accommodate the body. Together, they drop and roll it into the well.

The body plummets, lands with a dull thud far below.

Together, in the rain, they replace the stones.

Together, they hug and cry and promise each other everything will be all right, that none of this ever truly happened. And even if it did, it's over now. Bob Laurent is dead and buried and he won't be coming back. He can't hurt any of them ever again.

I closed my eyes and tilted my head back; let the raindrops tickle my face.

Most of my tears washed away, but just like the rain and all the horrors hiding within it, they kept coming. And as Betty's hand slowly slipped free of mine, I turned and saw the others standing behind us in the yard.

Through sheets of rain, there they were, children no more.

And in David Hamilton's hand, a knife, held down by his leg.

Betty left me, joined the others, and together they watched the woods behind me. Waiting…

My mind shattering, I slowly stole a look back over my shoulder.

Through the rain and darkness at the edge of the forest came an unnaturally white face. Striking blue eyes ringed in black opened wide in demonic delight as he glided between the trees, dancing like some sort of depraved marionette, his movements jerky and bizarre, arms up above his head and spindly legs prancing.

Without taking my eyes from him, I stumbled back across the yard until I also saw the others in my peripheral vision. The rain grew worse, falling in heavy diagonal sheets, but he was there, dancing, and when I looked at Betty and the others, what he'd done to them—all that unimaginable pain and horror—it was there too, branded on their faces like the mark it was. His mark. A mark of evil.

I stood in the rain, drenched and cold and unable to move as the creature danced deeper into the yard. And then he stopped, leaned forward, and with a wicked grin of a smile, pointed at me with a bony finger, the nail long and curved like a talon.

Slowly, very slowly, the finger curled back, summoning me. Once. Twice.

David handed Betty the knife. Once at my side, she held it out for me.

I took it, holding it tight with both hands, and stepped forward. Soaked and shivering, I looked back at my wife. She nodded, her lipstick running over and dripping from her chin like blood.

I reached out as if to touch her, but she was several feet away. In that moment I wanted nothing more than to put my arms around her and take her away from this awful place, but I knew that was not possible. This was my battle now, my demon to slay.

"Betty," I said, my voice a croak of a whisper beneath the rain, and then I turned and charged at him.

It opened its arm as if in welcome, head thrown back and mouth open to drink in the rain, the blood and the madness.

I crashed into him and together we fell. He vanished beneath me, and then I was hitting him with my fists, pounding him down deeper into the muddy earth. The thing writhed about and scrambled for purchase, struggling back up to its hands and knees, swiping at me with its claws. Flailing about, it smiled. It was happy. It was enjoying the violence, absorbing it. This was what it needed. But it was weak. Time had left it weak.

As it began to rise to its feet, I attacked again, this time with savagery I never would've believed myself capable of, slashing its throat with the blade then swinging it back around and burying it deep in the thing's gut.

Crimson sprayed from its throat wound and gushed from the jagged hole in its abdomen, but it kept rising, smiling demonically, eyes locked on me with something like love. But this wasn't love. This was sinister, twisted and evil.

Suddenly the others attacked, pulling it back to the ground and swarming on it like a pack of ravenous wolves. Betty ripped the knife from my hand and straddled Laurent. Raising the knife high above her head, she thrust it down again and again in a spray of blood and gore and endless rain.

It all seemed to happen so fast, and then they were drifting away, wandering off through the storm in separate directions, each covered in blood and entrails. Finally, Betty walked away too, leaving the body behind in the mud. She never looked at me, just turned her back on the fallen creature and stared at the ground as if she might find answers there.

Bob Laurent lay naked and broken in the rain, his clothes torn away, his body mangled. They'd ripped pieces of him away with their hands and teeth, nearly devouring him in their viciousness.

I realized then that the back light had been on the entire time. I looked back at the house. Light filled the kitchen window as well.

Someone stood there watching, peering out at the storm.

I felt my knees give out as I sank down and splashed into a puddle.

After a moment David and the others all came together again, wandering back into the light. The rain had washed away the gore, but none of us were clean. We could never be clean again.

I watched as David took the knife from Betty's hands. He leaned in, kissed her gently on the forehead then turned and walked away with the others.

As darkness swallowed them, Betty moved over to me—her face blank, her hair matted down and her clothes plastered to her body—put her arms around my shoulders and gently pulled me close. I fell into her, still on my knees. Her arms tightened around me and she dropped down to her knees as well.

We held each other awhile. There, in the rain.

When I opened my eyes I looked behind her, over her shoulder.

Laurent was gone.

Maybe he'd never really been there at all. Or maybe he'd been there all along. Real as the night, the rain, the blood coursing through my veins and the nightmares that refused to let me go.

7

All the stones have been put back in place. From below, submerged beneath the mud and rainwater, with dead eyes he sees, watches…listens…waits…rots. Scarred bones and fading bad dreams, nothing more…

Yet he haunts me still. Haunts us. As all good demons should.

I remember standing at a local junkyard behind Sully's Repair Shop. After a drawn out, somewhat confrontational conversation with the owner, he'd led me out to the bevy of dead and abandoned cars that had been towed and left there over the years, some dating back decades. One such vehicle was a truck that had once belonged to Bob Laurent. It had been found on a stretch of state highway a few miles outside town, parked in the breakdown lane as if he'd pulled over, shut off the engine and simply walked away. The truck had sat rotting and unclaimed ever since. As I looked at the rusted and rotted corpse that had once been Laurent's pickup, I told myself it didn't matter what was possible and what wasn't. The past was real. The evil within Laurent was real. I was real. My wife was real. Our pain was real.

Between the screams, the tears, the blood and violence, the lies and wounds, scars and those moments when I'd have sworn I'd come awake with my hands around Laurent's throat, gleefully choking the life from him, I dreamed of Betty sitting beneath a beautiful old oak tree, a noose hanging ominously from a branch above her, her clothes stained with Laurent's blood. And the faster I ran through the woods to her, to stop her from what she felt she needed to do to stop the things that had haunted her since childhood, the farther away she seemed to get. And when I could run no more, I knew I'd never catch her in time.

The wolf, he was there too.

But on this night of ghosts and memories, of tall tales and love stories, horrific demons in whiteface and a rain that crashed the Earth with ferocious anger, my nightmares parted and for just a moment there was peace.

No. Not peace.

Understanding…anger…pain…regret…loss…and yearning that will never leave me. But not peace. Not quite.

I closed my eyes and tried my best to remember the good. The joy.

And all I could see was Betty. My love. Forever. For always.

Why, baby? Why didn't you wait for me? Why didn't you tell me?

It's all right now. It's all right. The rain, it's stopped. Do you see?

Listen. Can you hear the quiet? Can you feel me there with you?

There's no one dancing beyond that dark and blurry window.

Not anymore. Not ever again.

It's only me now. Only me.

* * *

Even when the night began to die and a faint rumor of light burned through the misty fog in the distance above the trees, we remained in the backyard, on our knees and holding each other tight. The rain had stopped for a few hours but began to pick up again, falling heavily in twisted veils that curled and sprayed down on us. It was a warmer rain now, but just as telling. I ran a hand across Betty's face, cupped her cheek and lifted her chin from my shoulder so I could look into her eyes. She blurred through the rain, perhaps my tears.

"I'm sorry," she promised, but her eyes had grown sluggish and distant, and that effortless smile I'd always found so endearing, the one that curled just the corner of her mouth, now seemed forced and weary. "Do you believe me?"

I nodded and we kissed. It was a desperate kiss full of passion and fear, longing and the knowledge that it would be the last kiss we'd ever know.

There might be others, but not like this. Not here. Not now. Even as the rain crashed down on us and washed her away from me, I told her she was the most beautiful woman I'd ever seen, the only woman I'd ever loved and everything in the world to me.

I held on tight, wanting—needing—to keep her there with me, but she was already gone, already lost to the rain and mud.

In my arms I held nothing but old clothes. Her clothes from so very long ago I'd found beneath the floorboards of her bedroom closet along with those horrible photographs.

I bowed my head and cried like I never had before.

Eventually, I struggled to my feet. Somehow, my legs carried me as I stumbled across the yard. Fumbling keys from my pocket, I stopped at the stone walkway and took one look back at the old house. It sat silently in the storm, offering nothing more. It had told me its secrets, showed me its ghosts and now it too had fallen asleep.

It was time to go, there was nothing left here. It was all dead now, the good and bad and everything in between.

But before I could turn away, just for a moment I saw Betty as I'd seen her years before. Young and happy and vibrant and in love with me, hurrying out the door to see me, her hair flying in the breeze.

One day we'll be together again. Just like Pyramus and Thisbe. We'll die for love, not fear or pain or regret or because those old childhood wounds won't stop bleeding and become too much to hold in anymore, too painful to live with for even another moment, but for love, Betty, for love—and that's what will set us free. Finally, we'll be free. Together. Forever. Dreams no more.

Beneath the stones, beneath the earth, Laurent screamed, clawing at the sides of that old well. I forced him away, silencing his hideous screeches and pushing him back into the darkness as I clung desperately to what little remained of my sanity.

I focused on Betty, still there, so beautiful and smiling at me.

Sleep, my love. And when you open your eyes, I'll be there.

As the vision of her faded into the early morning mist, I wiped my eyes with bloody hands and whispered a final goodbye.

For just a second, I felt Betty's breath, warm and soft in my ear, telling me everything would be all right.

And for the first time since I'd lost her, I believed it just might be.

Without looking back, I left the dead to their graves and walked away through the rain, out of darkness and toward the slowly rising sun of a new day.

ABOUT THE AUTHOR

Greg F. Gifune is a best-selling, internationally-published author of several acclaimed novels, novellas and two short story collections. Called, "The best writer of horror and supernatural thrillers at work today" by New York Times best-selling author Christopher Rice, "One of the best writers of his generation" by both The Roswell Literary Review and author Brian Keene, and "Among the finest dark suspense writers of our time" by legendary best-selling author Ed Gorman, Greg's work has been published all over the world, translated into several languages, received starred reviews from Publishers Weekly, Library Journal, Kirkus and others, is consistently praised by readers and critics alike, and has garnered attention from Hollywood. His novel THE BLEEDING SEASON, originally published in 2003, has been hailed as a classic in the genre and is considered to be one of the best horror/thriller novels of the decade. In 2015 his short story HOAX was adapted to film, and starred Rodney Eastman (Nightmare on Elm Street series, I Spit on Your Grave) and was directed by Eric Shapiro (The Rule of Three). In 2016/17 Shapiro will direct a second film, FIRST IMPRESSIONS, based on Greg's short story of the same name. Also a respected editor with years of experience in the field in a variety of positions, Greg is Senior Editor at Darkfuse and at work on several projects. He resides in Massachusetts with his wife Carol, a bevy of cats and two dogs, Dozer and Bella. He can be reached online at gfgauthor@verizon.net or on Facebook and Twitter.

Available Books (in English)

Available Books

POPPY Z. BRITE – SELECTED STORIES
By Poppy Z. Brite
Collection – eBook Edition
February, 2016

Available Books

THE HITCHHIKING EFFECT
By Gene O'Neill
Collection – eBook Edition
February 2016

Available Books

SONGS FOR THE LOST
by Alexander Zelenyj
Collection – eBook Edition
April 2016

Available Books

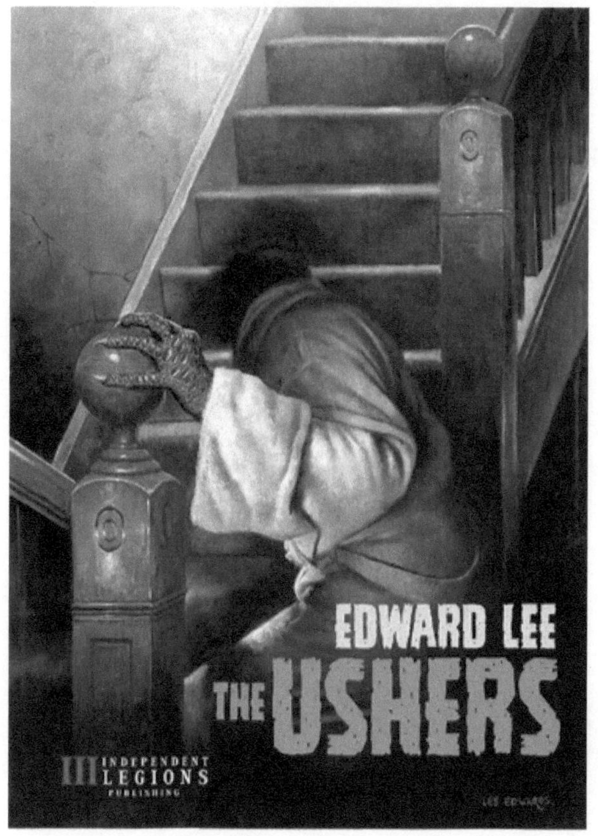

THE USHERS
by Edward Lee
Collection – eBook Edition
May 2016

Available Books

THE CRYSTAL EMPIRE - NOVELLA
by Poppy Z. Brite
Novella - eBook Edition
May 2016

Available Books

USED STORIES
by Poppy Z. Brite
Collection – eBook Edition
June 2016

Available Books

THE BEAUTY OF DEATH
by Peter Straub, Ramsey Campbell, John Skipp, Poppy Z. Brite, Edward Lee
and many others
Anthology – eBook Edition
July 2016

Available Books

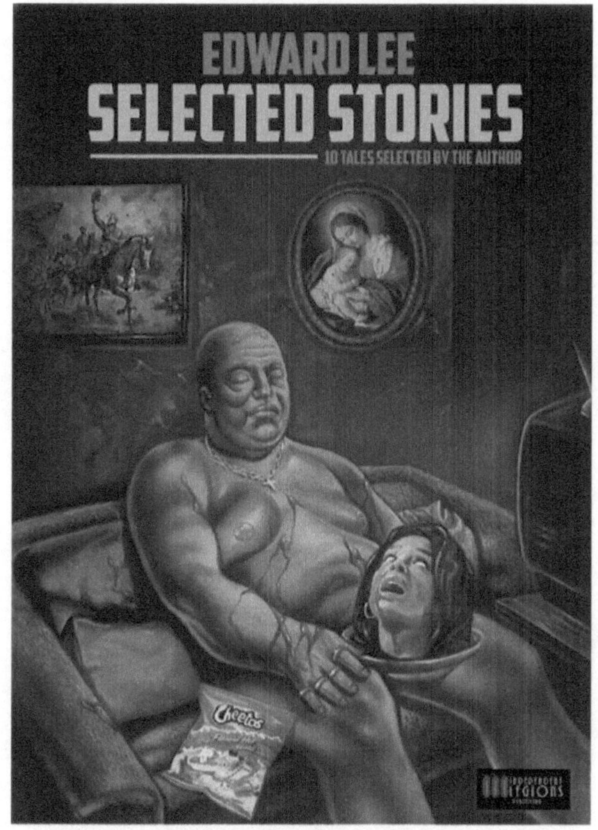

EDWARD LEE – SELECTED STORIES
by Edward Lee
Collection– eBook Edition
July 2016

Available Books

POPPY Z. BRITE – THE HORROR SHOW
by Poppy Z. Brite
Collection– eBook Edition
August 2016

Available Books

WHAT WE FOUND IN THE WOODS
by Shane McKenzie
Collection– eBook Edition
September 2016

Independent Legions Publishing
Via Castelbianco, 8 - 00168 Rome (Italy)
www.independentlegions.com
www.facebook.com/independentlegions

www.ingramcontent.com/pod-product-compliance
Lightning Source LLC
Chambersburg PA
CBHW032154190626
46814CB00005BA/1984

* 9 7 8 8 8 9 9 5 6 9 2 5 9 *